BEFORE I FORGET

Also by Tory Henwood Hoen

The Arc

BEFORE
I FORGET

A Novel

Tory Henwood Hoen

ST. MARTIN'S PRESS
NEW YORK

First published in the United States by St. Martin's Press, an imprint of St. Martin's Publishing Group

Designed by Donna Sinisgalli Noetzel

ISBN 978-1-250-27679-7

For my daughter

and

in memory of my father

What you can plan is too small for you to live.

—DAVID WHYTE,
"WHAT TO REMEMBER WHEN WAKING"

BEFORE I FORGET

Chapter 1

I am stuck between selves. Right now, I am no one.

I am also stuck, literally, in the mud, the wheels of my janky hatchback spinning in fruitless circles as they work themselves deeper into the earth. I should have known better than to drive up this particular road in this particular car at this particular time of year, but I forgot. It has been a while since I visited my father's house. More than a while. It has been nine years.

As I rev the engine, I recall his classic refrain: "If you visit during mud season, you must really mean it." In this area of New York—way upstate, farther than most urbanites are willing to go nowadays—there is this murky fifth season that falls between winter and spring, when everything is brown and dense, when the dirt roads turn soft and unruly as they thaw inch by stubborn inch. The other four seasons have their obvious charms, but mud season is a slog, palatable only to the locals and navigable only with the deepest of treads. My treads are inadequate, and I haven't been a local for a long time, which is probably why my five-hour journey has reached a premature conclusion here, a mile short of the house, where the cracked asphalt yields to dirt (or in this instance, sludge). I climb out of the car and wave my phone skyward, trying to get a signal so I can ask my older sister, Nina, to come fetch me in her sturdy Subaru. But again, I should know better—this section of woods is especially dense, and there is no hope of cell service. As the sun starts to dip behind the pines, I realize I'll have to start walking if I want to get to the house before dark. This would not normally be a problem—except my suitcase is on wheels.

I squelch my way around the car, pop the hatch, and dig through the miscellany that has accumulated in the back. If wealth were measured in complimentary linen tote bags, I would be a millionaire. I spot one that bears the logo of my employer, Actualize, and our tagline: WHAT WOULD YOUR BEST SELF DO?

"My best self can fuck right off," I say and then immediately feel bad. I apologize to the limp bag. "Sorry. It's not your fault. That was my quarter-life crisis talking." I'm convinced I have hurt the tote's feelings, so I grab it from the pile. Empathy is a good thing, but I might have too much of it.

I transfer a few essentials from my suitcase to the bag, then close the hatch and lock the car, although there's no need for such caution. Almost nobody comes this way.

The road snakes uphill, and I take a few steps in the sucking mud before finding a smoother groove where the dirt meets the undergrowth. It occurs to me that this is the exact time of year when the black bears are emerging from their winter sleep, and while I am an animal lover, I'm not looking to encounter any large wildlife at this moment.

"Hi, bears! It's me, Cricket! Just passing through! Nothing to see here!" I call out.

It's not far to the house: just a half mile up and then another half mile down toward the water. It doesn't take long for me to reach the crest of the hill, where I can see Catwood Pond stretching below—a ragged gash in the landscape formed by glaciers eons ago. Still partially frozen, its surface is mottled with patches of snow and inky soft spots, where water surges up from the ancient springs that feed the pond. Given its considerable size and depth, I always thought Catwood Pond deserved the designation of lake, but we don't always get what we deserve. The pond was supposed to have been named for some guy named Gerald Gatwood, who built the first camp in this corner of the Adirondacks. Someone's smudgy handwriting was to blame for the misrecording of the pond's name in official records, and no one ever bothered to correct it. Catwood it was, and Catwood it would remain. Sometimes our mistakes define us—that's just how life is.

The dimness settles around me as I walk, and the familiarity of this place seeps back into my senses. I know it's only a matter of time until I stumble upon the one memory that is too hard to bear. Instead, I think back to last week and the call from my sister.

———

"Do you have a minute? It's about Dad . . ." Nina had said.

I braced for bad news, certain that he was dead.

"Dead? No!" Nina laughed off my panic.

"Well, why would you say it like that? 'It's about Dad . . .'"

"Sorry, sorry. There's no crisis. It's actually good news. I got offered a postdoc," she clarified. My heart still pounding, I tried to convert my worry into excitement as she continued: "In Stockholm."

"Stockholm?" I didn't even realize she had been applying for positions, let alone considering moving abroad. Her PhD is in computational biology, with a focus on maternal health, and she has spent the last few years studying endometriosis at the molecular level. Biomarkers, DNA sequencing, protein networks—these are the terms she uses to explain her work.

I had naively assumed that she was content to analyze DNA on this side of the Atlantic, but I could hear the excitement in her voice as she said, "There's an institute in Stockholm where I can jump right into the next phase of my research. Unlike this country, Sweden actually funds women's health studies."

"Women's health? I think I've heard of it. But surely it can't be complex enough to merit *research*," I joked.

"Shocking, I know," Nina said. "And I'll be working with Elin Sundholm, so it doesn't get any better than that."

I had no idea who that was, but it had been a long time since I had heard Nina this energized. I knew there was no slowing her momentum, so I turned to logistics. "Okay . . . so how will that work? Dad will go with you?"

"I don't think that would make sense. It would be too disruptive for him, and not ideal for me."

"Right, of course. But who will take care of him?"

Nina was silent for a moment. "I've looked into our options. Dad's Medicare doesn't cover long-term care, so we'll have to pay out of pocket. Full-time, in-home help is way too expensive, so I think our only option is to move him into a private memory-care facility."

"Oh," I said, letting it sink in.

"There are some not too far from here, near Lake George," she continued. "They're not cheap, but we could swing it if we sell the house. Unless you want to take over."

I assumed she was joking about the last part. I live in New York City, and I barely have the wherewithal to take care of myself, let alone a seventy-four-year-old with dementia. I am only twenty-six, which means I am essentially a larva. In contemporary America, childhood can last well into one's thirties, forties, and even fifties. I've seen it happen. And besides, my father doesn't even know who I am anymore. He hasn't recognized me for at least three or four years—I don't know exactly when I faded from his memory, but I know I'm gone. "Me? Move to Locust? You're kidding, right?"

"Only half kidding. Honestly, I think Dad would love it. He always liked you best."

"That's not true."

"Yes, it is. Mom likes me more; Dad likes you more." Nina said it as if everyone agreed on this point. It's true that my father and I were once exceptionally close, but that seemed like a lifetime ago. She went on: "It could be good for you, too. Change of scene, change of perspective. Maybe Gemma would let you work remotely?"

"Doubtful. It's hard to bring someone their matcha remotely."

She snorted. "Fair enough." In the silence that followed, I could almost hear her weighing her words. "Listen, Cricket. I know Catwood Pond is a complicated place for you. But there was a time when you loved it here. It was your favorite spot on earth."

"I can't, Nina. We both know I can't."

She didn't push any further, and we eventually came to a mutual decision: find a long-term-care facility for our father and sell the house to pay for it. Really it was Nina's decision—she is our family's de facto leader—but she is skilled at including me without actually expecting anything of me. She has always known how to trick me into thinking I have agency. In that respect, she's an exemplary older sister.

———————

So that is why I'm here now, traipsing through the mud-laden woods in my flimsy canvas sneakers. This weekend, we will tour two potential homes for Dad. Nina leaves for Stockholm in two months, so we don't have long to get organized, but she had the foresight to wait-list him a year ago, just in case, so we know he is guaranteed a spot. My sister is always a step ahead.

As I round the bend toward the house, I am hit by the scent of April—mossy and metallic, comforting and melancholy, woodsmoke on the cold wind. I reach the driveway and pass the carved-wood sign that bears our last name, Campbell. The nails holding it flush to the spruce tree have rusted, and dribbling sap has stained it over the years.

The undulating surface of the long dirt drive is still familiar underfoot. I avoid the deep grooves worn by tires, choosing instead to walk along the elevated ridge of matted grass between them. Before long, I emerge from the trees to see the illuminated windows of the house, unblinking, watching my advance. I sprint the final stretch like I used to as a child. Back then, it was to outrun the werewolves. Now, it's to outpace the ghosts.

Chapter 2

The outer screen door drifts closed behind me, having lost its eager snap years ago.

"Helloooo?" I kick off my soggy sneakers and sock-creep through the mudroom, nearly tripping on a rusty fishing rod as I inhale the unchanged smell of the house: cedar, smoke, a hint of mildew.

"Cricket?" I hear Nina call in response. As I enter the drowsy light of the galley kitchen, she turns from her cutting board and comes in for a careful hug, extending her arms like a zombie so as not to smear me with her garlic-covered fingers. As usual, she looks like a more organized version of me: smoother hair, sharper features, better posture. Though we spring from the same source, I have always felt that she is the shiny floor model, while I am the problematic prototype.

My father shuffles in from the great room and looks at me with interest. "Well, hello," he says with a quizzical smile, as if he's pleasantly surprised to have a guest.

"Dad, Cricket is here," Nina reminds him with excitement.

"Ah, yes, of course," he says, matching her tone. I know he doesn't know who I am, but he does a good job of feigning cheerful familiarity.

"Hi, Dad." It has been over two years since I saw him in person, when Nina brought him to the city for a few days—and when I realized he didn't know me anymore. Now, I wonder who I am to him. The word *Dad* doesn't seem to faze him one way or the other. Perhaps he has stopped ascribing meaning to it and just assumes it is his name. I open my arms, and as we hug, I am shocked by how diminished he is. Over Zoom, I have noted that a little less of him exists each time we talk, but onscreen, it's difficult to pinpoint where the recession is taking place. Now, in person, it's clear how slight he is. He once stood nearly six feet tall, but we're essentially the same height now. I may even be a hair taller.

"I think I've finally outgrown you, Dad."

"Impossible," he says. We step back to examine each other before he concedes, "Well, you may be longer in the thorax, but never in the legs."

His white hair has thinned. What's left of it encircles his head like the wispy pappi of a dandelion, ready to be carried away on the breeze. His eyebrows, however, are flourishing. They look like two scraggly animals that have hitched a ride on his brow.

"Still rocking the wide wale," I note, referring to his olive-green corduroy trousers.

"We love a wide wale," confirms Nina as she resumes her chopping and stirring, efficiently moving from counter to stove, stove to counter.

My father looks down to contemplate the texture of the corduroy. "The only problem is, I think these are women's pants." He turns to Nina. "Is it possible that they're women's pants?"

"Those are most certainly your pants, Dad."

"They're mine. But are they *meant* for a woman?"

Nina and I chortle as she assures him, "No! You've had them forever. They're definitely men's."

He accepts this answer without protest, and then turns his attention back to me. "So, my friend, where are you in from?"

"New York City."

"New York City!" He seems energized by the idea of it, as if it were an alluring concept rather than the place where he spent the first half of his life. "Is that where you're living now?"

I've always lived there, technically, except for a few stints spent trying on different lives: a summer as a ranch hand in Wyoming, a winter as a ski bum in Big Sky, a spring as a ceramicist's assistant in New Mexico, and another winter as a waitress in the Florida Keys. Even if he didn't have Alzheimer's, I wouldn't blame him for not being able to keep track of me, given how aimless I've been since I dropped out of college six years ago.

"Yes," I answer. "I drove all the way up from New York. Five hours. Plus the time it took me to walk here from the main road."

"Oh no." Nina halts her chopping. "You got stuck?"

"It was inevitable. My car might as well be a go-kart."

"You drove the Raisin?" she asks, referring to the unfortunate purple-brown hue of my jalopy. "No chance of that car making it up the road. The mud is really bad this year."

"If you visit during mud season, you must really mean it," I respond, looking to bring the moment home, but I can tell my father does not recognize his own famous adage.

For a second, I feel a stab of sadness, and I clench down on it. Alzheimer's is a devious affliction. Not necessarily for the people who have it—who can say what their experience is, ultimately?—but for those who witness its machinations: a forgotten name or sacred memory, the lost thread of a story, the endlessly repeated questions. The ground is always shifting beneath us. Every time I speak to my father, I brace for minor heartbreak, but it still sneaks up on me.

"We can call someone to pull you out tomorrow," says Nina. "Do you want to go get your suitcase?"

"No need. I brought my desert-island items." I hold up my lumpy tote bag. "Excuse me for a moment. I'm going to primp." They know this is a joke. No one primps around here—it's a no-makeup, no-hairdryers, no-fuss kind of place.

As I leave the kitchen, I see the neatly painted sign my father created for our childhood dog, who had a penchant for nicking food off the table—or sometimes right out of our hands.

Crumpet's Rule
On the plate?
You must wait.
If it drops,
Lick your chops.

Crumpet died sixteen years ago, but her rule remains. I pass through the narrow doorway that leads to the great room, where the stone fireplace ripples with warmth, the flames casting spasmodic shadows on the ceiling, whose dark wooden beams are sturdy as ever. This house is well over a century old and was built according to the tastes of a long-gone generation that flocked to the Adirondacks in the late 1800s, erecting camps on the many lakes and ponds that dot the region. The Rockefellers and their ilk owned stately, sprawling properties, but more understated ones, like ours, were the norm. Many still don't have electricity or road access, which makes our main house—which is equipped with both—relatively modern. But it's nothing fancy, and it still bears the look and layout of a by-gone age: constructed from heavy spruce logs, with exposed timber dominating the interior. Today, people build houses with airy, light-filled kitchens that open to fluid living-dining spaces. But here, the aesthetic is darker and more cordoned off. All of the rooms in this house have doors, designations, decisiveness. They don't flow; they function. They endure.

I ascend the worn wooden staircase, whose landing jogs left and then leads up to a small central hallway. My room has a set of bunk beds, a separate twin bed, a single window that peers toward the pond, and a steeply sloped ceiling that I smack my head on every time I return. The walls are paneled with knotty pine, giving it the feel of a tree house or a squirrel's drey, cozy and contained, if a bit claustrophobic. I switch on the wobbly ceramic lamp that sits on the dresser. There is a framed photo of me and Nina standing on the porch of this house. I must have been around ten, with braces and a Speedo tan, which means Nina would have been sixteen. I am dramatically mugging for the camera, while Nina looks as though she is barely tolerating having her photo taken. She has one foot up on the railing as she ties her running sneakers. In those days, she was always either about to go for a run or just coming back from one. She rarely stood still.

Beside the photo sits a wooden box (also pine, always pine) with a *C* carved on the lid. Technically, *C* stands for Christine, my real name, but my nickname took hold almost as soon as I was born, because, as the story goes, I never cried—I chirped. The contents of the box have not shifted in the last decade: a tangle of woven friendship bracelets, a hair clip that's missing a few teeth, a smattering of coins, and a ring made out of a fishing fly with magenta feathers. I slip it on my middle finger, where it still fits perfectly. At the bottom of the box sits a slightly faded Polaroid. A blond teenager is airborne, having just jumped off a huge boulder by the edge of the pond. One of his legs kicks sideways and his wavy hair extends straight up over his head as gravity does its work. I remember waiting for just the right moment to snap this shot. Somewhere, there is an identical photo of me, taken by him. But that one is lost.

I remove the ring, put it back in the box, and slam the lid closed. Suddenly feeling cold, I move to the closet in search of a sweater. When I open it, I am confronted with the red swimsuit I used to wear as a lifeguard. It is faded now and starchy to the touch, its elasticity eroded. On the floor, my old Birkenstocks sit, bearing the imprints of my sweaty teenage feet. I take a green sweatshirt from a hanger, and as I pull my head through the neck, I notice the surprise that Nina has left on the pillow of the twin bed: it's Dandy, my beloved stuffed lion on whom I performed so many medical procedures (a tail reattachment, an eye replacement, a fluff realignment) that he now looks like an abstract approximation of a feline.

My phone lights up on top of the dresser, and I take a quick look at my texts. Nothing from Dylan, which is no surprise. We see each other when we see each other, without expectation. But I do believe he appreciates me, on some level, at least some of the time. And I feel the same way about him, more or less. There's a comfort to what we have. A sufficient compatibility. "It's not nothing," as he likes to say.

I know from experience that when people love you—*really* love you—they can end up in peril. So a long time ago, I resolved to date only people who didn't quite love me. It's not that they didn't *like* me, but there was no possibility of their making any kind of major effort or sacrifice on my behalf. To this day, I prefer a partner who values himself more than he values me. That way, I can protect us both.

———

"I'm glad to see Dandy is thriving," I say as I reenter the kitchen.

"He might be indestructible." Nina grins. "I found him in the attic. Never go up there, by the way. Unless you like mouse poop."

"Nothing wrong with a little mouse poop!" my father calls from the dining room. "It's fortifying."

Nina hands me two plates, and I carry them to the table where Dad is already seated and wearing an adult-sized bib whose pattern showcases a dizzying number of tropical fish.

"That's nice," I say. "Is it new?"

"New-ish," says Nina, settling at the head of the table. "And he looks great in it. Don't you, Dad?"

"It's very attractive," my father confirms, admiring his accessory. I realize that even if we had put a bib on him a decade ago, long before it was necessary, he would not have objected; nor would he have objected the decade before that. He has always been game for frivolity, delighted to oblige our whims and happy to laugh at himself. The opposite of our mother, who is ruthlessly goal-oriented and believes that any form of relaxing will lead to ruin.

"So what's the latest? What's been going on here?" I ask.

"Here? Mostly just birds," says my father. "Magnificent red birds."

"Cardinals," Nina specifies.

"That's right. Cardinals. We have all manner of wildlife here," he explains, as if I'm visiting this area for the first time. Then he whispers, as if disclosing a secret: "And soon it will be time to swim!"

Nina offers him a bowl of grated Parmesan.

"What in god's name . . . ?" My father examines the feathery shreds.

"It's Parmesan. You love Parmesan."

"Looks like Grandfather's eyebrows," he says conclusively before dumping a spoonful onto his plate.

He's not wrong, I think, although I have no idea which "Grandfather" he is referring to—his or mine. I only knew one of my grandparents—my mother's mother—and she died when I was five.

"The thing about surviving the winter here is that you must love to read, which I do. And you should also have a dog, which we don't. Do we?" my father asks Nina, who shakes her head and replies: "Just the cat."

"The cat, of course. And the wildlife. Just last week, a bear tore through our garbage bins . . ."

He begins a story, and Nina fact-checks him as he goes. ("That was last year.") I know she feels it's important to keep him tied to the truth with regular reminders and corrections, but I don't see the point. Even before he had Alzheimer's, my father never let himself be inhibited by facts. To the contrary, his creative interpretation of events always enhanced his storytelling. His reality has always been an abstract work of art; and perhaps that's true for all of us.

My father finishes his yarn, and then asks, "Is there anything more satisfying than a potato?" as he takes a bite of cauliflower.

This time, Nina doesn't have the heart to correct him, so we just nod in agreement and exchange an amused glance. Alzheimer's is not funny, except when it is, which is often. It has the capacity to be both devastating and hilarious, and those who witness it learn to live in limbo, because there's nowhere else to live.

As Nina and I catch up, Dad does a convincing job of following along. He nods and laughs when we do, though it's clear he doesn't always get our references or grasp whom we're snickering about. Nowadays, I only have superficial knowledge of the people in this town, but in the four years since Nina moved here to take care of our father, she has gotten a fuller picture. Still, there is not much local gossip to report.

"The Seavey house still hasn't sold," she says. "That's all I've got: news about what *hasn't* happened. Off-season is lethally boring here. I'll be glad for a change of scene."

Nina always had a meticulous plan for her life, and moving back to Locust was never part of it—but even she hadn't seen the pandemic coming. When the first cases of COVID were reported, she had been well-ensconced in her PhD program in Boston. But as 2020 progressed, we began to worry more about our father. His memory had been dwindling for a while, and when he backed his car out of the garage without remembering to open the door, it was clear he should not be living on his own any longer. Finding adequate at-home help was not feasible in those early days of the pandemic—the exposure risk was too high, as was the expense. So Nina quickly pivoted, relocating to Catwood Pond and arranging to write her dissertation from here while keeping an eye on our dad. Not long after, he was formally diagnosed with Alzheimer's.

At the time, I was working on a ranch in Wyoming, and though my responsibilities were few, the idea of returning to Locust never crossed my mind. Plus, Nina had stepped up without hesitation, and we all knew—without even having to discuss it—that she was the right woman for the job.

"More?" says Nina, offering me the bottle of Malbec we have nearly finished. Before I can answer, I feel a cloud of fur brush past my legs, and suddenly there is an animal on the table.

"Our beauty," says Dad, bopping the cat on the head. Dominic is a Maine coon of unknown age and origin. He appeared at the house the summer I was twelve and never left. That makes him at least fifteen, though he could be twice that for all we know. His voluminous coat gives him the look of a wolverine, and I notice that some fur has begun to clump around the base of his tail. For a time, he was my best friend. Now, he looks at me with skepticism.

"There you are!" I hold out my hand to stroke his forehead, but he dodges it. Maybe he doesn't recognize me, or maybe I've lost my touch. For most of my childhood, I was obsessed with animals and determined to become a veterinarian, but that dream fell by the wayside when I dropped out of school.

"Hey!" Nina snaps her fingers toward the cat as he nips a piece of chicken off my father's plate. Nina is not an animal person. "Stop it, Dom!"

"It's quite alright," says my father, giving the cat a head scratch. "We have an understanding."

"I guess Crumpet's Rule does not apply to cats," I note. "But I'm glad to see Dom's appetite is still robust. And that coat is glorious."

"Oh yes. She's a very handsome girl," says Dad, whose grasp of animal gender was always tenuous and is now completely fluid.

"*He,*" says Nina. "He's a boy."

"A boy?" My father looks incredulous. "With a name like Dawn?"

Nina and I burst into laughter, and my father slips another hunk of chicken to the cat.

"Carl will have his work cut out for him," says Nina, referring to a neighbor who has agreed to take Dominic when my dad moves to his new residence. Neither of the two homes we're touring tomorrow accepts animals, and Nina is in no rush to take the cat to Sweden. I certainly can't handle a pet right now, though the idea of re-homing Dom makes me sad. Or maybe it's the idea of re-homing my dad that is actually weighing on me. It's all mixed up together.

A lull settles over the table, and after a moment, Nina says, "Okay, Dad. Let's get you ready for bed."

"Already?" I look at my watch. It's only 8:30.

"He goes to bed at nine o'clock sharp, and he needs a bath tonight," she explains.

"A bath?" My father looks appalled. "During *mud season*? What's the point?"

He's joking now, and I am warmed by the fact that he is still himself. There are plenty of things he can't tell you—his birthday (March 1), the day of the week (Friday), what county we're in (Herkimer)—but his fundamental personality is intact, his sense of humor alive and well. And though he can't tell a long story without getting lost along the way, he can still deploy relics of his once-sprawling vocabulary: *querulous, bombastic, arcane, rambunctious, barf.* He still has moments of sharpness, his wit bubbling up to the surface.

"Do you need help? Is there anything I can do?" I ask as Nina removes our father's bib and helps him up from his chair.

"Don't worry. It's kind of a process."

"You sure?"

She waves me off casually. "We have our routine."

They shuffle out of the room arm in arm, and I am again hit by a pang of sadness as I envision the scene around me dissolving. No more dinners, no more cat, no more house, and, eventually, no more Dad. Before the sting behind my eyes can transmute into tears, I stand up and start to clear the table.

The kitchen here is functional and free of frills. The fact that we have a dishwasher at all is something to celebrate, although like most of the appliances in this house, it is decades old. When I turn it on, it hisses ominously and then begins to lurch, as if something inside is trying to escape. I wipe down the scratched butcher-block counters, put the kettle on, and start poking around in the drawers and cabinets, whose doors don't quite line up with their frames. Even with Nina living here full-time, not much has changed. She has kept the lights on and the water running, but when it comes to home improvements, she has insisted that she doesn't need "another project," the implication being that my father's care was project enough. Not to mention her PhD. From my vantage point, she has managed it all with her signature grace.

I search the contents of the cabinets: crackers, peanuts, oatmeal, Grape-Nuts, Metamucil. This is an exceptionally fiber-focused household. On one shelf, I come across a tub of crusty powdered Crystal Light with an expiration date of 1992, and eventually, I find the herbal tea.

By the time Nina returns forty-five minutes later, I am drowsing on the couch in front of the fireplace, where embers pop intermittently. She collapses into the armchair beside me, her body seeming to deflate with exhaustion.

"Thank you," I say.

"For what?"

"For taking such good care of him."

Nina waves me off for the second time tonight. This is how she accepts gratitude, compliments, offers of help—or rather, refuses to accept them. Nina is living proof of the theory that eldest daughters carry the weight of the whole family on their shoulders. Dutiful and disciplined—that's what she is. I don't think anyone would say the same about me.

"I wish I could have been more helpful these past few years," I say.

"Well, you're here now." Nina takes a sip of my tepid tea, then sticks her tongue out in disgust.

"It's a little late, don't you think?" I ask, wanting her to admonish me, or at least hold me accountable.

She shrugs in soft confirmation, but leaves it at that. We sit in the warm silence for a minute before I ask plainly: "Am I selfish?"

"No. You're twenty-six. There's a difference."

"But you stepped up. You've been there for him." Nina is six years older than I am, and while we were growing up, I always viewed her as neither child nor adult. She occupied a liminal space between the two groups; she could speak both languages. And although I eventually realized that actual adults were full of it, I never came to doubt Nina. She was my guide to the world, and even now, she remains my true north.

I always hoped I would become more like her with time, but as I reach certain ages she has already traversed, I see that our differences were never the result of our age gap. I have no chance of catching up or emulating her; we are on different tracks altogether.

"Cricket, I'm not going to guilt-trip you, if that's what you're fishing for. I had the flexibility to come and live here during the pandemic. It made sense, logistically. But now, with this opportunity in Sweden, I'm ready to do something for *myself*, to prioritize my own needs."

Needs—what a concept. I've never even been able to identify mine, let alone articulate and assert them. The fact that Nina can do all three of these things strikes me as superhuman.

"My god, you're evolved," I say. Nina has spent the last few years doing what is known as "the work": addressing her core childhood wounds, reparenting herself, integrating the aspects of her personhood that had once been at odds. I figure she's done enough therapy for all of us, and her progress will rub off on me at some point.

"Well, to be honest, I also need a break from all this," she says, waving vaguely toward our father's bedroom. "Caregiving is . . . a lot. And I think I've done what I can. I'm ready to have some fun again. I'm ready to be like you."

"What does that mean?" I wait for her to say *irresponsible*, but she doesn't.

"I don't know . . . freewheeling, spontaneous, adventurous."

These sound like compliments, but I know there's a less generous way to describe me: aimless, impulsive, noncommittal.

Nina gives me a sympathetic smile. "You don't need to feel bad, Cricket. You've been living your life. You're busy."

It *seems* like I'm busy, but really, I'm just lost. "I guess. But it's not like I'm off resolving the climate crisis. I work at a wellness company that occasionally poisons people by accident."

"What?"

"We had to recall our bee-pollen elixir last month. It's fine now."

"Well, don't be so hard on yourself. You've come a long way. And your life looks really fun to me—on Instagram, anyway."

Everyone's life looks fun on social media; that's the sorcery of it. Your soul may be slowly decaying, but there's a filter for that.

"We're doing the right thing—moving Dad to a home," Nina continues. "Maybe it's a little soon, but he'll have a chance to acclimate and find his groove. If we wait until he's really far gone, it will be too jarring for him."

"You're right. It just snuck up on me—the severity of his dementia. I always thought I would have a chance to mend things, but it never seemed like the right time. I can't believe it's been nine years since I was last here."

"I can," says Nina.

"I'm not even sure what I'm avoiding anymore—Dad's illness or Seth's memory."

For a moment, I feel myself return to that night—the frozen pond, the icy blue air, the sharp winter stars. It was ten years ago, but for me, it's still happening. If something doesn't shift soon, I could spend my whole life in this rut, just drifting from thing to thing, avoiding the possibility of heartbreak, avoiding possibility altogether. A hollowed-out, half-assed kind of life.

"Cricket? Do you think about him a lot?" When I'm slow to answer, Nina clarifies: "Seth, I mean."

"I know who you mean. And yes, I think about him all the time."

"Well, maybe this will be the closure you need," says Nina. "Finally selling the house. Really turning the page—and letting Seth go."

I know she means to comfort me, but it's not exactly closure that I'm seeking. It's something more complex: acceptance, integration, a metamorphosis. I want to be able to acknowledge the tragedy without reliving it. I want to be able to remember Seth without being haunted by him.

"Maybe," I say.

"It will be bittersweet, leaving here. But it's just a place. There are plenty of other places to live, things to see, jobs to do, people to love. Life is long, Cricket. The best things are still ahead of us, I promise."

When I look at her, she meets my gaze confidently. Nina possesses something I have never had: a determination to thrive. When I am struggling to believe in myself, I can always believe in her, and that's usually enough to get me through.

After she has gone to bed and the fire has died, I walk out to the porch that wraps around three sides of the house. The moon is on the wane, but its light is strong enough to silver the treetops and reveal the ice-covered pond down the hill. The landscape is still, as if waiting for something. My exhale creates a bloom of steam in the darkness as I descend the porch steps. Careful not to slip, I make my way across the sloped grass to the path, rippled with wet roots, that leads down to the water. There is still a drift of snow against the boathouse, and the wide rectangle of the dock is wet underfoot. Its splintered slats need replacing, but that will be someone else's burden to bear once we sell the house.

The end of the dock hovers a foot above the thin ice below. Leaning down, I turn an ear toward the surface. From deep under the ice comes a muted sound, like the noise a cartoon space-gun makes: *pew-pew-pew!* Fast and insistent. *Pew-pew, pew-pew!*

It's the sound of the thaw: water seething around contracting ice. It's the moaning and cracking of the pond as it wrestles with itself, reluctantly softening from solid to liquid. In the distance, a heavy crack rends the air and my heart leaps. Again, it's just ice shifting, but for a moment, I think I see a single headlight coming toward me from the distant shore.

It's an illusion, I tell myself. But there's an urgent energy in the damp air. Something wants me to listen; something wants to emerge.

Chapter 3

"So what did you think, Dad?" Nina asks from behind the wheel of her Subaru.

"Very nice," he says, gazing out the passenger-side window as we zip along the state route that leads from civilization back to our town.

"And . . . ?"

He looks at her blankly. He had seemed perfectly affable and at ease while we toured the two memory-care facilities, but now that we're back in the car, it's clear he did not really understand the intention of the visits.

"Which one did you like better?" Nina presses.

"Hmmm . . ." He doesn't elaborate. I sense that he can't distinguish between the two.

"Did you like the one with the screening room?" I offer from the back seat. "The movie theater?"

"Oh sure. You've got to have that."

"Figures. That's the more expensive one!" Nina bats his knee.

We drive for a few moments. I stare at my dad's wispy hair, his thin left shoulder in his plaid shirt. I miss him. I've missed him for a long time, but now there is more intensity to it. He turns his head as far as he can and says in my direction, "So when will you be moving in there?"

I lock eyes with Nina in the rearview mirror.

"No, Dad," she says gently. "Remember? Those are potential homes for *you*. Because you're going to move to a new place with lots of people and doctors and interesting things to do."

"Me?"

"Yes! Don't you think you would like to live there? With the movie theater?"

"That place? Certainly not."

"Why not?" she persists.

He furrows his brow. "It's full of old people."

Nina and I stifle our laughter, and I ask from the back seat, "How old do you think you are, Dad?"

He shakes his head. He may not have the correct number (seventy-four), but he has an answer: "Not *that* old."

Perhaps he is right. Maybe after a certain point, we get to decide how old we are. Or maybe there comes a moment when time starts sliding in all directions, revealing itself as an illusion, rendering age irrelevant.

I don't blame my father for not being enticed by the facilities we've seen. I found one of them bone-chillingly depressing. All the residents there seemed to be awaiting something—and not something good. The second one had a slightly more cheerful ambiance, but it still struck me as the wrong place for our father. It had no charm, no whimsy, and although the staff seemed perfectly capable of caring for my father, I wanted them to do more than just accommodate him—I wanted them to *appreciate* him.

Maybe Nina and I have underestimated just how attached our father is to his house, which is undeniably his natural habitat. Dad was raised in New York City, but he had spent all his summers in the Adirondacks. By the time he inherited the camp from his uncle in his late twenties, he was hooked on a visceral level. He always described our summers by Catwood Pond as "the great exhale." He said our bodies knew where we belonged; sometimes it just took a while for our minds to catch up.

"Well, I thought Orchard Hills was fantastic," coaxes Nina. I know she wants him to acquiesce so that she can move to Stockholm with a clear conscience. "Everyone says great things about it, and there are so many activities, great food, lots of eligible *ladies*."

My father waves his hand dismissively, not taking the conversation seriously, which is fine. It's not really his decision, but one that Nina and I will make—or rather, have already made. We turn onto the county road, whose two lanes are dappled with late-afternoon sun. Cresting and dipping through the woods, we wend our way towards Locust, where the road finally flattens out and intersects with Main Street. It's a blink-and-you'll-miss-it kind of town, perched on the south bank of Lake Locust, which draws tourists in the summer but dozes through the off-season. We don't see a soul as we pass the turn-off to the lake beach where I used to lifeguard, then Sal's hardware store, the Locust Inn, Deb's Depot, and Lorne's All-Day Diner. As we exit the center of town, we pass the community tennis courts. Puddles are pooled in the service boxes, and the posts look naked without their nets. I wonder if I can still swing a racquet.

A few minutes later, we reach the turnoff to our road. My little car is still there, nestled in the mud where I abandoned it—but there's something new on the windshield.

"Wait, slow down," I say. Nina stops and I hop out to examine the note that is tucked beneath the windshield wiper. In a messy scrawl, it says:

Happy to help pull you out. From Carl

No contact information. I crawl back into the car and ask, "Do we know a Carl?"

"He's our best friend," says Dad.

I look to Nina for verification.

"He's our neighbor. You know, the one who is adopting Dominic? He owns the cabin on the west bay—the old Ainsworth place," says Nina, skillfully navigating through the mud on our drive up the hill. I can picture the cabin. Catwood Pond only has about ten camps along its shores, and I know them all from memory. "Moved in about three years ago. Mid-fifties, maybe. Lives alone. I don't know him that well, but he comes by every few weeks to shoot the shit with Dad. It's kind of sweet."

"He's a skilled woodworker," adds my father. He seems to know more about Carl than he knows about himself.

"He's a former contractor. Now he makes custom furniture," adds Nina. "And he is always happy to help with odd jobs."

"Like a handyman?"

"Yeah, but for free."

"So he just does favors . . . for no reason?" I don't know why the idea of altruism arouses my suspicion. Maybe my life in New York City has warped me, but I'm not accustomed to people doing things without some kind of agenda or expectation of quid pro quo.

"He probably gets some satisfaction out of it. And he really likes Dad. Like he said, they're friends," says Nina, turning into our driveway.

"I didn't know Dad had friends."

"Of course I have friends!" our father interjects. "More friends than you could even dream of."

Since his diagnosis, my father's social network has atrophied. People aren't sure how to interact with him, so they just stop interacting at all. I don't blame them. I'm his daughter, and although I'm ashamed of it, I've avoided his illness, too. I backtrack, saying, "I know you have lots of friends, Dad. Carl sounds nice."

———

Later that evening, as the light falls, I find my father dozing in his favorite armchair, its leather shell cracked from years of wear. Beside him is the oversized cribbage board that doubles as a side table. Despite the many things he has forgotten, he still remembers the rules of this card game, according to Nina. It makes me think that there are chambers of his brain that are still fully functional, and maybe we should give him more credit. Maybe we should focus on what is still there, rather than what is lost. I sit down in the chair opposite him and start crawling my fingers along the holes in the table. Its surface is weathered, but with some refinishing, it could have a whole new life. Maybe with some refinishing, *I* could have a whole new life.

My father opens his eyes and sees me examining the table. "I made that," he says. I know this isn't true. It came with the house when he inherited it. This is where Nina would usually correct him, but I decide to go along for the ride, see what he comes up with.

"You did?"

"Yes. I built a lot of things here. The boathouse, for one. And the dock. In fact, I think I built this whole place."

It's a version of the truth. My father inherited this camp from an uncle when he was twenty-eight, not much older than I am now. Given its state of disrepair at the time, most would have considered it more of a burden than a boon, but Dad embraced the property and spent the next decade fixing it up. A civil engineer who specialized in water systems, he spent his weeks working for the City of New York; but he poured his long weekends and vacations into this property. He rebuilt the boathouse; revamped the guest cabin; fixed the dilapidated lean-to; and added running water and electricity to the main house. By the time he met my mother in his late thirties, the property was fully habitable, if a bit spartan. But most importantly: it was his own.

"I have all kinds of projects I'd like to work on when I get a chance," he says wistfully. "I really should rebuild the dock this summer."

I see no reason to contradict him. What's the harm in letting him think he's still capable of such a project? That he will still live here when summer rolls around?

He looks at me with renewed interest, as if he is trying to place me: "So, how long are you staying with us?"

"Just until tomorrow," I remind him.

"Is that all?"

"I wish it were longer. But I have to get back to New York."

"New York City? Is that where you're living now?"

I nod. Everyone talks about Alzheimer's as a decline, but that's not quite accurate. It's not a slope, but a spiral, like water circling a drain. Topics are trod over and over; questions are repeated; stories are retold. Maybe the word *decline* is too negative, too judgmental. Maybe there is a version of dementia that is liberating. I wonder what it would be like to be free of my memories, unburdened by the baggage of the past.

"Dad, do you remember Seth?"

"Seth . . ."

"Seth Atwater. My friend who lived here one summer." This is silly.

How could he remember Seth when he doesn't even remember me? But I go on, venturing a detail that might activate his memory. "He rode a snowmobile?"

"Hmmm, it's possible. I'm not sure."

I'm relieved. My father loved Seth and had been devastated by the accident, and maybe even more devastated by what came after—the distance that emerged between us. *Estranged* isn't the right word. It's more . . . *stranged*. While our relationship had once been so loving and natural—even conspiratorial—everything between us has gone, well, strange. I didn't mean for it to last nine years, but before we could find a way to truly reconnect, his Alzheimer's set in. Since then, it's like we've been on two separate ice floes, drifting in opposite directions. But I'm relieved that he is no longer tormented by the memories that still plague me.

He is quiet for a while before he asks, "You mean the blond kid?"

I nod. Seth was blond.

"Oh yes, I see him from time to time. He comes by."

I smile. There is a certain sweetness about my father's confusion. He picks up his abandoned glass of ginger beer from the cribbage table and takes a long sip. "Ahhh, that's good. Come, try a little fizz." He holds the glass toward me, and I take a sip. It's lukewarm but still snappy.

"Do you taste that spice?"

"Yep. It kicks you right in the esophagus."

He laughs and says, "Let me get you one. We have all kinds of wonderful drinks here."

As he shuffles toward the kitchen, my sadness shifts to curiosity. What if Alzheimer's isn't just a slow death? What if it's another dimension entirely—an ascension, even? We humans are so fixated on our minds that we see their loss as a tragedy. But what if it's a gift? Maybe the erosion of memory clears space for something truer. Maybe the intellect gets in the way of the heart, until little by little, it doesn't.

How freeing, I think. *For him—but also for me.* Maybe we no longer need to be tied by this gloom. Maybe it's advantageous that we have grown apart in recent years. Maybe we can see each other with a freshness. I can take him as he is, right now; and he can experience me as someone entirely new. A chance at a do-over (and over, and over). A chance to rewrite the narrative.

My father returns empty-handed, having forgotten why he went into the kitchen. He settles back into his chair, claps his hands on his corduroyed thighs, and shoots me a warm smile. "So, how long are you staying with us?"

Chapter 4

Nina has arranged for Carl to pull my car out of the mud the next day, and around noon, his blue pickup truck rolls into our driveway. From my room, I can hear him greet Nina and then my father, whose enthusiasm is palpable. "Carl, my good man!" I hear him say.

When I come down the stairs, they are all in the great room. Carl has a dark beard and shoulder-length hair that's gray at the temples. He wears a blue canvas shirt and workpants in a darker shade of blue. Blue on blue. His outfit is not unlike what many of my male friends in the city wear on a typical day, even though they work in graphic design or music production. Carl seems to wear his Carhartts out of actual pragmatism, rather than to build street cred.

"Hi, I'm Cricket," I say, shaking his calloused hand. "Thank you for helping with my car."

"Bold move—driving up here in that little hatchback."

"Yeah, I didn't quite make it across the finish line."

"Close enough," he offers kindly. "It shouldn't take much to pull you out."

It's time for me to leave if I want to get back to the city at a reasonable hour, and the melancholy of saying goodbye begins to set in. Not wanting to get emotional in front of Carl, I keep my farewells to Nina and my father brief. I plan to come back in a few weeks to help tie up loose ends and move my father into his chosen home. There will be plenty of time for crying and reminiscing then, but for now, I have a long drive and a busy week ahead.

"No bags?" asks Carl.

I have survived the weekend on the contents of my linen tote bag, supplemented by my old sweatshirt and a moth-eaten wool sweater that belongs to no one but the house.

"I travel light," I say, and Carl gives an approving nod as we head outside to his truck. I'm about to open the passenger door when I realize the seat is occupied by a large wolfish dog, who blinks at me with equanimity.

"Cynthia," Carl says, snapping his fingers and pointing to the back seat of the truck's cab. The dog complies.

"Thank you, Cynthia," I say, climbing into my seat and offering her my hand. She sniffs it, seems unoffended, and then pushes her forehead into my palm, inviting me to scratch her.

"Cynthia is a great name," I say.

"I named her after my mom. Well, my mom's middle name. She died a few years back, and I got this dog right after. I was in kind of a weird place. So yeah, now I have a dog named Cynthia." Carl throws the truck into reverse, then pulls forward up the driveway. His truck is worn-in but tidy. A string of Buddhist mala beads snakes around the neck of the rearview mirror.

"Well, that's a nice tribute," I say. "How does Cynthia feel about cats?"

Creases form at the corners of Carl's eyes as he smiles. "She's scared of them. Dominic will rule the roost in no time."

"It's really nice of you to take him in," I say.

"It's no bother. Happy to have the little guy," says Carl. We bump over the threshold of the driveway and onto the road, whose surface has hardened since I arrived. "So you came all the way up here just for the weekend?"

"Yeah. We visited two homes for my Dad. Orchard Hills and . . ."

"Dunbridge."

"That's right."

"Which one did he like?"

"Neither," I say. "He doesn't want to move. And he was appalled by how old the residents were."

Carl gives an amused snort. "I'm sure Arthur will come around. But I'll miss having him on the pond. He's an insightful guy. We've had some interesting chats over the years." We climb the hill and then start to descend again. "Did you ever think of moving up here? Looking after your dad when Nina leaves?"

It dawns on me that Carl doesn't know the reason I don't come here. He doesn't know that I'm a pariah in this town. He doesn't know that I'm irresponsible and unforgivable. He doesn't know *anything* about me. I simply say, "Nina thinks he'll be better off in a residence with medical staff and all that."

I'm struck that, based on his first impression, Carl assumes I'm capable of taking care of my dad. But suddenly it hits me: maybe I am. I feel a pit in my stomach as I realize that I'm only thinking about it now that it's too late. Maybe my father really *isn't* ready to move. Maybe we should be weighing his opinion more heavily. Maybe this is all happening too fast, too soon. But we've already made our plans.

"Right. And you're busy. I hear you've got a glamorous life in the Big Apple," says Carl as he slows the truck.

"I'm not sure I would call it glamorous. But yes, it's a life."

We reach the bottom of the hill where my car waits, and Carl maneuvers to the side of the road.

"There she is," I say. "The Raisin."

Carl nods. "If you could throw the Raisin into neutral, this should be quick." I hop out and do as he asks while he pulls a tow strap from the back of his truck and hooks it up to something under the bumper of my car. I should learn how to do these things, I tell myself, but driving has never been my forte.

I stand to the side of the road and Carl gets back behind the wheel of his truck. As he pulls forward, my tires slide easily out of the muddy grooves that had swallowed them two days ago.

"You made that look easy. Thank you so much."

"Happy to do it," he says. He seems unhurried, but I look at my watch and say, "Well, I'd better get on the road."

Cynthia has already resumed her position in the passenger seat of his truck, but Carl waits for me to get settled and start my car before he makes a U-turn that orients him back up the hill.

"Godspeed!" he calls and gives an efficient wave as we pass each other, headed back to our respective lives.

Chapter 5

_____

It takes me six hours to reach Manhattan, thanks to Sunday-evening traffic. Dylan and I have plans to meet at my apartment so we can order ramen and watch brain-numbing reality shows. I'm looking forward to a quiet night before the week begins, but when I walk through the door, I see there are a bunch of people in my living room. Two of them are my roommates; one of them is Dylan; and the others are people I vaguely recognize but can't name.

"Criiiiickeeeeet!" A tipsy Olivia greets me with over-the-top enthusiasm, as if I've been gone for two months rather than two nights. She, Tasha, and I live in a basement-level apartment on Canal Street. Our bedrooms have no windows, but we all agreed that natural light is a luxury, not a necessity. It's something you get in New York once you've really made it, along with a dishwasher and a washer/dryer. At twenty-six, we're not there yet.

"Hi, guys," I call, retreating to my bedroom. Dylan follows me, and as I put my things down, he pulls me toward him and kisses me, then lingers. I know that means he wants to have sex, but right now, I feel incapable of summoning any kind of enthusiasm. I start unpacking, and he gets the message.

"How was the drive?"

"Long."

"How's your dad?"

I don't know how to answer this question. My father is himself, but he's changing. He's alive, but he's dying. The ground is shifting, but in slow motion. There's nothing we can do about it, even if we wanted to. I'm tired, so I just say, "He's fine."

"Good." Dylan is satisfied with my answer and eager to rejoin the crowd in the living room, now that he knows I'm not in the mood to hook up.

"I wish you had come with me so you could have finally met him," I say.

"I met him that one time on Zoom," says Dylan, sounding defensive. "And he wouldn't have remembered me anyway, right?"

I feel every sinew in my body stiffen. I want to say, *He doesn't remember me either, but that's not a reason to discount him.* Does he really think the only reason to interact with someone is to have them acknowledge and validate you? It strikes me as an exceedingly myopic way to view relationships, a sad way of keeping social score. But maybe I'm being too harsh. Dylan's parents are in their late fifties and brimming with health. I can't expect him to know what I'm going through. I barely even know what I'm going through myself. So I try to give him the benefit of the doubt. "Yeah, you're probably right."

"And you know I had to work all weekend," he continues, but now, I wish he would stop talking and just order us some ramen.

Dylan works in ad sales, and when we met just over a year ago, I was attracted to how disarmingly normal he seemed. He was smart but not arrogant, ambitious but not grandiose, affectionate but not smothering. But lately, something has shifted. He spends more and more time on social media, and on multiple occasions, he has asked me to film him doing viral TikTok dances. I thought he was joking at first, but now I realize that he is actually attempting to become an influencer. He seems confident about his new career direction, even though he has no clear income stream. I didn't see this coming, and although people are allowed to change, sometimes that change is hard to watch. These days, Dylan seems to calibrate his efforts based on whether they will produce an image or a video that will generate likes, shares, or his favorite accolade: fire emojis. Maybe that's why he is so ambivalent about getting to know my father. Alzheimer's isn't exactly share-worthy.

Dylan is talking about a meme he finds particularly compelling, and I tune him out, pulling my chin-length hair into a low, stumpy ponytail. My brown roots are growing out, and the rest of it, which I bleached six months ago, has taken on a hay-like quality. I was happy when my new hair felt like a possible reinvention, but now I have no idea what to do with it, so I do nothing. My mother once told me I was too passive, but I prefer to think of myself as patient. Some problems solve themselves if you simply wait a while.

"Cricket!" I hear someone yell from the living room, and I follow the call. There are beer bottles all over the place, and something red and sticky has congealed on one corner of the coffee table. I flop down at the end of the stained couch, and someone offers me a vape, which I decline.

"My parents are so embarrassing," says a girl I don't know as she scrolls on her phone. "My dad just asked me if I know any nepo babies . . ."

Another of the unknowns tries to one-up her by saying, "Well, my dad is coming to town next week and he insists on taking a carriage ride in Central Park. Like, firstly, that's unethical. Secondly, it's for tourists. Thirdly, it's *cold* out . . ."

I want to shake her and say, "Just do it. Indulge him while you have time. You'll regret it if you don't." But I don't even know her name, let alone her situation. And more importantly: the advice I want to give her is really the advice I want to give myself. I don't actually want a carriage ride in Central Park, but I wish I could complain about my father making me do something like that. I wish he had the capacity to come into the city and embarrass me. I wish he could retain where I live, what I do, who I am. I wish he weren't disappearing.

Olivia stands up and grabs my hand. "We're going to Silicon Sally's. You're coming."

"There's no way. I'm exhausted." Silicon Sally's is a cocktail bar that specializes in artisanal moonshine. I hate it there. Olivia leans back with all her body weight to pull me up, but she's tiny, and I don't budge. "I just drove six hours, guys."

They all make noises of protest, but eventually I convince them I'm serious about staying in. As they grab their phones and throw on their jackets, Dylan looks at me. I can tell he wants to go out, despite our plans to watch trashy TV. And the ramen is still unordered.

"Go," I say.

"You sure? You don't want me to stay with you?" It's not a genuine offer; just a gesture so he can *say* he offered. But if I accept, he'll sulk for the rest of the night.

"You should go," I say. "I'm going to pass out soon, anyway."

He gives me a perfunctory kiss and then follows the others as they stream out. The door closes behind them, and I listen as their footsteps echo in the concrete stairwell before spilling out onto the street. Even six months ago, I would have happily followed them to the bar—or maybe led the charge. But lately, I'm finding that I rarely want to do what they do on any given night. Our interests are diverging, and it leaves me with a lonely feeling. Everyone always talks about finding "your people," "your tribe," "your chosen family." I don't mean to be ungrateful; I like my friends, and we keep each other entertained. But lately, I feel like more of a lone wolf—or maybe I'm just running with the wrong pack.

I rinse out a few bottles and take them over to the recycling bin, which is predictably full, so I place them on the floor with the rest of the overflow. My roommates have left three scented candles burning, and I blow them out, one by one. I have a vague feeling that, when it comes to my life, not only am I sitting on the sidelines, but I'm playing the wrong game altogether. As I look around at the leftover mess from the weekend, I think: *I'm ready to be something other than young.*

Chapter 6

On Monday morning when I enter my boss's office, she is hanging upside down from a metal apparatus that looks like a huge praying mantis.

"Do you want me to come back later?" I ask, unsure what I have interrupted.

"No, no. I'm just going to stay inverted while we do our check-in if that's cool with you. Need to let my chakras breathe a little."

"No problem," I say.

"Don't you ever get that urge to be upside down? It always helps energize my vessel."

I know Gemma well enough to know that her *vessel* is her body. And though I generally avoid speaking in her particular patois, I am fluent in it after working at Actualize, the wellness company she founded, for the past two years. When I met her, I was at a notably low point, working in the Theater District as a merch seller at *The Phantom of the Opera*. Before each show, I would traverse the aisles trying to sell as many mugs, masks, and T-shirts as I could before the lights went down and the synthesizers boomed. On my off days, I worked as a TaskRabbit doing odd jobs, and it was in this role that I was summoned to the home of Gemma Dwyer. She had just launched her company, and she needed help boxing up samples to send to key social media influencers. Gemma instructed me on how to artfully arrange the oud-scented soaps, the LED masks, the face mist infused with magnesium-rich water from a Japanese hot spring. We sealed each box with a twine bow and a lavender sprig, and over the course of the day, we got to talking. I had never met anyone quite like her. She seemed to have a cure for every ailment, a solution for every problem, a mantra for every worry. I was impressed by her confidence and conviction—two things I was lacking. When you are full of questions, you are drawn to people who look like answers.

When Gemma asked me to be her full-time administrative assistant, I was elated. It meant finally being on the path to a sustainable career. Gemma didn't care that I lacked a college degree and a coherent résumé. Her only prerequisite was that I believe unflinchingly in the mission of her company. And I did believe, at the beginning. After all, I was the one who applied the decal with the phrase WHAT WOULD YOUR BEST SELF DO? on the wall outside this very office. I was the one who ordered the linen tote bags inscribed with the same motto. I was convinced we would help make the world a better, healthier place—and that, through osmosis, I would become a better, healthier person. I didn't just drink the Actualize Kool-Aid—I chugged it.

Gemma was clear from the beginning: "We don't sell products; we sell *healing*." And I cannot deny that the consumer appetite for healing is insatiable these days. Our nervous systems are rattled; our auras are dim; our energy is erratic—everyone is convinced they're in peril. And then along comes Gemma to assure them there is hope. Whatever your ailment, real or imagined, there's a tincture for it, and if not a tincture, then an oil, a supplement, a tea, a bath salt, a crystal that you charge under the full moon and then put in your vagina, an ionic cocoon that helps you sweat out your demons, or a red-light mask that makes you look like a serial killer but feel like a deity. There is a filler you can inject into your face to "look as young as you feel"; and then there is a treatment to dissolve that filler once you realize you have overdone it.

But after two years, I no longer believe in Actualize's mission. I'm convinced that Gemma's version of wellness is really just a form of narcissism, a way to divide the body—sorry, the *vessel*—into infinite components that all beg to be lavished with money and attention. Did you know your earlobes need their own skincare regimen? And your kneecaps, too. You could spend all day exfoliating, lifting, moisturizing, resurfacing, deep conditioning, buffing, harmonizing, depilating, and rejuvenating your myriad bodily surfaces, but at the end of that day, your soul will still ache for what it really wants: freedom from the consumptive cycle of never feeling or looking quite good enough. We've conflated health with vanity. It's not that I don't believe in healing; I just don't believe you can buy it for $78 an ounce.

"How was your weekend?" I ask as I try to decide where to sit, given Gemma's current upside-down orientation. The taut skin of her face has turned fuchsia and her normally waist-length hair now pools onto the cream-colored rug. (Everything in this office is either beige or cream, and all the furniture has rounded edges because Gemma believes sharp corners are hostile to the psyche.) I choose a chair that allows me to face her, or at least face her knees.

"So nourishing," she says. "I went to a friend's farm on the North Fork. Did a ton of foraging and forest bathing and sea immersing." If you met Gemma today, you would assume she has always been a clean-living earth child whose energy field has been humming at full capacity since the day she was birthed. That's what she wants you to assume. But I know that much of this identity is self-styled, as is her accent, which sounds vaguely English but also Southern Californian, even though she grew up in a voluptuous McMansion in New Jersey. "What about you, mama? What did you get up to?"

"I visited my dad in the Adirondacks."

"Oh, that's right!" She makes an upside-down sympathy-face. "How is he?"

That question again. "Not great, but okay."

She puts her hand on her heart, and then her eyes light up with an idea. "Has he tried lion's mane? I've heard it's great for cognition. You know, I bet we could do a whole line for memory health. The dementia market is huge, and it's only going to grow as boomers age."

The dementia market. I decide not to be offended by her abrupt shift into business mode. She can't help it. In addition to being a self-proclaimed "healer" and "seeker," Gemma is the most cunning saleswoman I've ever met.

We eventually turn to the reason for the meeting, and as I give updates on our current projects—what is progressing, what has stalled—I realize there is not one item on my to-do list that is remotely interesting to me. My motivation has run dry. After two years, I am still stuck in my administrative role, and though I do have bigger ideas I've tried to share recently, Gemma doesn't see me as a *creative*. That's her domain.

"Are we set for the rollout of Twelve by Twelve?" she asks, referring to the new product line we're launching: a twelve-step skincare routine designed for tweens. Gemma believes you're never too young to start addressing aesthetic anxieties you don't yet have.

I check my list, feeling my moral core tremble in objection. "All set. Preview event is this Friday; digital and out-of-home campaigns roll out next Tuesday. Influencers are set to start teasing it this weekend."

"Perfect."

We run through a few more items and once our meeting concludes, I finally notice the objects piled on Gemma's desk: a soap on a rope, an old-timey wooden bucket, a linen rag, and a few other items.

"What's all this?"

"Oh! Let me show you." Gemma raises her arms, and the plank of her body flips upright on the inversion machine. She goes completely still for a moment, and I worry she might be unconscious; but she soon regains her equilibrium, unhooks her ankles, and rushes over to the desk. "For Holiday, merch is working on a Back-to-Basics Bundle. Close your eyes." She waits until I comply. "Okay, picture it's the 1800s. You're a pioneer woman, crossing the country in a wagon, sleeping around a fire, bathing in streams—but make it luxury. Now open your eyes." She picks up the items one by one. "All you need is a gorgeous boar-bristle body brush, a natural sea sponge, a linen hair towel, and a handmade ash bucket. So fucking cute, right?"

I must be making a face because she reacts to my expression with: "Uh-oh. Our resident skeptic isn't sold?"

"It's just . . . I don't think the pioneer lifestyle was considered to be all that glamorous—or even hygienic. I get the sense there was a lot of hunger, illness, death. They were really up against the elements, those pioneers."

"Yeah, but aren't we all? Who says the struggle can't be chic? Plus, homesteading is huge right now."

"Go West, young man . . ." I start to say.

"What?"

"It's a quote from Horace Greeley. 'Go West, young man, go West and grow up with the country.' It was about westward expansion. You know, manifest destiny?"

"Oh my god . . . *that's* what we'll call the collection: Manifest Destiny." A dreamy look comes over her face as she says, "Go West, young woman, go West and *glow up* with the country."

I cringe, but Gemma is alight with a sense of her own brilliance. "Actually, can you write that up real quick? Like a mini marketing strategy that I can share with the team. It's April, so we need to get going if this is going to happen for Holiday."

Right. We only have six months to persuade people to buy a $130 bucket come November.

"Actually . . . I can't." I am suddenly overcome with a sense of resistance.

"Oh," says Gemma, confused. I've never denied a request from her before. "This afternoon, then."

"No, Gemma. I can't do this anymore." The words leave my mouth hastily, and as they do, I feel a jolt of excitement, a fundamental rightness coursing through my veins. "I quit."

Gemma looks dumbfounded. "What? Cricket . . ."

It is so impulsive that I feel as though I am learning of this plan right along with her. It's as if the decision has made itself, and I'm just being pulled along in its wake. I feel a frenzy within, then a surge of certainty.

"I know it seems sudden, but there's somewhere else I need to be." I stand up from the cream-hued chair, walk past the sand-toned couch, and leave my boss dumbstruck, her hand still clenching the boar-bristle body brush.

I escape the Actualize office and immediately call Nina. She doesn't pick up at first, so I ring her twice more as I pace the sidewalk, my heart pounding.

When I finally get through, she sounds worried. "Cricket? Is everything okay?"

"Yes. Sorry to stress you. Just have a question. Have you listed the house yet?"

"No, that's next week, once we take the photos."

"Okay, good. Don't. I don't want to sell it."

"Um, okay . . ."

"I want to move there. I want to take care of Dad."

"Cricket." Nina pauses, and I can sense her taking a deep breath. "That's a really generous thought, but do you know what that would actually entail?"

Of course I don't. But I'm tired of being underestimated, underutilized. "I can learn."

"It's a lot of work, and it's only going to get harder as he gets sicker. He's really slipping," Nina explains. "It's a huge burden to bear. And a few days ago, you seemed pretty clear that you weren't up for it."

"I know, but things changed."

"Is it that you're feeling guilty? He'll be perfectly happy at Orchard Hills once he settles in."

"But he doesn't want to go. He wants to be at home," I say. "Shouldn't we take his wishes into account?"

"He'll acclimate. And more importantly, he'll be safe."

"I can keep him safe." Neither of us speaks for a moment, and then I say plaintively: "I want more time with him."

"But we have no idea how much longer he'll be himself. What if you rearrange your whole life, and then he completely forgets who he is? Caregiving is nonstop, and it's not glamorous. Dad can be a real pain in the ass, you know. A few weeks ago, he decided to do the laundry while I was out, and he poured an entire liter of detergent into the drum of the dryer. The *dryer*, Cricket."

"Ooof." I didn't know that. Nina and I speak every week, but I realize she has been sparing me the details of her day-to-day, probably in an attempt to protect me.

"Stuff like that is happening more and more often," she says.

"I get it. I can handle it." I don't know how to explain my rationale, other than there is an urgent energy flowing through me. I have a sudden conviction that my father and I have things to do together, and that this is our last chance to do them.

Of course Nina, being Nina, is focused on the practical. She bombards me with a slew of questions, finally landing on: "What about money? Dad doesn't have a lot of savings, and you know his licensing deal expires at the end of this year, right?"

Our father sold a series of patents in his thirties and secured a lucrative deal for one of them—a nanofiltration membrane that removes bacteria from water—that has provided royalties ever since.

Nina continues: "That's another reason why this is a good time to sell the house. We need to make sure we can cover his expenses going forward."

"What about his pension? And social security?"

"They're modest. They won't pay for a home or a significant amount of in-home care, should he eventually need that."

I hadn't considered any of this, but it all seems surmountable. "I'll get a job. I can find something remote, or even local. You know me. I'm scrappy. I can always find work."

"That's true."

"I'm not saying this will be our long-term solution, but let me give it a try. If things aren't working by this time next year, we can sell up and move him into a home. At least we will have given him one more year in the house that he loves."

Nina is quiet as she considers my idea, then she says, "You're really ready to leave the city? What about Actualize?"

"I just quit."

"You just . . ."

"I know this is sudden," I explain before she can protest. "But I'm not like you. I don't make decisions by *thinking*."

"Clearly. And we love that about you, but . . ."

"But what?"

"You know you can't save Dad, right? There's no chance of a happy ending here."

"That's not what I'm after."

"What *are* you after?"

I think: *I want a new life. I want to rebuild myself from the ground up. I want to return to the place where things went wrong so that I can make them right.*

But before I can answer, Nina proceeds. "I hope you're not doing this out of some feeling of obligation or heroism."

"It's not that complicated, and I'm not that altruistic," I say, finally finding the simplest and truest explanation. "I just want to be with my dad."

Chapter 7

It is easier to leave New York than I would have thought. The city I grew up in seems to spit me out with disconcerting ease. Even those with whom my life is most intertwined don't put up a fight. After her initial shock, Gemma wishes me well and sends me off with yet another linen tote bag full of free samples, including a vial of snail mucin (a fancy term for slime) that she swears will "change my life." Dylan says he'll miss me and we should leave things "open." He also reminds me that his lease is ending and asks if he can take over my room as soon as I vacate it. Olivia and Tasha do an appropriate amount of pouting, but eventually they accept my decision and cede my room to Dylan. ("We'll evict him if you ever decide to come back," Olivia assures me.)

The only person who kicks up a fuss is my mother, and I should have seen that coming.

"Why in the *world* would you do that?" she asks when I call to break the news. These days, she lives in London with her second husband, George. At sixty-two, she is still working full tilt at a major management consulting firm. "After everything you went through in that godforsaken town? Besides, you're a *city* girl. You have *ambitions*. Not to mention a fabulous job, finally."

When I landed at Actualize, my mother seemed to let out a breath that she had been holding ever since I quit school. Not only is she a fan of the company's face-tightening serums and plush bath towels, but she thinks Gemma is a visionary who I would do well to emulate.

"That woman is going places" is a refrain I've heard more times than I'd like.

"Nina did it," I say. "She took care of him for years."

"Yes, but Nina is . . ." She pauses, and I wait to be offended. "Nina is on a clear track. You have yet to establish yours."

"Maybe my track leads back to Locust."

My mother sighs. "You have no obligation to Arthur, you know."

"It's not about obligation," I reply. "I just feel . . . called."

"*Called*? To what? To eschew civilization?" Her distaste for Cat-wood Pond has only grown in the years since she left it once and for all. Despite my father's abiding love for the camp, my mother never warmed to it. She always found it too rustic and remote. She prefers cities, action, movement, noise. After growing up in a gray Midwestern steel town, she always wanted a big, busy life—the kind that is always just out of reach, but keeps you grasping nonetheless. For the past few years, I have tried to live the life she always encouraged. But now, I want the opposite.

"I don't understand," she says.

I don't expect her to.

———————

A month after making my decision to leave, I drive north in the Raisin with two and a half suitcases and room to spare. It's mid-May, one of the most beautiful times of year in Manhattan and, as I'm only remembering now, the start of black fly season in the Adirondacks. Not ideal. But as the grimy outskirts of the city give way to more rural surroundings, I begin to breathe again. Hours later, when I finally take our exit and turn onto the route that leads to another route that eventually bends toward Locust, the forest engulfs me quickly. *Green* is the obvious word for this landscape, but it is not adequate. Without taking my eyes off the road, I can spot at least ten different greens; if you go searching with intention, you will find dozens more. The bright ferns, the deep firs, the pale lichen, the vibrant moss—enough shades to constitute an entire palette. As I pull into our driveway and get out of the car, I am met by a final shade of green: Dominic's eyes are luminous in the late-afternoon sun as he lazes atop the woodpile by the back door.

"I'm home," I say, approaching him to scratch him under the chin. This time, he seems to recognize me. He stands, stretches, and then rams his fluffy head into my shoulder, as if to say, *Finally*.

———————

I have one month to learn the ropes of caregiving before Nina leaves for Stockholm in June, and she approaches the handoff as if she is leading a presidential transition—no box left unchecked. In the four years that she has taken care of my father, she has established firm routines and protocols: wake at 7:00 A.M., nap at 2:00 P.M., bed at 9:00 P.M. He plays piano every afternoon. Outings are on Saturdays. Grocery runs are on Mondays. Nina sticks closely to this schedule to minimize surprises and stress. Her thinking is that if she can keep our dad's routine consistent, she can slow his cognitive decline. It all seems overly rigid to me, but I know it's easier not to question Nina's policies. At least, not until after she leaves.

I anticipated some of my new responsibilities (giving my dad his morning and evening medications, scheduling and attending his doctor appointments, managing the household) and some I did not (getting him to floss his teeth properly, disposing of the diapers that he wears overnight). The hardest part, however, is the monotony. The conversations that repeat; the sense of a momentum-less existence. Groundhog's Day, Nina calls it. She was right to warn me that I was taking on a lot, and there are moments when I second-guess my ability to handle this new role. On the other hand, it feels good to be needed. It feels good to no longer be selling luxury snail slime to people whose faces look just fine.

As the days tick by, we do our best to prepare our father for the upcoming transition. But as my sister cedes more of her duties to me and spends more time out of the house, my father's most-asked question is, "Where's Nina?"

She assures me that this is to be expected, that he just needs time to adjust to the new normal. But I worry about the void she will leave.

———————

As her departure for Stockholm approaches, I begin waking earlier and earlier. Today, it's only 6:00 A.M. when I decide that sleep is a lost cause. I creep downstairs, and when I enter the great room, I see that Nina is already there, perched on the couch and much more awake than I am.

She glances up from her laptop. "Come look at this."

I plop down next to her and peek at the image on her screen. It is a riot of color—iridescent blues and greens, punctuated by streaks of magenta and a repeating pattern of red orbs.

"What do you think that is?" She grins expectantly.

It could be anything: an oil spill, a piece of contemporary art, the glittery remnants left on the dance floor after a rave. But knowing Nina's field of study, I make an educated guess: "Bacteria?"

"Some of it is!" She pauses for dramatic effect and then says, as if delivering a punchline: "It's a colon."

I look more closely, still lost in the explosion of psychedelic color.

"An extremely thin slice of a colon, and each color is a different biomarker."

"Are you getting into the digestion game?" I ask.

"I'm looking at different inflammatory mediators to see whether gut microbiota interacts with endometriosis." She realizes she has lost me. "But seriously, isn't it beautiful? These images are just so . . ." She shakes her head in awe. She's not wrong: there's something other-worldly about the blobs and swirls on the screen. It turns out a sliver of colon is an entire galaxy unto itself.

I envy Nina for having found her calling and doggedly pursuing it. I don't know many people who have this kind of conviction—and derive this kind of joy—from their work. But thanks to Nina, I know it's possible.

She closes her laptop. "Let's go swimming."

I hesitate. The sun isn't even up. "I need coffee."

"No, you need a sunrise swim."

She's right, of course. This is the best time of day to be by the water: before anything has stirred, when the pond is an unbroken sheet of glass and the light creeps over the eastern tree line, revealing the world, one detail at a time. We change into our swimsuits and throw on our tattered "pond robes." These bathrobes are older than I am and have hung in the closets of this house since the seventies. Nina's is red-and-white striped, while mine is beige, or perhaps a yellowed white. They have thinned in places, but my father never believed in replacing things just because they were worn. "Perfectly good" was always how he described our possessions, no matter how stained or rusted or out-of-date we girls deemed them to be. His philosophy has cast a distinct patina over this house and its collected objects.

Nina and I scamper down the path and reach the dock, where the gentle thud of our footsteps cuts the silence. I lean over the edge to look down into the water, which is clear enough to reveal the rocks piled on the floor of the pond eight or nine feet below. A silver fish darts one way, then the other, its movements sharp but indecisive. On the near shore, a fallen birch lies half submerged in the sapphire water as if living a double life, its pearly bark blue and ghostly beneath the surface. Unlike river-fed waterbodies, which absorb whatever floats their way from upstream, Catwood is replenished solely by springs that filter up from the bottom of the pond, infusing the water with a mineral quality that leaves the skin feeling silky and renewed. In the summer, the house shower goes mostly unused, it being no match for the type of purification you feel after a swim in the pond.

"Ow!" I slap my arm where a black fly has just left a bloody streak. "You little butthead."

"Yeah, they're bad right now. Only one way to save yourself," says Nina, swinging her arms and diving from the edge of the dock. She breaks the surface in a clean line and disappears, barely making a splash. I drop my robe and follow her, clenching as I am swallowed by the icy water. By the end of summer, the pond will reach an acceptable temperature of seventy degrees. But now, in these early summer days, it hovers closer to sixty. Some call it bracing; some call it torture.

Nina and I pop out of the water and scream, as is our custom, cracking open the quiet of the morning. For a moment, I forget that I've been away. It feels like we are just kids again, flipping around like otters, churning up the water to keep the pond monsters at bay. I can hear my mother telling us we're too far from the dock; I can hear my father telling her to let us be.

––––––––

My parents were married for twenty-seven years, and my mom used to joke that they fell in love in the New York City sewer system. When they met in 1988, my mother, Tish, was a twenty-six-year-old management consultant and my father was a thirty-eight-year-old engineer who worked for the NYC Department of Environmental Protection. A work project brought them together: my mother's firm was tasked with streamlining my father's department, and my father was called in to help inform where cuts should be made. In the end, he made such a compelling case that my mother's firm recommended the city *expand* his budget, and somewhere along the way, he and my mother struck up a flirtation.

They were an unlikely couple from the outset. Armed with an MBA, my mother had come to New York brimming with ambition. As the only female in her division, she was determined to both play the game and beat the odds, and she approached the early years of her career as if she were storming a fortress. Along the way, she had a tumultuous relationship with a fellow consultant who was not her boss but not her professional equal. A pinstriped yuppie, he found unending ways to remind her of his relative superiority. Sexism was so rampant in her workplace that she took it for granted, and when she met my father, she was jolted by his sense of egalitarianism. As she put it, "He wasn't trying to be a hotshot"—and she liked that about him. Much later, she would come to wish he were more financially ambitious, but at first, she was comforted by what seemed to be his innate sense of integrity and balance.

For his part, my father was taken by my mother's moxie and curiosity. Known to his colleagues as the "water whisperer," he could troubleshoot anything from a faltering dam to inadequate storm-surge systems. His work could be dry, but Tish absorbed it with interest, asked creative questions, assessed the challenges that faced his department, and then gave what amounted to a meticulously researched and fair recommendation. He was as impressed as he was smitten.

They began dating, and soon after, my father sold his first patent. Their lives appeared to be opening up, and within a year, they married. It was the late eighties—my mother was energetic and irreverent; my father was warm and witty. Her hair was permed; his khakis were pleated. As newlyweds, they settled on the Upper West Side, not far from where my father had grown up in Morningside Heights, but a considerable distance from the small Midwestern town that my mother had left behind. For a few years, they tore around the city like it was their own personal playground. But my father's favorite thing was to take her up to his camp in the Adirondacks, where he taught her how to paddle a canoe, scale a fish, and identify the Big Dipper and Orion's Belt. It wasn't her comfort zone, but at first, she did her best to summon enthusiasm for the deep-woods life that he loved so much. She considered the camp a quirky addendum to their real life in the city.

A few years later, Nina was born. My father loved parenthood right away; my mother was more ambivalent. Her maternity leave made her feel claustrophobic, and when she finally returned to work, she found that her position had been downsized and her path to promotion all but blocked. Outraged, she left the firm and resolved to find a new job, but doing so with an infant proved harder than she thought. A year passed, then another. She promised herself she would return to work when the time was right, and in the meantime, she tried to embrace her role as a stay-at-home mother.

In the following years, my father sold a few more patents, and my mother was heartened by their expanding financial horizon. Six years after Nina was born, I came along, and a few years after that, my father secured a licensing deal for his latest invention: the nanofiltration membrane. At this point, my mother suggested moving into a bigger home—a townhouse, at last. But my father thought our original apartment was adequate, and he preferred to put any extra capital into the maintenance of the camp. He hoped to retire early from his job with the city, explaining that they could live off his patents, as long as they lived within their means.

"What more do we need?" was my father's outlook.

"Where do I begin?" was my mother's.

When it came to material wealth, my father had already achieved what he thought necessary; my mother was just getting started. But more importantly, my mother was perpetually frustrated by her own unrealized earning power. My father was happy to provide for her, but she had never wanted to be reliant on him financially. She still clung to the idea that she would restart her career; she resented that my father seemed to have forgotten she ever had one.

When I was seven, my father retired early in order to spend more time at the camp and more time with us. That same year, my mother finally landed a job that would put her squarely back on the corporate path she had abandoned a decade earlier. As my father's career wound down, my mother's ramped up. He wanted to spend more time in the Adirondacks; she wanted to spend less. He wanted to give his daughters large swaths of unstructured time in the woods; my mother wanted to give us the resources she believed would lead to conventional success (good schools, high-paying jobs). It wasn't long before my mother's income far exceeded what my father's had ever been. As the financial power balance shifted, their divergent values came to the fore, and cracks began to form. At first, they were determined to make it work, despite their conflicting priorities. Summer remained my father's domain. We spent the whole season at Catwood Pond, with my mother visiting for just one week each August before returning to work in the city. Conversely, during the schoolyear, my mother called the shots and set the schedule. This divide-and-conquer approach worked well enough, but eventually, it was clear that it wasn't just a parenting strategy. My parents were leading separate lives. The unraveling of their marriage happened over time, as it often does, until the winter I was sixteen, when the tenuous thread binding them together finally snapped.

Chapter 8

On the morning Nina is to leave for Stockholm, I wake in my creaky twin bed from a confounding dream: I coughed up my own heart. One quick retch and there it was in my hand, continuing its steady, purple thud.

Bewildered, I thrusted it toward hazy passersby, asking, "Can I live without this?"

They all shrugged—not knowing, not caring, or both.

Can I live without this? Perhaps I don't need my heart after all, my dream-self decided, so I threw it toward the frozen pond, where it fell through a hole in the ice and sank.

Over breakfast, Nina attributes my dream to nerves. She never has dreams herself (no time), and she has little patience for the details of my nighttime phantasms.

"Do you think it means I'm heartless?" I press. "Or emotionally arrested?"

"Something like that," she says, distracted as she rinses her plate and verifies something on her phone. It's easy to see that she wants to get moving toward her new life.

"Goodrich is going to mail you a physical copy of Dad's will," she reminds me. "And they'll keep a copy at their office as well."

I nod. Last week, we updated my father's will and switched the power of attorney designations from Nina to me, putting me legally in charge of my father's finances and medical decisions. "It's just a precaution in case something happens unexpectedly," Nina had assured me. "But it should be you, since you're local."

Now, as she prepares to leave, I feel the heaviness of the responsibility begin to descend. She takes a final walk through the house, where she has left a profusion of lists and labels meant to guide me from here on out, and that's in addition to the digital files she has shared with me: spreadsheets, documents, and a calendar that she will be able to monitor from abroad.

I help Nina load the last of her things into the Subaru—which will now be my car, with the Raisin being demoted to backup. Nina closes the trunk, checks her watch, and looks around. "Where's Dad?"

"He was just here." I turn and go back into the house, where I find my father in his room, changing back into his nightshirt.

"Dad, what are you doing?" I ask.

"I think I'll have a rest," he says.

"That's fine, but can you rest in the car? We have to drive Nina to the airport."

"The airport? Where is she going?"

"Stockholm."

"Stockholm!" He looks both excited and concerned.

"Yes, she's leaving today," I say. "And I'll be staying here with you." He looks me up and down, skeptically.

"Can you change so we can go?" I say, holding up the beige turtleneck I had helped him put on less than thirty minutes ago. "We don't want to make her late for the plane."

"I don't see why I can't wear this," he says of his knee-length linen nightshirt.

We negotiate for a moment, and when we finally make it out to the driveway, he is wearing his nightshirt over a pair of jeans. For footwear, he has chosen lime-green Crocs.

Nina raises her eyebrows but says nothing, and we pile into the car. The nearest international airport is in Burlington, and on the three-hour drive, we have plenty of time to review every last detail of my father's care. By the time we cross into Vermont, Nina's task-mastering has given way to a jittery optimism.

We park and walk to the terminal, where Nina checks in and requests an upgrade. Persuasive but not pushy, she succeeds. Business class it will be. We watch her neatly packed suitcases float away on the conveyor belt, bound for New York and then Stockholm. With all her to-dos done, she finally relaxes enough to become tearful, hugging my father as if this is their final goodbye. I suppose the version of him she meets next will be changed, but that's true of all of us, to some extent.

"There, there," my father pats her back, seeking to ease her distress, though he doesn't understand its source.

Nina sniffs assertively and squeezes her eyes closed as if to halt the flow of tears. When she opens them again, she looks purposeful.

"You've got this, Cricket," she says to me, grabbing my shoulders and giving me a little shake. I nod, which seems to satisfy her. With that, she turns. We watch as she breezes through the short security line, moving buoyantly in the direction of her future.

———

Back in the short-term parking lot, I find myself scanning the rows for the Raisin before I remember: I'm a Subaru woman now. I open the passenger door and stay close as my father effortfully climbs into his seat, clinging to the roof of the car for balance, or for dear life, or both. By the time I get into the driver's seat, he is grumbling in frustration.

"This damn thing . . ." He wrestles with the seat belt, pulling it at the wrong angle and in the wrong direction.

I lean over and slide the belt across his torso, but just before I latch it, he grabs it from me and pushes it into the buckle as if delivering the final blow in a battle. Once it clicks, he relaxes and his annoyance quickly dissipates.

"So, where to?" he asks.

I let him know we are heading home, but the drive will take a few hours. We pull away from the airport, and only now does the weight of my new role finally hit me. I wonder if this is how first-time parents feel when they bring their newborns home. It's not that my father is as fragile as an infant, but he is dependent on me. It's terrifying to finally be in charge.

"Have you ever been to Sweden?" I ask, knowing that he has, several times.

"Not yet." My father shakes his head. "Someday, perhaps. Although I'm quite busy. And why would I go all the way to Sweden when I could go to . . . Saratoga?"

I laugh. "Or Scranton?"

"Or Scarsdale."

"Or Saskatoon?"

My father smiles, his watery gray eyes bright in the midday sun. He says, "This is where I belong. There's really no place better."

This far north, there is a voraciousness to early summer, brief though it is. The season snaps into action, flashing its brazen greens, knowing it must exist to the hilt. It's not like the lazy, wilted summer of the South, nor is it like the long, abundant, sun-soaked California version. In the Adirondacks, summer is an ecstatic, too-bold season that, even when in full swing, already seems to long for itself.

"Will you miss Nina?" I ask.

"Certainly," he says. "But she deserves a nice trip."

Though we have tried to prepare him, he doesn't seem to grasp that Nina has moved away and that I am her replacement. I could tell him for the hundredth time, but instead, I just agree, "She does."

He begins poking at the control panel in search of a radio station, then grows frustrated with the touchscreen he can't decipher. "This damn thing . . ."

I help him scan the channels, pausing so he can react to each and finally settling on a station playing Roy Orbison. We pick up speed as Roy warbles about heartbreak, and within minutes, my father is asleep.

Chapter 9

Over the next few days, we settle into something of a rhythm. When my father asks about Nina, I try out an array of responses. "She moved to Stockholm" proves too jarring for him, so I experiment with "She's on a trip" and "She's out for a bit." Those explanations land better, and I see that my job is to find answers that will satisfy him without telling outright lies. I am the filter through which his reality now flows.

In addition to getting reacquainted with my father, I am also re-acquainting myself with the home and the land I once knew so well. Everything is smaller than I remember: the house itself, the lawn, the pond, the sky. I remember it all stretching on forever, huge and wild and a little bit treacherous. But now, everything feels scaled down and approachable, like I'm living in a miniature of the past.

Our days are long and slow. I have plenty to do, but nothing is urgent, and I have time to revisit my old haunts. There is the lean-to, where we often slept as kids—sometimes six or eight of us in a row of sleeping bags, crammed together like cigars in a box, our giggles echoing over the water until the last of us fell asleep. There is the guest cabin, which I always avoided, believing it haunted. There is a patch of blueberry bushes where I once "ran away" at the age of seven. Using a dishcloth and stick to fashion a bindle, I took off up the driveway until I reached the bushes, which were still within earshot of the house (I wanted to observe the eruption of concern once my family realized I was gone). Waiting in the warm soil, I could hear my parents talking about the car needing work; hear them say something about "that jackass Rod Seavey"; hear them go silent as they turned back to their preoccupations; but I did not hear them mention me. Not only were they not frantic with worry, but they hadn't even noticed my absence. After an hour (which felt like three days, by my count), I grew bored. I grabbed a handful of damp dirt and smeared it across my cheeks. I mussed my hair so I would look like a proper runaway. I gripped my bindle and limped back toward the house, throwing the door open so they could not possibly miss my dramatic return. I remember my mother saying something like, "Cricket, I need you to clean up your art supplies. They're all over the porch." She didn't notice my dirt-smeared face, my knotted hair, or the fact that I had been away for *years*. In that moment, I realized that my mother never noticed me when I was good, or even when I was gone. She only noticed me when I made a mess that somehow inconvenienced her. But my father caught on and indulged me: "What do we have here, a little orphan in from the cold?" Validated, I dropped my bindle and ran into his arms.

Then there is the narrow boathouse where our aluminum boat still bobs, knocking lightly against the dock. Mostly unused these days, its eight-horsepower engine is small but capable. My father taught me to drive it when I was only eight, which horrified my mother, but she did not intervene. On more than one occasion, I went for a spin by myself when I was barely old enough to see over the bow. Only once did I run out of gas in the middle of the pond and need to be rescued by Nina, who towed me back with the canoe. That summer, my mother only stayed at camp for six days, and I missed her. To combat that feeling, I took a jar of her fancy face cream and smeared it on the door of the boathouse. I still remember the sensation of my fingers digging into the thick cream and then dragging four long streaks, like oil paint, across the chipped paint. The streaks are still there on the door nearly two decades later—waxy, hardened, but unmistakable.

When I was nine or ten, some trees were cleared in the wooded area behind the house to afford a better view of the pond. A series of dry stumps remained, and from them, I created a world. I transformed the clearing into a fast-paced animal hospital, where stumps became operating tables and recovery rooms. Someone was always in crisis, and as head surgeon, it was up to me to save them. Though I specialized in treating exotic mammals (ocelots, lemurs, reindeer), I would take any patient who came through the door: ponies, stoats, dragons.

The hospital was well-equipped. In the hollow of a tree, I had hidden the receiver of an old rotary phone, whose curly wire hung loose, not connected to anything. A large rock functioned as the front desk, where frantic patients explained their plights. I had somehow acquired a vintage doctor's bag that I stuffed with supplies (bandages, string, kitchen tongs, knitting needles). A crumbling rock wall was my office, where I was *not* to be disturbed, except in the case of emergency—and there was always an emergency. A skunk might need stitches, an alligator might need a C-section, or a zebra might need a tail amputation. There were quieter days, too: routine checkups for dogs and cats, the braiding of horses' manes, the clipping of lions' claws. I did it all while managing a sizeable imaginary staff, who were all incredibly deferential. All but Alex, my promising but unruly protégé who happened to be a squirrel.

"For Christ's sake, Alex," I would bark into the tree phone. "This is the third time you've been late this month. I see so much potential in you, but I can't work with potential alone."

Alex hated to be held accountable, but it was necessary. I spent long hours in the hospital, high on my own authority.

Now, when I visit the clearing, all I see are stumps. I miss my imaginary world, just as I miss my childhood self.

One morning after I give my father his breakfast and morning medication, I find myself wandering the shoreline. Catwood Pond being long and narrow, there is only one other property that is visible from our house. Directly across the water, I can make out the shapes of the now-empty Seavey camp: the two-story boathouse, the vast lawn, the sprawling main house. It all sits, hot and still, as if waiting for something. I place my hand on a tree, thick as an elephant's leg, and run my fingers over the bulging sap bubbles. Although I know better, I can't resist pressing my nail into one that is big as a grape. Its viscous insides burst over my finger and slide down the bark, leaving a lazy trail. I press the tips of my fingers together and indulge in the sticky resistance as I try to pull them apart. A dormant feeling begins to stir. It's more than a memory; it's like a portal. Suddenly, I remember exactly what it felt like to be sixteen. My senses have held on to this version of me—the self who thrummed with a chaotic mix of optimism and defiance and fear and brazenness. The self who, one summer, collided with a boy named Seth.

Chapter 10

———

June 2015

The year I was sixteen, I failed my driver's test but passed my lifeguard certification. By the time Memorial Day arrived and opened the door to summer, I had secured a job at Lake Locust, which was ten times the size of our pond and bustled with tourists from June through Labor Day. It was only four miles away and an easy enough bike ride to the lake from our house, but I stewed each time I set out, knowing that I could have been driving a car, if only it weren't for that botched K-turn. And the forgotten turn signal. And the rolling stop. All minor infractions, in my opinion, but enough to leave me bike-bound for the foreseeable future.

On the first real day of summer, I hopped on my rusty Trek, wearing a red one-piece swimsuit, some tattered running shorts, and my green JanSport backpack. As usual, my mother barked at me not to wear Birkenstocks while riding my bike, but I ignored her as I pedaled up our driveway, my toes and heels bare in the breeze.

My route to the big lake took me past the town tennis courts, and as I approached them, I could hear the rhythmic pop of a ball being smacked back and forth. I slowed to see who was playing and sighed with dread as I realized it was Greg Seavey. When he saw me, he caught the ball in his right hand, abruptly halting the rally.

"Cricket Campbell. Nice wheels."

I rolled my eyes and came to a stop. Obviously, Greg had heard about my failed test, just as I had heard about his new BMW, which bore a vanity plate that read: BOOYAH. He walked over and looked me up and down through the chain-link fence, channeling his disappointment.

"You don't have to look so devastated," I said. "It's fine. I'll retake the test when I feel like it."

"No, it's not that. It's just . . ." Greg shook his head regretfully. "You had *all year* to grow boobs."

Greg loved nothing more than to shine a spotlight on people's insecurities, and my chest size had been a preoccupation of his since we were twelve years old.

"And you had all year to fix your personality," I fired back.

Greg's tennis partner laughed at my quick retort. Only then did I really notice him: cute, a bit taller than Greg, with messy blond hair.

"Hi, I'm Cricket," I said, with a cautious smile.

"Seth." He had a relaxed air about him that was very different from Greg's agitated cockiness. It was what I could only assume was genuine confidence—a rarity in anyone our age.

"He's my cousin," Greg interjected, as if this fact somehow ranked Seth below him in the social hierarchy. But Greg was now superfluous to this conversation, and neither Seth nor I turned to look at him.

"Are you here for the summer?" I asked.

Seth nodded. "That's the plan. Teaching at the tennis camp. You?"

"Yeah. Lifeguarding at the lake." I checked my watch and realized I was already two minutes late. "Shoot. Gotta go. I'll see you around?"

"For sure . . ." Seth began.

"Beers tonight at Sully's dock," interrupted Greg. It was more of a command than an invitation. Technically, Greg and I were friends. Or at least, we were tethered by a shared circle of friends who spent every summer here. I didn't like him much these days, but now that we were in high school, the social dynamics were churning so swiftly that it was better not to write anyone off, even if he was an inveterate ass named Greg Seavey.

"We'll see," I said as I pedaled away, suddenly feeling a little off-balance as my sandals slapped against my heels. I knew how to handle

Greg. It was the unexpected arrival of Seth that had thrown me for a loop.

————————

A few weeks later, on the night of the solstice, my friends gathered at Greg's. We knew it was the longest day of the year, but time didn't mean much to us that summer, when our future spilled out before us like an eager tide that we believed would never ebb. While my family's camp was an example of Adirondack understatement, the Seaveys' property was the opposite. It had been one of the great historic camps, once owned by a former president. But when the Seaveys acquired it, they modernized it and depleted it of its original charms. They expanded the two-story boathouse, adding large docks on either side. Their three motorboats and two Jet Skis were always on display, and it was rumored that Mr. Seavey was looking to add a seaplane to his fleet. A stone firepit was built into the hillside and was "architecturally significant," or so Greg told us. Up the hill, the main house asserted itself as one of the biggest in the area, and the rest of the estate comprised four guest cabins, each one decorated in an over-the-top way that imitated Adirondack charm rather than embodied it: mounted moose heads, cashmere blankets that were over-luxurious, and decorative signs that said things like LIVING THAT BACKWOODS LIFE.

Pretension aside, the Seaveys' was a convenient place to party. Greg's parents were notably permissive, and they encouraged him to host in the hope that it would make him popular, which it did.

I could easily boat to Greg's from my dock, but that night, I arrived by car with my best friend, Chloe—who had passed her driver's test and had access to her mom's SUV—so that we could stop by Deb's Depot on our way. Deb had no qualms about selling alcohol to minors, as long as those minors had passable fake IDs, and we used ours to buy bright-pink wine and a case of the cheapest beer available.

As we ambled down Greg's well-kept lawn, I could see there were already at least fifteen kids gathered on the dock. The firepit threw sparks into the air, and a few people stood around an ice-filled cooler by the boathouse. Chloe and I approached to unload our haul, and as I transferred the beers from their box to the cooler, Greg plucked one from my hand to inspect it. He had recently taken up drinking obscure craft beers, so he now scoffed at the humble varieties he had been perfectly happy to guzzle last summer.

"You know why drinking light beer is like having sex in a canoe?" he asked. None of us responded, so he continued with a grin: "Because it's fucking close to water!"

A few of the boys chortled. I rolled my eyes and tried to smile knowingly. I knew it was just an expression, but the truth was: I had no idea what sex was like, in a canoe or anywhere else.

Suddenly I felt a pleasant electricity, and I turned to see that Seth had sidled up in time to hear Greg's punchline. He smiled at me and shrugged, taking a can from the cooler. "Well, I like light beer."

"Me, too," I said, feeling a sense of relief. I still didn't know Seth well, but I wanted to. In the few weeks since I had first met him at the tennis court, he had become an object of fascination to me. Privately, I was cultivating what I hoped was a shared connection, but what could easily have been a humiliatingly one-sided crush.

What I knew about Seth: he was a year older than Greg and me, which meant he would be a senior in the fall. His mother and Greg's mother were sisters, though I heard there had been some kind of feud between them. Something about money—one of them having too much of it, the other not enough. Seth was not a "summer person" like most of us were. He lived in the Adirondacks year-round, though a bit farther north in the direction of Lake Placid. His parents were divorced. We had only spoken a handful of times at gatherings like this, but he always seemed relaxed, unconcerned with how he was perceived and uninterested in the teenage drama that embroiled the rest of us. I noticed that he only laughed when he was actually amused; and he seemed to treat everyone with easy equanimity.

I didn't realize I was staring at Seth until his eyes turned to me. I looked down, but before I could come up with anything to say, the moment was punctured by a scream. Greg had thrown Chloe over his shoulder and was lumbering toward the end of the dock.

"Greg! Don't you dare!" she yelped, half annoyed and half thrilled to be the target of his antics and the center of attention. I happened to know she had spent an hour choosing her outfit and putting on makeup, something I never did. Tonight, she had painstakingly applied tiny gemstones to the outer corners of her eyes. That's not the kind of thing Greg would have taken into consideration as he barreled toward the water. We all thought he was going to dump her in, but he stopped just short of the edge of the dock and put her down, his point made. She slapped his shoulder and walked back toward the firepit, shaking her head. We all understood that this kind of interaction constituted flirtation.

As it was the longest day of the year, the sun disappeared around 8:45 P.M. that night, but the sky did not fully darken until closer to 10:00 P.M. By then, everyone was tipsy and looking for boundaries to test and trouble to stir up. Our friend Sully had grown tired of toasting marshmallows over the firepit and was experimenting with roasting a full Snickers bar. Another kid had hopped on a Jet Ski and was tearing back and forth between the boathouse and the far bay. Greg made another attempt to drag Chloe into the water, and this time, he meant it. They both tumbled in, and others jumped in after them. Soon the shallows were frothing with teenagers, their shrieks and cackles echoing through the warm summer air. Those who were still dry began sprinting toward the end of the dock. I was near the back of the pack, and before I got very far, I felt a hand slip into my palm and pull me out of the fray.

"Shhhh." Seth held his finger in front of his lips, and we scurried around the boathouse and into the woods along the shoreline. As I navigated the uneven forest floor in my sandals, I felt a fiery pressure within—excitement and fear comingling. Was this really happening? And if so, what *was* it, exactly, that was happening? Seth seemed to have a destination in mind, and he led me with confidence past the darkening trees. We could still hear the whoops and splashes from the dock, and I was elated to have broken from the group, to be on a stealth adventure with Seth.

We passed first one, then another of the guest cabins, and finally wended our way through the woods to an enormous boulder that sat on the shoreline, partially submerged in the pond. It was twice my height and big as a whale.

"Are you okay to climb this?" Seth asked.

"Of course," I said, as I looked for a foothold.

"I'll give you a boost." Seth knit his fingers together, and I stepped into them. He lifted me high enough to start my ascent. It only took a few seconds for me to summit the boulder, but when I reached the top, my heart was pounding.

"Have you ever been up here?" Seth asked.

I shook my head, and we made our way to the edge, where the rock sloped sharply down to the water below. Seth sat and let his calves hang down, and I followed suit. He pulled a beer out of his pocket, cracked the tab, and offered me the first sip. From our perch, we could see our friends cavorting on the far dock, their restless shapes backlit by the fire.

"Do you have FOMO?" Seth asked.

"Not at all." I had been to a version of this party dozens of times, and I knew that the most exciting things happened around the edges of the action.

We passed the beer back and forth in what felt like an unrushed rhythm, and I was relieved to have something between us to absorb the pleasant tension that was growing.

"Why haven't you spent the summer here before?" I asked.

Seth shrugged. "I usually work at one of the tennis clubs near Saranac. But my mom thought I should take a job here this year."

"And she didn't want to come with you?"

"She has to work. She can't really take much vacation. But she thought I should spend some time with this part of the family. Maybe so she doesn't have to."

"You're her proxy?"

"Something like that."

It made me wonder if my parents did the same—used my sister and me as a shield, a means of avoiding their own marital stagnation. To me, that strategy seemed more complicated than it was worth, but I knew adults had the capacity to twist themselves into knots rather than face the hard truths of their lives. I hoped that would never happen to me, that my loyalty would always be to reality, no matter how painful it might be.

"My mom is cool, though. You would like each other," said Seth. I appreciated this vote of confidence, which had a forward-looking quality to it.

"What about Greg?" I asked, feeling bold. We both knew it was a leading question. "I know he's your cousin, but do you actually *like* him?"

Seth smiled. "He's my cousin."

"Such diplomacy." I grinned in the darkness.

"If you're asking whether I would be his friend if he *weren't* my cousin, well, probably not. But we get along. I understand him, even when I don't agree with him."

"That's fair."

A familiar song carried over the water from the dock. I looked down into the black expanse and heard the lazy lap of water against the boulder beneath us. This time, when Seth took the beer from me, he set it down and looked into my eyes. On fire but paralyzed, I had to summon all my courage to hold his gaze.

He leaned in and kissed me, confidently but quickly, then pulled away to gauge my reaction. I must have smiled or blushed or seemed otherwise receptive, because when he leaned in again, it was more purposeful. More artful. I felt my body melt into the rock beneath us, everything blurring as my world shifted on its axis.

This was hardly my first kiss; that had happened a few years prior, when I was thirteen, with none other than Greg Seavey. But all I remember from that experience was too much saliva—his or mine, I still don't know—and Greg telling me a few days later that I wasn't his type. No, this was something altogether different. This was my first kiss that felt like something more than an experiment; my first kiss that made me think I was finally doing it right; my first kiss that I could actually envision leading to sex in a canoe (or perhaps somewhere more hospitable).

Until this moment, I had never even considered sleeping with a real-life teenage boy. With a movie star? Yes. A rock star? Of course.

But those people were conveniently out of reach, so I could cultivate the fantasy from a safe distance. The thought of sex with an actual peer horrified me—until now. Now it started to seem possible, and maybe even desirable. Still, it was terrifying: to be aware that you're living the most exciting moment of your life as it happens. To be fully present but also out-of-body, overcome by a pleasant quaking. *I feel alive*, I thought. And even more astonishing: I felt deserving.

Eventually, having exhausted the ways we could make out on a boulder without injuring ourselves, we climbed down and headed back to the party. But we took our time, stopping along the way to kiss against the odd tree. By the time we got back to the dock around midnight, most everyone had dispersed. Chloe and Greg were nowhere to be found, and none of my remaining friends were in any condition to drive me home, even by boat. I was already late for my 11:30 P.M. curfew, which left me with only one option. Nina was twenty-two and had just graduated from college with the highest of honors. She would head to her Peace Corps post that fall, but for the summer, she was here. And she had a car.

When my sister arrived twenty minutes later, I left Seth by the dock and scampered up the lawn, propelled by giddiness and beer. As I dove into the passenger seat, she raised her eyebrows, intrigued.

"What?" I asked defensively, though I knew I was radiating excitement.

Nina reached over and lifted a lock of my hair that was matted with balsam sap. "Fun night?"

I touched the snarl proudly. She grinned but didn't pry as she backed the car up and performed a perfect K-turn. The whole way home, I let my right hand fly out the window, watching it rise and fall in the clean night air. In that moment, I felt absolutely certain that everything in my life was going to work out just fine.

Chapter 11

Something is not right with Dominic. In addition to his clumping fur, I notice that he is getting grumpier, even just in the month that I've been here. When I call Nina to ask when he last saw a vet, she says, "Hmm. Well, his checkups lapsed during COVID." When I press her further, it's clear he hasn't had an annual in over five years, maybe more. "He always seemed fine," she insists, but I make him an appointment nonetheless.

On the day of the visit, I wrestle Dominic into his carrier, which my father keeps on his lap during the forty-five-minute drive to the nearest clinic. The appointment costs $180 and takes all of fifteen minutes.

"All in all, Dominic looks good," says Dr. Raymond, feeling the cat's abdomen and then taking a look in his ears. "Except for his teeth, which isn't unusual for a cat of this age."

"What's wrong with his teeth?" I ask.

"Not a thing," says my father, in Dominic's defense.

Dr. Raymond pulls the cat's lip up to show me his inflamed gums. "Periodontal disease, and at least one rotten tooth. I would suggest a full dental cleaning, and at that time we can take X-rays and remove any necessary teeth. It's completely up to you—but it will make him much more comfortable."

"Okay, let's do that," I say, without hesitation.

"Great," says Dr. Raymond. "It takes a few hours—we have to put him under to do the procedure. But I believe we have some openings toward the end of the month."

The receptionist is only able to give me a vague estimate of what

Dominic's dental work will cost, explaining, "We won't really know until the day of, once they assess the X-rays. We can give you an estimate then. It's typically about $100 per extraction."

I figure I can afford a tooth or two, so I schedule the appointment, but I make a mental note to begin my job search in earnest this week. I have no savings, and for now, we are living on my father's income. It's enough to keep us afloat, but we certainly don't have money for extras or emergencies. And when his licensing deal expires at the end of the year, I will need to step into the role of breadwinner, in addition to caregiver.

On the drive home, my father asks again about Nina. "Where did she go? That woman who used to live with us."

"Stockholm. She's on a trip," I say.

"How nice." After a moment, he adds, "Though it's a shame she had to leave before the loons come back."

"The loons?" I ask.

He nods with certainty. "Any day now."

Loons were a fixture on the pond when I was growing up, but Nina says that in recent years they have not come. Perhaps the changing climate has pushed them elsewhere, or perhaps they prefer the larger lakes of the region, where they can claim more territory. Whatever the reason, we have no more loons and haven't for some time. But I don't want to tarnish whatever memory my father is holding on to, so I go along with it. "Yes, it's a shame she had to leave before the loons come back."

———

That afternoon, my father wakes from his nap in a sprightly mood. According to the schedule Nina left us, this is his designated window for playing the piano, but before I can suggest that, he chirps, "Time for a swim!"

I can tell he is determined, and as his caregiver—I'm still getting used to the term—I decide to prioritize his real-time interests over Nina's dictates. I feel a sizzle of rebellion.

"Okay, let's find your swimsuit," I say.

"Swimsuit? Who needs it!" he says punchily as he beelines for the door. I saw my father naked once, by accident, when I was a child. I was so horrified that I vowed never to see an unclothed man again.

"I think you'd better put it on, Dad," I say, hoping this doesn't become a struggle. *What would Nina do?* I wonder.

He looks at me for a moment as if to challenge my authority, but then quickly acquiesces. "Very well! Now, if I were a swimsuit, where would I be . . . ?"

We locate his forest-green trunks on the back of his bathroom door, and I leave him to change into them. I know there will come a time when even this task will require my help, but for now, I encourage him to be as independent as possible.

Once in my own bathing suit, I wait in one of the wicker armchairs on the porch, my feet up on the railing, which is supported by two diagonally crossed logs that form an elongated X, as is the architectural style in these parts. My father is taking a while, and I wonder if I should go check on him. But soon enough, he emerges and calls, "Pond-ward, ho!"

We walk arm in arm, my father setting the pace with his careful shuffling. There are five stairs to navigate, plus a stretch of grass and then the sloped dirt path. As a child, I could hurtle from the porch of this house to the pond in thirteen ecstatic seconds, my sprint culminating in a triumphant splash. Today, we take our time, pausing to examine a flamboyant mushroom that has sprung up beside the path and then to analyze the song of a bird overhead. Dad was once an expert on such avian matters, but now his guesses are as arbitrary as mine. A whippoorwill? A warbler? Probably. Who knows.

When we reach the dock, the slats are warm from the sun, which lingers heavy and orange above the trees across the pond. We hang our robes on the rusted hooks of the boathouse wall. My father approaches the ladder and turns, backing down carefully. I'm glad that I recently took the initiative to clean the algae-coated steps so he won't slip. It was an absolutely disgusting job, and one that would have made me squirm in my youth, but now, algae removal is simply a part of my existence. It's up to me to keep my father safe.

"Here he goes . . ." my father announces. "The mighty amphibian!"

He releases his grip on the ladder and wafts gently backward into the water. These days, he is light enough to bob like a raft. He commences the elementary backstroke. His range of motion is smaller and joltier than it used to be, creating an uneven wake as he moves away from the dock.

"Aaahhhhh, that's refreshing." He closes his eyes and lets the pond hold him, indulging his arthritic joints in a moment of weightlessness.

I dive in and shoot through the dark water, eventually emerging beside him. The surface ripples and reacts, but soon settles around us. My father scoots further and further out. He is still a competent swimmer, but I stay near him just in case.

"You know, you taught me to swim right here," I say.

His face is tilted up to the sky. "Is that right?"

"Yep," I say as I tread water. "It took a while. You were very patient with me."

"Oh, good. I'm glad I was."

It's true: we spent hours upon hours here in the shallows, me floating on my back, then my front. I loathed when my feet touched the silty bottom of the pond, where who-knows-what was lurking. My father held me so I wouldn't encounter the murk, but sometimes he let me drown a little, just to get a feel for it, before supporting me again. Once I got the hang of swimming, the real fun began. There was no end to the elaborate aquatic games my father invented. There was Dolphin Show, where I played the part of the trained dolphin who did tricks on command. There was Feeding Frenzy, where we pretended to be sharks and circled Nina menacingly. And then, of course, there was Whale Ride, where I would hold on to my father's shoulders as he swam deeper and deeper into the cold depths, me trailing behind him like a remora fish.

I've already told him all this a few times this summer, but he doesn't hold the information long before he forgets. Even a brief conversational lull can wipe the slate clean. It's not lost on me that I now have the power to control our shared narrative, to pick and choose which aspects of the truth I want to unearth or bury. Our family story is mine to craft now. If I don't like the version I relay to him today, I can always tweak it tomorrow. The truth, whatever that is, seems more fungible than ever.

We glide our way back, and I hoist myself onto the dock as Dad slowly ascends the ladder. Donning our robes, we sit in the flimsy aluminum folding chairs that have been here forever. The sun is now gone, and the sky is a hazy pink over the blackening trees.

We sit for a moment as the pond stills and finds its balance, mirroring the sky. It has never occurred to me until now that this must be why it's called evening. The *even*-ing, when the ragged edges of the day soften into something more calm and reciprocal. The air holds a hint of humidity, and the quiet is commanding and layered: the chirping of insects, the steady drill of a woodpecker, the occasional crack of a twig along the shoreline, my father's deep nose-breathing.

Then suddenly, an interruption: *Aaaa-ooooooooo-looooh. Aaaa-ooooooooo-looooh.*

It's a distinctive call—strong, searching, spectral. I run into the boathouse to grab the binoculars we keep hanging on a hook. Returning, I peer toward the center of the pond. There's no mistaking it: a loon.

"Look," I gasp, handing my father the binoculars. "Do you see?"

He fumbles with the focus and I help him adjust it. After a moment, he whispers, "What a fine fellow . . ."

We watch as the loon cuts a sharp course through the water, then dives and disappears. After a moment, it emerges even closer to us. Now we can see its white spotting, the reddish cast of its eyes, the sharp dagger of its beak.

"Dad, you called it."

"What's that?"

"Earlier, in the car . . . you said something about the loons coming back. I had no idea what you were talking about because they haven't come here for years, but you predicted it."

He looks into my eyes plaintively: "Did I? How clever of me." The loon calls again, and from somewhere we can't see, his mate answers. My father picks up the binoculars and peers through them again. "If I were a loon, this is where I would make my home, too."

————————

If it had just been the return of the loons (the mate eventually revealed herself, with a fluffy gray loonlet in tow), I wouldn't have paid it much mind; but over the next week, my father has a series of other minor premonitions. At least, I think that's what is going on. It's also possible that I'm losing my grip on reality, although I didn't expect that to happen so soon. Yes, we are isolated in the woods, but I was hoping to maintain my sanity until at least midwinter. We haven't even hit July yet.

The next prediction comes a couple of days later. We wake to a torrential downpour, but Dad assures me we will be able to go out in the canoe that afternoon. The forecast indicates otherwise, but sure enough, the sun breaks through just after 1:00 P.M.

Then there is the evening we are watching *Jeopardy!* and a smug, bespectacled contestant from Bethesda takes an early lead. "He won't win," my father says. "Not with a smirk like that." The smirker increases his sizeable lead until the final question, when he overconfidently bets it all and is defeated by a plucky history teacher from Des Moines.

And the afternoon when my father announces: "It's time for blueberries." I know it's far too early in the season, but we walk up the driveway to check the bushes anyway. Sure enough, the first berries have just ripened from green to purple. They're tart, but promising—and weeks earlier than usual.

Dad always forgets his predictions by the time they are realized; I'm the only witness. But it occurs to me that Nina must have experienced this phenomenon as well, so the next time she calls, I ask, "Did you ever notice that Dad has a sixth sense? Like he can foresee things?"

"What kind of things?"

I tell her about the loons, the unexpected sun, the *Jeopardy!* upset, the early blueberries.

"Those sound like coincidences to me," she says, seeming distracted. I hear street noise and people twittering in Swedish in the background.

"So you never noticed this? You don't think he's even a *little bit* psychic?"

"Oh boy," Nina says. "You might need to get out more."

"I know they're little things. It's just that they don't feel like coincidences. I mean, the loons? After years of no loons? Maybe he's tuned into something."

"Cricket, he's not psychic; he's confused. And your imagination is running a little wild."

"Okay. Yeah. You're right." This is why I need Nina; she brings me back to earth. The summer solstice is almost upon us, and it must be making me loopy—I'm seeing prophecies where they don't exist.

"Cricket, do you have anyone to hang out with other than Dad?"

"Carl has come by a few times," I say, but this doesn't satisfy her.

"What about your friend Chloe? I think she's still around in the summer. Have you tried reaching out?"

I haven't, and I'm not ready to.

"I will," I fib. "That's a good idea."

Chapter 12

I'm not exactly sure what I expected, moving back here. In my more naive moments, I had probably hoped for a sense of renewal, if not an all-out catharsis. A sustained feeling of fulfillment. And of course, I had hoped for some kind of reconciliation with my father—or at least, a chance to apologize for the horrible way I acted as a grief-stricken teenager. But he doesn't even know that I'm his daughter, so I'm not sure how I expected that to work. Maybe Nina was right: what I signed up for was caregiving, but what I sought was a miracle.

If you had told me a year ago that looking after my dad would soon be my day-to-day, I would have congratulated you on the great joke. And if you had asked my dad, fifteen years ago, who would be taking care of him in the twilight of his life, he likely would have suggested anyone but me. But here I am, doing it. We continually surprise each other. We even surprise ourselves.

For the first few weeks after Nina's departure, I do my best to adhere to her instructions: I wake my father at 7:00 A.M. He brushes his teeth. I give him his morning pills (Flomax, Aricept, baby aspirin). We select his outfit for the day. Physically, he can still do most of this on his own, but I need to be there to keep him on task. Otherwise, he gets derailed and wanders into the great room with no pants on. I've seen it happen.

But it isn't long before the carefully conceived schedule that Nina left us falls by the wayside; and by the time July rolls around, I have all but discarded her timetables and spreadsheets. I just don't see the point in waking my father up if he is tired, or putting him to bed if he isn't. That doesn't mean we are doing anything particularly wild, only that we might go to the dump on Tuesday rather than on Friday. We might hit the post office on Wednesday rather than on Saturday. We never have much to throw out, and we don't receive much mail, but we enjoy the adventure of tossing our trash and the subtle drama of opening our P.O. box to see what might lurk inside.

Sometimes it occurs to me that I should at least attempt to cultivate a social life here, but the prospect is daunting. I'm worried about running into people I used to know, about having to recap the last decade. What is there to say? I haven't been back, but I haven't moved on.

I had set a goal to find a job by the end of June, but my search is proving trickier than I expected. I inquire at a few local businesses (the Locust Inn, Lorne's All-Day Diner) about part-time positions, but most have already hired their summer staff, and the ones who still have openings would need me to work early mornings or late nights. I can't manage that while also taking care of my father, who needs steady supervision, lest he decide to wander off or take the boat out. There are unending ways to get into trouble at Catwood Pond—I would know. My next thought is to try to find an at-home aide to stay with him while I work, but I quickly realize the cost of hiring someone would cancel out whatever I could make in a local service job. For a moment, I wonder if *I* should get a job as a home aide—it seems like a decent gig—and then I realize the nonsensicality of becoming a care worker so that I can hire a care worker, like a snake eating its own tail. The truth is, looking after my father is already a full-time job, albeit an unpaid one. I need something that allows maximum flexibility— and some degree of mental stimulation.

That leaves remote work, which I figure I could do from home while also keeping an adequate eye on my father. But as I search various job boards online, it's clear that most of the roles that interest me require a college degree. Suddenly, I fear that I might be wholly unemployable, which is ironic given the diversity of gigs I've had in my life. I've managed to shapeshift from cleaning stalls on a ranch to waiting tables at a Michelin-starred restaurant. And although I'm still willing to do all manner of work, being my dad's caregiver means I can't be as flexible as I once was. I can feel my stress mounting, but I tell myself I have time. We have enough money for now.

One afternoon, my father and I are sitting on the porch. He used to spend hours with a book here, but reading has become tricky for him. He will pick up the newspaper or a magazine out of habit, but put it down before long, defeated. I know he still has the capacity to read—he sometimes recites a headline to me—but it seems he can no longer follow a narrative thread for long enough to get through a whole article, or a chapter, or even a paragraph. So we have a new afternoon tradition: I read poetry aloud to him, and he promptly falls asleep.

As I leaf through a heavy anthology, my dad looks at his watch and says, "Carl should be here soon."

"I don't think he's coming today," I say gently. I happen to know that Carl is out of town and isn't expected back until next week. Letting my finger land on a random page, I commence reading Theodore Roethke's "The Waking." By the time I get to "We think by feeling. What is there to know?" my father is asleep—his mouth open and emitting jagged snores at uneven intervals.

From here, I can see across the pond to the far shore, a mile away. In my lifeguarding days, I could easily swim there and back, but I haven't attempted it since the summer after Seth's accident, when grief made me restless, and constant motion was the only thing that kept me from disintegrating. I had once heard that if a shark stops swimming, it dies. And maybe I feared the same would be true for me. Or worse—that stillness might mean aching like that forever. So I lived the next decade in a feverish effort to keep moving: new relationships, new experiences, new distractions.

This is the first time I've sat still in years.

Suddenly, I hear heavy footsteps on the stairs of the porch, and Carl appears in his summer uniform: brown work boots, navy pants, blue T-shirt.

"Hi there," I say. "This is a nice surprise. I thought you were still out of town."

"Came back a little early," says Carl softly, not wanting to wake my dad. He hands me a basket of colorful heirloom tomatoes and a huge jar of honey with the comb half-submerged. "My friend up north keeps bees."

"Oh, wow. Thank you," I say, getting up and gesturing for him to follow me inside.

I wouldn't say I know Carl well, but we have established an easy rapport since I arrived in May. A month and a half in, it's safe to say he is my best local friend—not to mention my only local friend. As we stand in the coolness of the unlit kitchen, I pour us some iced tea and cut two fat wedges of lemon.

"Plans for the weekend?" he asks.

"Oh, you know us. We're going to get crazy," I say. I think about my friends in the city, who are inevitably hopping between outdoor bars and backyard barbecues and rooftop parties now that summer is in full swing. I feel a pang of anxiety about missing out on something, losing ground, drifting into orbit, never being heard from again. "We'll probably take the canoe out later."

"Perfect day for it," says Carl. He seems to pick up on my listlessness. "You doing okay, in general? This must be a big change for you. Living here."

"I'm fine." My knee-jerk response. But then I actually consider the question. "A little lonely, I guess. I used to have a big group of friends here when I was younger, but we're not in touch anymore."

He nods, then surprises me by asking: "Are you practicing self-care?"

I nearly spit out my iced tea. When I worked at Actualize, I heard that term about ten times a day, but I haven't thought about it since I moved here. I would never have pegged Carl as the self-care type, but his question makes me think.

"I guess I think more about my dad's care than I do my own. But I'm having a nice enough time. We love the dump—we went yesterday."

"Going to the dump is your self-care?" Carl asks, and we both laugh. But then he says seriously: "Doing this for a parent can become all-consuming. Just don't forget to take care of yourself, too."

We stand in silence for a minute, but Carl doesn't seem to be in a rush. He never is. Eventually I say: "It's weird—my dad said you would come by today. I told him he was mistaken because I thought you were out of town. But here you are. This keeps happening."

"What does?"

"He keeps making these little . . . predictions. Or prophecies," I say. "But I'm sure they're just coincidences."

"Why are you sure of that?"

"I mean, he's not exactly on the pulse. It's hard to know where he is, mentally. But every once in a while, he has a conviction about something—like he knows what's going to take place, and then it does. It's happened more times than I can count this summer. Just little things."

Carl doesn't look surprised or skeptical. In fact, for a moment, I think he is about to reveal something, but he just nods and walks to the sink to rinse his glass.

"Have you noticed it, too?" I ask.

"Absolutely. He's tuned into something. I've always thought so."

"Nina disagrees. I mean, she doesn't think he's psychic."

Carl shrugs. "It's subtle. Sometimes what he says is vague, or it takes a while to make sense. But he has a definite awareness. For instance, he knew you would come back."

"What do you mean?"

"Sometimes when he would mention you, he would say 'When Cricket moves back . . .' or 'When Cricket comes to live with me . . .' like it was inevitable. And this is for as long as I've known him. Three years ago, he was saying that."

"But I had no intention of moving here until a few months ago. This was never the plan."

Carl shrugs again. "He thought it was."

"So weird. Nina never mentioned him saying that. But maybe she didn't notice. Or maybe she just discounted it because of his Alzheimer's.

I mean, he doesn't even know who I am. He doesn't understand that I'm his daughter."

"Maybe not in the day-to-day, but on some level, he knows." Carl seems certain in a way that assuages my skepticism. "Arthur's memory is faulty, but I've always felt he's still working with the fundamental truths. He has even helped me process some things. I once joked that he's my own personal oracle."

I snort my iced tea. "Ah, yes. The renowned oracle at Catwood Pond . . ."

Carl laughs softly, his crow's feet crinkling.

"Well, I'm relieved to hear I'm not going crazy," I say.

"You're far from crazy," says Carl. "You might even be onto something."

After Carl leaves, I putter around the great room, not so much decluttering as moving the clutter from place to place. I rearrange some of the bookshelves that surround the fireplace; I dust the standup piano; I reset the pieces on the backgammon board; and I twirl the burnished wooden globe on its stand. "Adventure calls. Where should I travel next?" I ask as I spin the orb. Then I close my eyes and drop my finger like a pin. I take a deep breath and look: the Adirondacks. My finger has landed exactly where I already am, and I have to smile at the anticlimax.

I look out the window and see my father's head resting against the back of his chair, his hair puffing in the breeze. After a moment, he begins to stir. He stands up and starts for the door, but then seems to reconsider or forget what his aim was, and he moves back to the chair, where he sits and trains his gaze on the pond. I wonder what occupies his mind in this moment. I didn't used to think of "sitting" as an activity, but we do a lot of it these days. Sometimes just watching the busyness of a squirrel can fill an hour. The anticipation of a rainstorm can occupy a whole afternoon. I've never been into meditation, but I think this is what meditators are after: the ability to do nothing but feel everything, to hold on to life so lightly that it has a chance to bowl you over.

As I watch my father watching the water, I am hit with a future-ache about the time when he will no longer be here. I've heard it called *anticipatory grief*, but that's too clinical for me. There's no adequate label for this feeling of something eating away at you, the growing realization that someday you will be devastated—so why not start now? Get ahead of it. Beat your heartbreak to the punch.

I retreat to the kitchen and cut up two of Carl's tomatoes—one that is streaked with orange and yellow, and one that is so red it's almost purple. I sprinkle them with olive oil, a little salt, and then carry the plate out to the porch.

For a moment, my father is surprised. He looks as if he's trying to place me. "Well, hello."

"Hi, Dad," I say, hoping to reorient him to who he is, who I am, who we are to each other. "Did you have a nice snooze?"

"Did I ever!" he says, clapping his hands onto his thighs. "What do you have there?"

"You were right again. Carl *did* stop by, and he brought these," I say, holding the plate out to him.

"Well, will you look at those beauties! You know, you can spend all summer waiting for one sensational tomato."

He pops a slice into his mouth, contemplates the flavor, and then nods. "That's it. That's the one."

Chapter 13

———

A few days later, I wake to find my father already up and at his writing desk, which is strewn with papers and abandoned drafts. His handwriting, once neat and artful, is now large and wobbly.

"What are you working on, Dad?"

"Some correspondence," he says. He seems to have forgotten all about email and smartphones. In his new mind, the telephone (a landline, naturally) and the post office are his only portals to the outside world. He sometimes becomes preoccupied with "staying in touch," but it's unclear with whom. He occasionally mentions specific people—a man named Rip Chastain, an acquaintance named Beverly Hauser—but I have no idea who they are, if they're still alive, or if they ever existed. I peer over his shoulder and see that he has started a few letters.

Dear Gillian, Are you still . . .

Dear Antoine, How are you? I think . . .

Dear Leonard, Has it really been . . .

He hasn't gotten very far on any of them, and when I inquire about their recipients, he isn't quite clear on who they are.

"I really need to get to the post office today," he says with some urgency. We were there just two days ago, but I have no reason not to indulge him. I suggest we write to Nina.

"Nina?"

"Your daughter. The one who used to live here with you."

"Right. Yes. Where has she gone?"

"To Stockholm." The truth no longer upsets him, which I hope means he has grown comfortable with me as his main "person."

"Stockholm! Good for her."

We make some coffee and English muffins and then install ourselves on the porch. There's a slight wind, and the water is rippling
westward as if it has somewhere to be, unlike us. We rarely have
anywhere to be, other than where we are. I'm not sure if that's sad or
ideal.

I grab a pen and begin to craft our own clumsy version of Mad
Libs. I provide the narrative arc of the letter, prompting my father to
fill in the descriptive details as we go.

Dear Nina,

We're here on the porch, and <u>we couldn't be happier</u>. The sun is <u>still</u>
<u>there, where it usually is</u>. The woods are <u>fresh and fitful</u>. We miss
you very much and we hope you <u>miss us too</u>. Did we tell you about
the loons? We think they are <u>a handsome couple</u>. They seem to <u>have</u>
<u>the world on a string</u>, and they sing like <u>Maria Callas</u>. Their young
loonlet is <u>finding her way in the world</u>. The most exciting thing
that happened this summer was <u>that tomato. You know the one</u>.
All is well here. We are looking forward to <u>going to the post office</u>.
And we hope to <u>have a visit from our friend Seth</u>.

This last fill-in-the-blank stops me in my tracks. "Did you mean
Carl?"

"No," my father says matter-of-factly. "Seth."

I choose to omit this part, and I quickly sign and seal the letter. *It*
was a slip of the tongue, I tell myself. We finish breakfast, dress for the
day, and make our way out to the car.

After we reckon with my father's seat belt, he relaxes and says, "So,
where to?"

"To the post office, Dad. It was your idea!"

"Ah, yes. Right you are." He is skilled at pretending to remember
something once reminded.

When we arrive, Warren the postmaster is jamming a few odd
envelopes into overstuffed P.O. boxes whose owners haven't come
by in months, or maybe years. He moves at a slow pace and seems

overwhelmed by even the small amount of mail that comes and goes under his watch.

"The Campbells two times in one week?" He grins when he sees us, surprised that we are breaking our usual cadence. "What a nice surprise."

"We decided to get a little crazy, mix things up," I say.

"Arthur, come have a look at these yellow warblers." Warren motions for my father to peruse the new limited-edition stamps that have just come in. They marvel together as I check our mailbox. I fish out a promotional flyer from AARP, a credit-card offer (my father has been preapproved), and a Sharper Image catalogue.

"Nothing too momentous in there," Warren calls to me. I choose not to let it bother me that he has so thoroughly analyzed the scant contents of our box. But I am a little disappointed that there's nothing of importance, because I thought my father's interest in coming to the post office might have been another premonition. I'm looking everywhere now, but maybe Nina is right: I'm getting carried away.

I join my dad at the counter, where we purchase the warbler stamps and post our letter to Stockholm. ("Is that where she's living now?" my father asks me, amazed.) But as we turn to leave, the door swings open and an elegant older woman blows in like a gale. She has long steel-colored hair with a white streak in the front, and she wears a black full-length bodysuit under a sheer cheetah-print caftan. Not the typical deep-woods wardrobe. As she whisks past us with purpose, I recognize her as Paula Garibaldi, the flamboyant dance teacher of my youth.

"Warren, my love!" Her raspy voice conveys confidence as she plops a heavy pile of flyers on the counter. "Be a darling and get these distributed today? My enrollment is untenably low."

I glance at the top flyer, which advertises: MISS PAULA'S DANCE BARN: TAP, JAZZ, BALLET, HIP-HOP. ALL AGES, ALL GENDERS, ALL SKILL LEVELS—THE MORE, THE MERRIER.

"Paula." Warren sighs. "How many times . . . I can't just put them in the mailboxes. It's illegal. The USPS isn't a charity. You have to pay for postage."

"Cut the crap, Warren," she says. "I don't need the government's blessing to teach tap dance."

"This is the *last* time," says Warren as he picks up the flyers. I have a feeling he has said that many times before and will likely end up saying it again.

"You're a doll," says Paula, before finally noticing her rapt audience. "Arthur Campbell? Is that you, dear? It's Paula . . ." She presses her manicured fingers to her chest.

"Paula!" My dad conveys his usual enthusiasm, but I can tell he doesn't know who she is.

Paula looks at me and a smile comes over her face. "Cricket Campbell . . ."

I feel exposed, but also warmed by the fact that she recognizes me.

"Where have you been hiding? It's been years and years. Look at you! Finally back for a visit."

"More than a visit. I moved here in May," I admit.

"May? You've been hiding for two months? We need to get you out of the house. I always hope Arthur will come see me, but he never does, the cad," says Paula, with a hint of flirtation.

"We're working with some memory issues, so he may have forgotten," I explain.

"I understand. So, Cricket, you're here for good?"

"For a year, at least. We'll see how it goes."

"You're a saint. My daughter would rather see me eaten by wolves than become my caregiver."

Suddenly I feel bold. "Paula, you don't by chance need administrative help, do you? I'm looking for work. I could assist with things like email marketing, social media, your website . . ."

Paula laughs. "I would love help with my website—if I had one! I'm not really an internet person." She points to the flyers. "This is as far as I've ever gotten with marketing."

"Well, I don't want to mess with a good thing," I say. "It's just a thought."

Paula looks at my legs. "Are you still dancing?"

I can't help but laugh at this question. I hung up my jazz shoes long ago.

"Well, you should be. I teach a class for adults now. Tuesday nights at seven in the barn. You'll love it. Come next week—we can talk business afterward."

Her forcefulness could be viewed as abrasive, but I am reassured by it. I'm still getting used to my newfound authority—I have become my parent's parent—and sometimes, I miss being told what to do. Paula pecks my father on the cheek and then grabs my forearm as she fixes her dark eyes on me. "I'll see you Tuesday, Cricket."

She floats out the door before I can respond.

"Quite a minx," my father says.

We turn to see Warren beginning to distribute the flyers Paula has left. He shakes his head in amused exasperation. "Hell on wheels, that one."

Chapter 14

As I drive to Paula's dance class the following Tuesday, I call my mom. I'm on a stretch of road where I know I will have exactly five minutes of reliable cell service: the perfect amount of time to check in and speedily exit the conversation before she starts giving me life advice.

She picks up after one ring. "Cricket! Perfect timing. I was just telling George we should have you here for Thanksgiving this year. Nina could pop down from Stockholm."

My mother met George Ratliff-Jones, a very British man with a very British name, on a red-eye from New York to London four years ago. They were seated next to each other on the overnight flight, and to this day, they like to joke that they "slept together on their first date"—a quip that I could do without. At the time, my mother's consulting career had her regularly commuting between New York and London. They struck up a transatlantic romance, and when COVID hit just a few months later, they decided to go all in. My mother moved into George's house in St. John's Wood, and less than a year later, they were married. I still don't know him well, but he seems like a good match for her. And it's fitting that, whereas she met my father in the sewers of New York, she met George in business class at thirty thousand feet. It's where she always aspired to be.

"Thanksgiving—that's months away," I say. "And I didn't know you still celebrated, now that you're English."

"We don't, usually," she muses. "But we could approximate it this year. Remind me: Do you like quail?"

"It's a nice idea, Mom, but I can't leave Dad here alone."

"Of course you can." She doesn't seem to understand that I have a real responsibility now. I am neither as flexible nor as persuadable as I used to be. "You don't have a job yet, do you?"

"Actually, I might. A consulting gig. I'm heading to a meeting right now to iron out the details," I say, embellishing just enough.

"Fabulous! For whom? Where?"

"A local business in Locust."

"Oh." Her voice falls.

"Do you remember my old dance teacher, Paula Garibaldi?"

"Vaguely." She swiftly moves on. "Have you thought about Europe? You know, George could easily find you something here. In fact, I was just . . ."

"Mom, I can't hear you. I think you're breaking up." I timed things perfectly. She says something about *taking your future more seriously* and then something about Nina, and I hear her say *quail* again before the line goes dead.

Though we speak almost every week, she still won't acknowledge that I have made a commitment here. It's as if my choosing to live at Catwood Pond somehow offends her on a personal level. She still thinks I should want what she wants and do as she does. She has never really seen me for who I am.

A few minutes later, I turn onto the dirt drive that leads to Miss Paula's. Carl has agreed to hang out with my father for the evening while I "do something for myself." I keep my expectations low as I envision myself doing sad jazz hands in the mirrored barn where I used to prance in my youth, but I figure that, at the very least, a little exercise and human interaction can't hurt—and if some employment comes out of it, all the better.

As soon as I park, I can feel a distinct energy in the air. The door to the barn is slightly ajar, and I tentatively poke my head in. The space is as I remember it: rustic but clean, with low lights and a huge mirror taking up an entire wall of the structure. There are four people inside: Sal from the hardware store, a middle-aged woman, a gangly teenage boy, and, of course, there is Paula, who is dressed in sheer black tights and a low-back tiger-print leotard. Her hair is loose, and her powdery purple eyeshadow fades artfully into her brow bone. The Pointer Sisters' "Slow Hand" drifts through the air, and Paula calls out to me: "Jump right in! We're warming up!"

I drop my bag, kick off my shoes, and take a place in front of the mirror, where everyone is slowly writhing, hips revolving, shoulders rolling. For a moment, I regret my frumpy sweatpants and oversized T-shirt, but as I look around at the other outfits—denim cutoffs on Sal, a teal unitard on the teenage boy—it seems that anything goes here.

"Listen to the words. What's she saying? *I want a lover with an easy touch.*" Paula dips her pelvis and answers her own question: "So make it easy!"

She throws her upper body toward the floor in a half-fold, and then slowly rolls up, dragging her hands over her torso inch by inch. Everyone follows suit. This is a far cry from the bubbly modern jazz of my youth. Honestly, I don't know *what* this is—but I like it.

The Pointer Sisters gives way to a smooth Janet Jackson jam, and Paula purrs in her authoritative rasp: "For our newcomer, we have only one rule for the next hour: no thinking. Let your body take it from here."

The other three members of the class whoop in excitement, and Paula starts to call out dance steps that I used to know by heart. "To the right: *chassé, chassé, passé*, and body roll! To the left . . ."

This could be my opportunity to *chassé* my way right out the door, but I drove seventeen minutes to be here, so I decide to surrender to the experience.

Everyone seems to know what they're doing. I try to follow along, but I'm always a few steps behind. When Sal (who is next to me in his short-shorts) swiftly changes direction during a sultry hip roll, I almost run into him. He gives me a forgiving wink, and I feel myself relax. There's no question that I am by far the worst dancer here—my wild flailing in the mirror confirms this fact—but it's equally clear that no one is keeping score. A moment later, we're crawling across the floor like pulsating leopards, then popping up and spinning to the far wall. I had wanted a new life, and here it is: I'm 350 miles north of New York City, deep in the woods, shimmying around a barn with four people who are taking this just seriously enough. Suddenly it hits me: this is the most fun I've had in years.

By the time we finish our cooldown, I'm glossy with sweat and giddy from adrenaline. My fellow dancers come up to introduce themselves, and suddenly I feel like I'm part of a gang of unruly misfits. As they trickle out of the barn into the night, Paula approaches. "You've still got it."

This is beyond generous, but I accept the compliment and say, "That was so fun. Were your classes always this saucy?"

Paula shakes her head. "I've gotten much saucier with age."

"Well, I really needed that. It's been an adjustment, moving here. But maybe I just needed to dance."

Paula nods proudly, like a guru whose student has finally begun to see the light. "You know, I'm a Manhattan transplant, too. Years back. Way before I taught you the first time around."

"Really? I don't think I knew that. You don't miss the city?"

"Of course I miss the city. I'd give my eyeteeth for one more run on Broadway, but you've got to dance where you are, baby." She begins walking around the barn, tidying up and turning off lights. "So, let's talk admin. I need all the help I can get to bring in new students. Word of mouth used to be sufficient, but I know I should be doing more. I've just never been a computer person. I mean, I do email—I love email— but that's about it."

"I get it," I say. "I can definitely help. It won't take much to set up a website, start building your digital mailing list, and maybe get you on Instagram, if you're up for it."

We settle on an hourly rate that feels modest but fair, plus Paula says I can come to any of her classes free of charge.

It's not a career, but it's a move in the right direction. I gather my things, and as I approach the door, Paula adds: "I'm glad you've come back, Cricket. You can have a nice life here if you're willing to get a little creative."

Chapter 15

———

As July unfurls, my father and I maximize our time on the water. One evening, feeling ambitious, we decide to go for an after-dinner canoe ride. Taking the motorboat out would be easier, but this late in the day, we prefer to paddle so we don't disturb the peace. Getting into the canoe is no small feat for my father, but I've devised a system that works well enough. I haul the boat as far up the wooden slip as it will go. He sits down on the dry part of the slip, inches over, and crawls into the boat one body part at a time: arm, leg, hips, other leg, other arm. It takes a while, but once he is settled, I push the canoe out into the water, and I leap in from the dock.

"Whoooaaa-ooohhh!" my father whoops as we rock left and right. If we were working with a newfangled lightweight canoe, we would tip in an instant. But ours is an antique wooden model, as heavy as they come. We're not going to win any races in it, but it's nearly capsize-proof, as long as we're sitting and centered.

We begin paddling eastward, planning to skim the full perimeter of the pond. After a few minutes, we see the loons are out, diving and popping up in a small inlet, finding and losing each other over and over again. Their loonlet bobs on the surface, patiently observing her parents' activities. Just as we pass, her mother surfaces with a fish in her beak. She brings it to her baby, who receives it with an open gullet.

We round a small peninsula and proceed along the length of the pond, passing a boathouse every so often. Although the town of Locust is alive with seasonal bustle, Catwood is sleepy this summer. With so few camps on the pond, the activity ebbs and flows as generations come and go. When I was growing up, there was a critical mass of youngsters who were always darting from shore to shore. But this summer, I have barely seen another boat. As we pass the beaver dam, we cease our paddling and search for signs of activity. Suddenly, up ahead, I notice something that looks like a branch, although it's moving too quickly along its course to be inanimate. As we near, I realize it's not just a stick, but a beaver carrying a stick. It scoots faster, and as we pass, it slaps its tail, creating a walloping kerplunk before it disappears.

"Same to you!" says my father.

We start paddling again, instinctively following the line of the shore as we begin to turn westward. From the back of the canoe, I provide both steering and the majority of our propulsion. My father sits up front, dipping his paddle intermittently. But what he lacks in strength, he makes up for in wonder, in his enduring ability to be awed.

"Spectacular," he says as we coast past another inlet, where a lanky blue heron stands at attention. "How lucky we are to live here."

We skirt the shoreline, and before long, we come to the Seavey property. The once-flashy camp now seems to droop, having been unoccupied for years.

"Who is it that lives here?" my father asks.

"The Seaveys," I say, curious to see if the name will mean anything to him.

"Strange. I don't think I know them."

He certainly used to, and he never liked them, given their propensity for flouting rules aimed at preserving the pond's delicate ecosystem. I'm relieved that this property doesn't bring anything up in his recollection.

"Just as well. They never come anymore. I've heard they're trying to sell," I say as the main house comes into view.

"Good luck to them. Who would want to buy that monstrosity?" His feelings on ostentation have not changed with time.

We glide on, past the expansive boathouse, the docks, the crumbling firepit, the forested shoreline. For me, this landscape is loaded with nostalgia and regret, longing and guilt. Up ahead, a formidable boulder juts out into the pond. How many times did Seth and I leap from this rock together that summer? Twenty? Thirty? How many times did we plunge, synchronized, into the blue water? How many times did we pop up, breathless and wild-eyed, calling out for each other like loons?

Chapter 16

———

July 2015

By the time summer was in full swing, Seth and I were officially in love. Most of my friends were thrilled that I finally had a real boyfriend. The only person who seemed skeptical was Greg, and his increasing huffiness about my relationship with his cousin only made it sweeter for me.

I still couldn't believe Seth actually liked me. Sometimes when I saw him from a distance—glimpsing him at the tennis courts, or spotting him out in a boat, or catching his gaze across a bonfire—I thought to myself, *Who is that?* And then it would hit me: he is mine.

In those days, cell service in Locust was practically nonexistent. As a result, we all made plans via landline or in person, and we often left our smartphones by the wayside when we got together. You couldn't Google anything anyway, and there was no reason to document or Instagram the action. In many ways, this gave us what amounted to an old-fashioned youth. We had to talk to our friends' parents on the phone when we called their houses; we had to wait for one another to arrive without having an exact ETA. As a result, we moved more slowly and with more patience. We lingered longer. And when the moment was good, we relished it, knowing there was nowhere else to be.

One afternoon, we all gathered at the Seaveys' dock to swim. Some came in motorboats, some in canoes, some by car, and one kid named Mick had waterskied behind Sully's boat. We alternated lazing in the sun and leaping into the water, and at one point, Chloe's canoe was capsized so we could turn it into a cavern. This was a game we had all played since childhood—flipping a canoe so that it retained an air bubble big enough to let you breathe freely if you swam underneath it.

"Meet you in there?" said Seth, winking at me before he dove into the water and disappeared. I had always found this canoe game a bit claustrophobic, but I followed, slithering under the side of the canoe and bobbing up into the cavity within. It was dark, but a few streaks of light reflected off the water, creating stripes on the bottom of the boat and across Seth's dripping face. I pushed my hair back and found my footing in the silty bottom of the pond.

"Hey," I said, wincing as I realized how loud my voice was as it reverberated off the walls of the boat. In a whisper, I tried again: "Hey."

"Hey." Seth moved closer to me. Our chins touched the water, and there were just a few inches of space between the tops of our heads and the floor of the canoe. It felt like being in the belly of a whale—both intimate and scary.

He pulled me toward him and kissed me. In the darkness, in the water, it felt as if we were suspended in a netherworld of our own making. I laced my fingers together behind Seth's neck as I felt his hand move up my thigh. Feeling bold, I reached for the waistband of his swimsuit, but just then, we heard a scream. Then another.

We ducked out into the open to see what was happening. On the lawn, Greg and Chloe were inspecting something. Greg had a stick in his hand, and I could tell that whatever he was poking at was alive—and likely scared. I splashed my way out of the water, and as I neared them, I saw that the object of their interest was a green-and-black garter snake that had become entangled in a piece of duct tape. Greg lifted it with the stick and then dropped it back onto the grass.

"Stop it!" I yelled. "Why are you poking it?"

"I'm seeing if it's alive," said Greg, as the snake whipped its tail in an effort to escape the tape.

"It's obviously alive," I said, as Seth caught up with me. "You're hurting it."

Greg shrugged. "Chill. It's a snake."

"It's a sentient being." I looked around for a way to free the animal, but it was well-adhered, and some of its skin had begun to come off on the tape. "Can someone find a box?"

"Don't tell me you're going to do CPR on a snake," Greg said. "Just throw it in the water and let nature take its course."

But Seth was already jogging toward the boathouse, and when he returned with an empty cooler, I gently lifted the snake, tape and all, into it. Its scales had a delicate softness that I knew well. I had volunteered at a local animal sanctuary the previous summer, where I helped rehabilitate quite a few snakes (not to mention birds, rodents, and even a fox).

Chloe looked into the cooler and squealed. I thought I saw the reptile fix one of its tiny black eyes on me, conveying a clear call for help.

"Will you pull my boat around?" I asked Seth, who took off in the direction of the dock where it was tied up. I carried the cooler to the end of the dock, and as Seth slowed, I hopped into the front of the boat. We took off across the pond at full speed, like EMTs on a mission.

By the time we reached my boathouse, I had a plan. We docked and carried our patient up to the porch, but when my mother—who was in residence for the week—saw us trying to come inside with a snake, she said, "Oh no you don't." So Seth waited with the cooler while I went inside to look for something I could use to loosen the tape's grip.

I returned with a jar of coconut oil, and set to work inching my fingers along the snake, carefully dabbing oil in the places where the tape met its scales. Slowly, my diligence began to pay off. The tape gave way a millimeter at a time, taking none of the snake's skin with it.

"It's working!" said Seth, watching with rapt attention.

"Getting there," I said. "Come on, little Coconut."

"You can do it, Coconut," whispered Seth, embracing the name I had spontaneously given the snake.

Our patient was surprisingly compliant, and it stayed perfectly still as I navigated the final section of its tail. When I finally lifted the tape off, it was mostly free of scales.

"Nice," said Seth, relieved. "He's going to be okay."

"I think so, but see how that part of the mid-body is a bit swollen? We need to keep him contained for a day or two so he can recuperate in safety," I said with a sense of authority I didn't know I could muster.

I found a suitable box, and Seth gathered some grass and rocks, which we added to the makeshift enclosure for ambiance. Finally, we left a small bowl of water, lest Coconut get thirsty. When we were confident that our patient was comfortably resting, we finally looked at each other.

"Nice work, Dr. Campbell," said Seth. "I'll be your vet tech any day."

It was thrilling to have someone I loved see me at my best—and to reflect back both who I was and who I could become. Somehow, Seth's love for me ignited a feeling of love toward myself. When he delighted in me, I delighted in myself. When he laughed at my jokes, I believed in my own hilarity. If I ever had a *best self*, she flourished that summer—and Seth was the primary witness.

A few days later, when I had nursed Coconut back to health and released him in a safe place on our property, I decided it was inevitable: of course I was going to be a vet someday. If Seth believed it, so did I.

Chapter 17

My father and I drop Dominic off for his dental procedure at 9:00 A.M., and when the vet's office calls a few hours later, I leap for my phone. General anesthesia can be fatal for cats of advanced age, and I pray that the news is good.

"He's doing really well," says Dr. Raymond. "But the X-rays show that the tooth decay is worse than we thought. There are nine teeth that require removal."

"Nine teeth," I say, trying to do the math. "So that's $900?!"

"I'll transfer you to the front desk for an exact estimate, and you can let them know how you'd like to proceed. Again, it's your choice . . ."

"But he'll be much more comfortable," I say.

"Exactly," says Dr. Raymond. "Hold, please."

A punchy Rod Stewart song comes on, and, just as I am starting to enjoy it, I hear, "This is Kathy at the front desk. So for nine teeth, plus the cleaning, the anesthesia, the meds, the X-rays, the pre-surgical bloodwork . . ."—I can hear her acrylic nails flying around the keyboard—"that will come out to $2,300. And we include a complimentary nail trim."

For a moment, I can't breathe. "$2,300?"

"Yes. Oh, wait. Do you need an Elizabethan collar? To prevent him from agitating the wound once he's home? If so, that will be . . . $2,306."

After a moment of stunned silence, during which I envision a loopy Dominic catching his cone-of-shame on the doorways of our house, I remember that I have a decision to make.

"Would you like us to proceed with the removal of the teeth?"

I don't have the money, but I can't bear the thought of Dominic waking up only for me to tell him, "Sorry, buddy, but we opted to let your teeth rot." And besides, he is my father's beloved companion; we need him healthy.

As I begin to sweat, Kathy says something about a payment plan. Four installments. Over time. Zero interest.

"Okay," I say. "Yes, you can proceed."

I know I'm doing the right thing for our cat, and, by proxy, for my dad. But when I hang up the phone, I immediately panic. Even with my new gig doing Paula's tech and admin, it will take me months to pay off this bill. I have to figure something out fast, and though it's hard to stomach, there's only one logical option. I open my laptop and compose a new email.

Subj: Freelance help?

Gemma,

Hello! I hope you're well. I've been eagerly following Actualize's announcements and social feeds—looks like business is booming! No surprise there. Things are busy here in the Adirondacks as well. I'm writing because I have an opening in my schedule to do a bit of freelance work, and I immediately thought of you. Any chance you need remote help with strategy or marketing? No worries if not.

All my best,
Cricket

I hit send with a wince. Writing to Gemma feels like crawling back to an ex who you know is bad for you. But at the same time, I know what makes Gemma tick, and I hope this will be a path to a quick paycheck or two. Just enough to cover Dominic's dental bill, then I will move on from Actualize for good. I close my laptop, sigh, and call to my father, "Dad? It's time to go get the cat."

My father wanders into the room and looks around. "The cat? Where is she?"

"She's at the doctor," I say. (Gender is a construct.)

When we arrive at the vet, I reluctantly hand over my credit card to Kathy, and the vet tech eagerly hands over Dominic, who is lolling in his carrier, docile and high on painkillers.

"He did beautifully," the vet tech says with a smile, as if Dominic has just aced the LSAT rather than drained my bank account.

"Thanks for taking such good care of him," I say. It's not lost on me that I once dreamed of being the veterinarian on the other side of this transaction. Maybe in my next life.

When we get home, I open my email and see there is a response from Gemma.

Re: Freelance help?

hey lady! Was just talking about you! Funny you should write. Ella is leaving 😞 and we need help with product copy asap
Cc'ing Adelaide to provide details
xoxoxo
G

Adelaide informs me that they need descriptions for thirty new products. Copywriting wasn't part of my job previously, but having been one of her first employees, I know Gemma's sensibilities better than anyone, and I'm confident I can pull it off. When Adelaide says they can pay me a flat fee of $500 for the rush job, I immediately accept. It's nearly enough to cover one of our payments to Dominic's vet.

When we hang up, I pour myself a large whisky and contemplate the irony of my financial situation. Somehow, I've landed two gigs in the past week, and yet I'm deeper in debt than ever.

———

A few days later, a hefty box arrives from Actualize, filled with samples to help inform my writing. Gemma wants me to "live the products" so that I can fully articulate their value to the customer. I lay everything out on the dining table. Among the samples are the ash bucket and accompanying accessories I had spied on Gemma's desk back in April. It's a full-circle moment that leaves me feeling conflicted about being back in Gemma's web, but at the same time, I need the money.

My father and I spend the rest of the day trying out serums, oils, creams, botanical tinctures, crystals, and infrared devices. I know I can trust him to be both candid and creative in his assessments.

"What the devil is this?" he says, holding up a comma-shaped object that's dripping with liquid.

"It's an eye mask. To depuff this area," I explain, placing it under his eye, along the curve of his cheekbone. I hold up a mirror to show him his reflection.

"Looks like a leech!"

Though his commentary isn't necessarily fodder for marketing copy, it does keep me amused as we move through the products. He doesn't like the algae-infused mud mask ("like being licked by a slug") but he loves the wildflower emulsion I rub onto his temples ("makes me feel like a fawn in a field").

Finally, it's time for me to start writing. As I wait for the words to come, I pick up the ash bucket one more time and sniff it. I will admit, it has a nice earthiness. I run the boar-bristle body brush along my arm and squeeze the sea sponge in my hand. Channeling Gemma, I open my laptop and swallow my pride.

Why should bathing be a chore when it can be a sacred ritual? Our "Manifest Destiny" collection takes inspiration from the pioneer women of yore, who traversed an untouched landscape, soaking up the elements along the way. Think cold mountain streams, sage-scented crosswinds, and soul-soothing sunsets. Perfect for trailblazers and trad wives alike, this collection will transport you to a purer place and a simpler time. Go West, young woman! Go West and glow up with the country.

A few days after I send the assignment in, Gemma writes back to tell me I nailed it: Were you this good when you worked here? LOL.

I was, though I never got the chance to write copy or do anything remotely creative in my former role. I was merely Gemma's hench-man, a job I don't miss.

She's wondering if I'm willing to do another round. It's a slippery slope. I have a vision of myself on my deathbed, decades from now, wondering how I ended up working for Gemma Dwyer for the entirety of my life. Then again, if I do four more of these copy projects, I will have made enough to pay off Dominic's dental bill. I say yes, but promise myself I will focus on finding more meaningful work once I'm out of debt.

Chapter 18

August 2015

There was no shortage of places in Locust for Seth and me to steal off to. Though we both had obligations (our jobs, the occasional evening with our respective families), we shared the same overriding goal: to see each other as often as possible. We met on docks, in boats, at the tennis courts. We met in the morning before work, during lunch breaks, and at night under the star-pierced sky.

Seth came by our house often, and my father took an immediate liking to him. My mother was less enthusiastic when she met him during her annual visit to the camp, but I sensed it had less to do with Seth than it did with her own dissatisfaction that week. Nothing seemed to impress or amuse her anymore. She was exasperated by every mosquito, every raindrop, every spiderweb. She was aggravated by the clunking dishwasher, the splintery dock, the sagging roof. Her patience with the woods had run out, and she spent her days in Locust running unnecessary errands at the closest strip mall, which was almost an hour away from our house. When it came to me, she was dismayed that my father didn't seem to be enforcing my curfew, and during the week that she was in residence, she noted the hour of my return every night. Once she left, my father's more laissez-faire parenting style resumed, and as usual, my curfew began to feel more like a suggestion than a mandate. One night, I stole Nina's car and went to a movie with Seth. We took our time coming home, and when I arrived at 12:30 A.M., my father was still up reading in his chair. I saw a flicker of relief cross his face when he saw me come in, but all he said was, "Nice night for a drive."

Though I didn't miss my mother's watchfulness, I was occasionally overwhelmed by the autonomy my father afforded me. With no boundary to push against, I began to feel a rising anxiety. Seth and I had not talked about having sex, but the subtext was always there. Our relationship felt like it was barreling toward something, and I figured it had to be that, but I was terrified—not just of the actual act, but of how it might change our dynamic. Or maybe how it might change me. What would happen when I crossed that threshold? I feared I would lose the little control I felt I had, so I preferred to stay on this side of the experience, where everything felt charged with a sense of anticipation. Within this emotional landscape, everything Seth and I did was thrilling. Simply browsing the shelves of Deb's Depot took on an air of exhilaration. Tennis became a way for us to dispel some of the tension that was building. My hormones had never been wilder; my forehand had never been better.

"Why don't you just do it already?" Chloe asked me one afternoon while we were stretched out on her dock.

"Do what?"

She looked at me like it was obvious, which it was. She and Greg had been having sex since last summer, and she seemed determined for me to join the club.

"I'm scared," I admitted.

"Why? It's no big deal. Just get it out of the way."

"Is that how it worked for you and Greg?" I asked.

"Yeah, pretty much."

"And then what? After you . . . got it out of the way."

Chloe shrugged. "You just keep having sex."

It wasn't the most enticing pitch. "So it's not really out of the way. It's more like it . . . becomes the focus."

"I guess, but at least you're over that initial hurdle. You know what you're dealing with. And then you realize sex is just a means to an end," Chloe explained. "The point is to keep him fixated on you. If you don't have sex, he will eventually get bored and become interested in someone else."

Boredom was the last thing I felt with Seth; I had never considered he might eventually feel it with me.

"Seth has had sex before, right?" asked Chloe, sitting up as if this was pivotal.

I nodded. Seth had admitted as much the one time we broached the topic.

"So there you go. It's no big deal for *you*, because you don't know what you're missing. But Seth is living without something he used to have. See? That's the tricky part."

It was just one tricky part of what was becoming an increasingly confusing matrix. To satisfy Chloe, I said, "Okay. I'll think about it."

And I did. Before long, I thought about it constantly. I tried not to let Chloe's words get to me, but she had planted a seed of anxiety. A clock had started, and from then on, it would always be ticking in my mind, marking time until one of two things happened: I mustered the courage to have sex, or Seth decided to leave.

I wrestled with my fears until I couldn't be alone with them anymore. One night, when Seth and I had taken my boat to the easternmost part of Catwood Pond, where there were no houses and no lights, I finally looked at him and asked, "Do you think we should have sex? I mean, not this minute. But like, before summer is over."

Seth looked a little shocked, then intrigued. "I mean, that would be nice."

I felt my heart sink, realizing I had hoped he would say it was inconsequential to him.

"Did I say the wrong thing?" he asked. "Do you not want to?"

"No, I do," I said. "Or I think I want to. Or I think I'm *supposed* to want to."

Seth smiled. "Well, why don't you give yourself time to decide which one it is? There's no rush."

"But . . ." It was already mid-August. After Labor Day, Seth and I would go our separate ways, and then who knew what would happen? I took a breath. "Okay."

I wrapped a blanket around myself like a cocoon. Seth looked at me and then reached down and opened a tacklebox that was on the floor of the boat. He rummaged around and pulled out an ornate fly, with magenta feathers shooting out from a white-and-black speckled body. He then took a pair of scissors and began to pry off the hook.

"What are you doing? Isn't it a little dark for fishing?" I could barely see the shore behind him, and all we had in the boat was a small solar-powered lantern.

"You'll see," he said, tying off a piece of fishing line. After a moment, he said, "Give me your hand."

I held out my palm, but he flipped it over and then gently slid the fly—which he had fashioned into a ring—onto my middle finger. It looked as if a dragonfly had alighted on my hand.

"See?" he said.

"See what?"

"There's no pressure. I'm already hooked."

As we bobbed under a starry sky, Seth took the blanket I was clinging to and wrapped it around both of us. I leaned into his shoulder, and he assured me that what we were currently doing—and not doing—was just fine with him. I did my best to believe him.

———

As Labor Day approached, the exultation I had felt about my first love had given way to angst about what would come next. Seth was entering his senior year near Lake Placid, and I would be a junior at my school in New York City. It was one thing for me to steal the car for the occasional illicit spin around Locust, but I wasn't brazen enough to venture on a five-hour drive on the interstate without a license. It seemed unlikely that we would be able to see each other until next summer, and that was if Seth returned to Locust at all. By then, he would be on the verge of college and would probably have more important things to do than teach tennis in a tiny lake town.

When I asked Seth how he saw things evolving between us, he seemed confident that we would figure it out. But I was consumed by worry.

Eventually, Nina noticed my fretting and asked what was up. I admitted to her I wasn't ready to have sex with Seth, but that I worried he would forget about me if I didn't.

"That's not true," she said. "Don't do anything you're not ready to do."

This advice came as a huge relief, and I found myself breathing more easily. But Nina's next idea threw me for a loop.

"Why don't you just take a break over the school year? Sometimes the best way to keep someone interested is to break up with him."

"Really?" This seemed just as confusing as Chloe's strategy.

"It's counterintuitive. That's why it works."

I didn't understand her logic, but I knew from experience that Nina was always right. Plus, she had had several boyfriends, and she seemed to have been firmly in control of each of those relationships.

"Break up with him so I can eventually get him back . . . I think I get it," I said. "Like loons?"

"What?"

"You know how loons migrate south, but they come back to the same lakes every summer to reconnect with their mates? They're monogamous, but they spend the winters apart."

"Sure, yes," said Nina. "Like loons."

I was so attached to Seth that, to my teenaged brain, this actually started to feel like a sensible solution—not to mention a necessary way to protect myself. I could see adulthood looming on the horizon, but I wanted to linger in childhood for a while longer. Plus, I had heard an adage that went something like "If you love someone, set them free," which sounded romantic to me. So I took Nina's advice.

On the day Seth was to leave Catwood Pond, I broke the news. His mom was on her way to pick him up, and we only had a short window before she would arrive.

"I don't want you to feel tied down," I said as we sat on the bed in Seth's cabin.

"But I *like* being tied down," Seth protested, a band of sunlight cutting through the dusty air between us.

"But that could change once you're back in your normal routine," I said. "I want you to have your freedom."

I didn't say the other thing I wanted: *for you to use that freedom to pine for me until next summer, when we can pick up where we left off.* I yearned for a day when we could be together again, when I was a little bit older and more ready for this kind of emotional intensity. In the meantime, I wanted to hit pause.

"I don't get it," said Seth, looking distraught. "Don't you love me?"

"Of course I do," I said, realizing I had underestimated how much this would hurt him. I was so caught up in my long-term plan—our joyful reunion next summer!—that I had miscalculated the near-term pain it would cause.

"Why are you acting so blasé about this?" Seth said, searching my face for a clue. "If you love me, then why would we break up?"

Because Nina said so, I thought. The logic of my plan was starting to feel shaky, but there was no going back now. I had already inflicted the wound. In an effort to sound confident and mature, I said: "Because it's just what I need right now."

"Okay," said Seth, his voice cracking with emotion. "I don't get it. But okay."

In that instant, I became aware of my own power—and not in a good way. Guilt-ridden, I felt tears start to come. "This doesn't necessarily have to be the end," I said lamely. "I just need some time."

"Okay," Seth said again, looking destroyed. It broke my heart to see that his usual ease and chattiness had turned brittle. He seemed scared of me as he said softly: "Whatever you need."

I left his cabin feeling hollow and unsteady. Everything in my body wanted to undo what I had just done, but I stayed the course, hoping that Nina's full-circle theory would eventually bring us back together. After all, I was supposed to be the heroine of this love story. So why did I feel like the villain?

Chapter 19

———

"What could possibly be in here?" my father asks, examining the latest package from Actualize as we drive home from the post office.

"I'm sure it's stranger than we can even guess," I say, letting my left hand fly out the car window. We have passed Labor Day, and the air is warm and hazy as summer drags its feet. Cooler days are coming, but for now, we are suspended between seasons.

My father contemplates the box again. "It must be an armadillo."

When we get home, we sift through the contents of the package. There are the usual powders and potions. There is a deck of Actualize-branded tarot cards. There is an oblong canister containing piñon-scented incense from Arizona. Eventually, my hand lands on a round, textured object: an armadillo. Or to be more specific, an armadillo-shaped incense holder.

I look from the armadillo to my father. A coincidence, or a premonition? There's still no way to be sure.

Over lunch, we explore the deck of tarot cards. Despite the recent upswing in tarot's popularity, I don't know much about it. I have friends who used to pull out their decks as a party trick, but I never thought to take their readings seriously. As I glance at the guide, my father makes his way through the deck, and when I look over, he has chosen three cards.

"Already pulling cards I see! What do you think those mean?" I ask.

He examines them. "Well, this one is you," he says, pushing the Fool toward me.

"Of course," I say.

"And this one must be me," he says, selecting the Hermit for himself.

I scan the guide and read aloud: "The Fool represents new beginnings, adventure, possibility." A much better outlook than I had feared. "And the Hermit represents wisdom, introspection, spiritual enlightenment. That does sound like you, Dad!"

He holds up the third card, the Lovers, and I read the explanation: "Connections, kindred spirits, important choices. So whose card is that? I'm guessing Dominic?"

My father examines the card for a long moment, then puts it down and looks at me with certainty. "That one is Seth."

I don't know much about oracles or clairvoyants or soothsayers, or whatever we're calling them these days—but I think my dad might be one.

Historically, I've been skeptical of self-styled prophets. I'm aware that there's a long tradition of seers in nearly every culture of the world; but I also know that a psychic on MacDougal Street once charged me $50 just to tell me that my soul was "dangerously adrift"—and I could have told her that for free. During my years at Actualize, I heard Gemma claim on many occasions that she herself had "intuitive gifts" and could "see our auras," but I always thought that was just her way of subtly threatening people.

Undoubtedly, there are charlatans out there who seek to exploit other people's uncertainties and insecurities. But the psychic glimmers that my father has demonstrated feel different from all that. They pierce our monotonous days with little flashes of magic. Plus, his mini-prophecies are legitimate; I've seen them come true before my very eyes. Even Carl has affirmed that my father is uniquely prescient, which makes me wonder: Did he have this gift when I was growing up? I don't think so, but it's possible I wasn't attuned enough to notice it. It's also possible that his Alzheimer's is clearing out stale information to make way for some kind of higher knowledge. It's also possible I'm going insane.

After we put away the tarot cards, my father lies down for a nap. I start a load of laundry, empty the dishwasher, and realize this is the second time he has mentioned Seth in the last few weeks. He doesn't seem to remember the accident, but Seth clearly occupies space in his subconscious, and it seems like something is surfacing.

The afternoon is slow, golden, and in no rush to become evening. My father is still asleep when I pull out my laptop to search: *Can losing your memory make you psychic?* The results are chaotic. Rather than travel down a series of dubious internet tunnels, I decide to seek a more historical perspective. I type: *Oracle at Delphi.*

I first learned about the famous oracle during our Greek mythology unit in sixth grade, but I need a refresher. Was the oracle a person? A python? A rock that emitted wisdom?

My research yields the following: the oracle was a woman, or rather, a series of women, who each served for a time as the High Priestess of the Temple of Apollo at Delphi in ancient Greece. People would come from far and wide to seek her counsel—the pilgrimage itself was an integral part of the experience. Upon arrival, these visitors, known as "supplicants," would make offerings. Next, they would enter a meditative state and ask their questions. Finally, the oracle would respond. There are conflicting accounts about exactly what form her response would take. Some claim it was abstract rambling that required interpretation, but there was widespread faith that the oracle's prophecies were well worth the journey. Wars were waged, alliances formed, marriages consummated, plans made, and projects abandoned—all based on the oracle's visions. Her prophecies were enigmatic, but so what? If the truth was in the eye of the interpreter, then maybe incoherence was the point. An oracle doesn't just hand you the answer; she nudges you toward finding your own meaning.

Chapter 20

_____

It begins as a game.

When I ask outright if my father thinks he might be an oracle, he laughs and says, "Me? An oracle? Well . . . I don't see why not." So I devise a project: for each day in the month of October, we will try out a different form of divination. It turns out there are more to choose from than I had ever imagined. There are the well-known ones, like palmistry (palm reading) and tasseomancy (the analysis of tea leaves). But then there are the more obscure varieties: scarpomancy (telling someone's fortune by studying their worn-in shoes), tyromancy (the reading of cheese), and apantomancy (the interpretation of chance encounters with animals). There are some we decide to forgo, like anthropomancy (which involves human sacrifice) and umbilicomancy (the reading of umbilical cords), but most are fair game. The format of this project works well for us because it is open-ended. Unlike games with complicated rules or films with opaque storylines, our divination process allows us to interpret the signs as we see fit. My father can ramble in any direction. There is no need for logic or linearity. We are free to make our own kind of sense.

Sometimes the results are whimsical. On the day we try bibliomancy—foretelling by choosing a random passage from a book—we begin with a simple question: "What does the universe want to tell us today?" I have my father close his eyes and select a random book from the hundreds of spines that line our shelves. We ready ourselves for profundity, but he somehow bypasses the deep thinkers (Kafka, Rumi, Laozi) and lands on a faded cookbook of Canadian recipes, where his hand fumbles before falling on the page for "Nova Scotian Hodge Podge." We laugh at the name for what is essentially a vegetable stew, but not wanting to defy the fates, we make it for dinner that night.

Then there is the day we try favomancy, which involves throwing a handful of beans on the ground and interpreting the pattern in which they fall. Dad is in a low mood on this day, and although his bean toss reveals what looks like a rainbow to me, his eyes well up with tears when I ask what it means to him.

"I shouldn't be alive," he says, weeping. "See?" He points to all the beans but one. "All of my friends are dead. I'm the only one left."

My instinct is to try to talk him out of his sorrowful interpretation, but that wouldn't be in the spirit of our project. He sees what he sees. So I comfort him, assure him I am happy he is still here with me, clean up the beans, and make him a cup of cinnamon tea. Within a few minutes, he is his usual upbeat self. For him, it's as though nothing happened, but for me, it's a flash of his hidden inner world. There's so much still bubbling there—fear, despair, delight, awe—if only I knew how to access it.

Nina thinks our divination project is ridiculous. I try to keep her in the loop when we have our weekly catchups, but she has little patience for my *dispatches from the occult,* as she calls them. She says I'm over-taxing our father and compromising his remaining capacity. I explain that it's a creative pursuit—it gives us new things to talk about and helps me meet Dad on a different level where he can be an authority.

"But he's not an authority," she says one day over the phone. "Just remember that."

"How do you know? He's insightful and inventive. He's not just a lesser version of his former self." I can tell she thinks I'm in denial, and it's possible she's right, but I continue: "I just don't see why Alzheimer's has to be so depressing. Why is it all about decline? Why can't it be about creation, too? It's not like I'm making him do things he doesn't want to do. He enjoys it."

I can hear Nina sigh.

"Anyway, we're almost done with it," I say. "October is nearly over. Then we'll move on to something else."

"How about something rooted in reality next time?" she suggests. I realize that Nina is having trouble relinquishing control of my father's care, even from across the ocean. But the more time I spend here, the less I subscribe to her philosophy of trying to keep him "on track." It seems more humane—and interesting—for me to go where he leads, not the other way around.

When we hang up the phone, I stare out the kitchen window. It's true autumn now. Long gone are the bright days of September that might as well still be summer. Now is the brown crispy time when death is in the air. There's an urgency to it (savor every fleeting moment of sunlight) but also a futility (winter is close at hand). I sift through a bowl of apples and bite into one that tastes both fresh and fermented, rich with a hint of decay, like the season itself.

"Who was that on the telephone?" my father asks from the doorway of the kitchen. I hand him an apple, and he crunches into it with gusto.

"Nina," I say.

"Nina. Nina . . . Now, who is Nina?"

I noticed he had stopped referring to her a few weeks ago, but I wasn't sure if that meant she had left his memory entirely or if he just couldn't remember her name. I don't have the heart to say "She's your daughter" for the thousandth time—it feels too confronting. So I offer another version of the truth: "She's my sister."

That satisfies him, but I know he doesn't comprehend the relational web that connects us all. "I didn't know you had a sister. We should have her over sometime."

"Good idea," I say, as we chomp our apples. Then I venture a question I have not yet had the courage to ask: "Do you know who I am?"

"Of course." He pauses as if second-guessing himself, but then continues with confidence: "You're my comrade. My canoe partner. My aide-de-camp . . ."

He never does land on *daughter*, but I'm okay with all of these descriptors, as long as he sees me as a benevolent and welcome pres-ence. This is more of a relationship than we've had in a long time.

He takes a final bite of his apple and concludes: "We're a good team, you and I."

———————

Halloween marks the final day of our divination project, and we have worked our way to sciomancy—the interpretation of shadows. With the autumnal equinox now well behind us, the evenings are falling earlier and earlier, and we decide to seek out shadows down by the water. I help my father into one of his thick wool sweaters and I put on a puffer vest, and we make our way to the pond. The flamboyant hues of early fall have mostly given way to a more restrained palette of crimson, brown, and gray. But along the shoreline, a wall of spruces encircles the water, stalwart and evergreen.

At the dock, we arrange our chairs so that we can see both the pond and the long expanse of the boathouse wall, where the late-afternoon light dances over the chipped paint. As is our routine, I read the definition of today's form of divination to orient my father. It's clear he is not tracking our project, but that's my job. His job is simply to participate, and participate he does.

"Okay." I clear my throat. "Sciomancy: a form of divination through shadows, taking into account their size, shape, movement, and appearance."

My father nods, and we both become pensive as we study the flickers on the boathouse wall, reflections of the lapping water below.

"What do you think, Dad? What do the shadows mean?"

"Well, sometimes a shadow is just a shadow. They come and go. It's best not to take them too seriously."

Fair enough. We watch as the flickering slows, and the distinct light-shapes start to coagulate into a more unified blob. One side of the boathouse is now covered by a large shadow that encroaches at a diagonal angle.

My father breaks the silence: "Oh, he's gone."

"Who's that?"

My father points to an area of the wall and traces an outline. "Your friend. The blond kid. He was just here, but he left when he saw you."

"What do you mean? Where?" My heart thuds, and I can't take a breath. This is the type of joke my father might have played twenty years ago, but he's not capable of that kind of deliberate trickery anymore. He doesn't even know I'm his daughter, so how could he remember Seth well enough to conjure him for fun?

"Right there. At the edge of the dock. He must be in the boathouse now."

I get up and run around the corner, pulling open the door and half expecting to come face-to-face with a teenager who has been dead for ten years. But there is nothing but the boat in its bay, the open mouth of the boathouse, and the water beyond. I try to catch my breath.

He's confused, I tell myself. He's mixing memories, maybe even hallucinating. Perhaps we need to abort this project before it dredges up all kinds of chaos.

I return to the dock shaken, but I try to shrug it off. My father is completely at ease as he looks out over the pond. We sit in silence until the sun dissolves and the dancing shadows on the boathouse solidify into a straightforward, even shade of green.

Later that night, when I am in bed, I look up *sciomancy* once more. Shadows, shadows, the reading of shadows. But then there it is—an alternative definition that I had missed during my preliminary research. It's not only the reading of shadows. Sciomancy can also be a form of divination that leverages the help of ghosts.

Chapter 21

December 2015

My plan didn't work. I had wanted Seth to pine for me, but instead, I spent that entire fall pining for *him*. We spoke a few times and texted occasionally, but his tone had cooled and I could tell that I had shaken his confidence in us, if not sabotaged the relationship entirely. We discussed the possibility of visiting each other, but the logistics were too complicated. Between our busy school and sports schedules, there was not a single weekend that worked, even if we met halfway—somewhere around Poughkeepsie. By the time winter break rolled around, I was convinced I had jeopardized the one thing that meant the most to me.

I spent a quiet Christmas with my parents in the city. The day after, my mother went to visit Nina in Nicaragua, where she was posted for the Peace Corps. It was decided that I would stay home with my father so I could study over the break. I had come close to failing two subjects that fall, and my mother was already convinced I wouldn't get into any good colleges the next year. We all agreed it was time for me to get serious about my schoolwork. But a few days after my mother's departure, I received a text from Chloe.

Chloe: NYE plans?

Me: None to speak of. Why?

Chloe: Greg's having a party in Locust. Can u find a way up here?

My family didn't often go to the Adirondacks in winter. In fact, the last time we were there in the snow, I was little enough to be bundled up and pulled around the frozen pond in a plastic sled.

Chloe: Seth will be there

She knew how to motivate me. I began to have a vision of a dramatic reconciliation: *Our eyes would meet, and it would be like no time had passed. I would apologize for having broken up with him, and he would forgive me instantly. My fear would dissipate, and we would finally have sex. Everything would be okay again. No—everything would be perfect.*

For the next few hours, I turned my plan over and over in my mind, cultivating it like an oyster does its pearl. Finally, I asked my father if we could go to Locust for the remainder of the break.

"You're supposed to study," he reminded me.

"But I can study there."

I could tell my father was torn. He was always keen to go to Catwood Pond, but my mother had been explicit. I persisted, threading the needle just so, and as usual, my will won out. By December 28, we were on the road to the Adirondacks.

I spent our first two days there diligently studying, only taking occasional breaks to tramp around outside. It was witheringly cold, and the pond was hidden under a smooth expanse of snow, marked only by the tracks of cross-country skis and paw prints. Directly in front of our dock, I noticed the fresh marks of a rabbit, whose long strides had doubled back on themselves before changing direction. Perhaps she was evading something, or maybe she suddenly had a better idea. *It's okay to change your mind*, I told myself. *It's okay to admit you were wrong.*

Invigorated by the icy air in my lungs and the imminence of seeing Seth again, I felt I was on the verge of something momentous, as if I had found the portal to adulthood. Whatever qualms had burdened me the previous summer now seemed muffled and surmountable. Maybe Chloe had been right about having sex for the first time: I just needed to get it out of the way. I felt bold and ready to grow up. At least, that's what I thought I felt.

What I didn't know then: coming of age isn't something you can choreograph, and it doesn't happen all at once. You start the process; you stall; you regress; and then comes another growth spurt. Eventually, your path looks like a series of paw prints in the snow—layered, as if compelled by confusion or curiosity—that double back before veering off in the direction of destiny.

On the day of the party, Chloe and I spent an hour on the phone discussing what we would wear. Summertime in Locust was always a casual, low-stakes affair, but New Year's Eve felt more consequential. As usual, I hadn't brought the right clothes.

"When in doubt, wear black," Chloe asserted.

"I didn't bring black," I said.

"Okay, when in doubt, wear navy."

"Didn't bring that either."

"Gray?"

We settled on a green sweater and jeans. Chloe planned to wear a black jumpsuit that was "slutty in a good way." She reminded me to wear some makeup. "Seth will like it. It will show him that you've evolved."

"Okay. But how much? Just some mascara or . . . ?"

I was clueless, but Chloe was someone who collected beauty products and watched YouTube tutorials for fun. "Keep it simple. Go for like a French coquette look. Like a thick cat-eye and a nude glossy lip. Think Jane Birkin or Françoise Hardy."

I didn't know what she was talking about, but I set to work by the dim light in my bedroom. I had found a tube of liquid eyeliner in Nina's room, and though I had to wipe it off and start over a few times, I eventually managed to trace a steady black line on my upper lids. As it dried, I blinked at myself in the mirror and tried to see myself from Seth's perspective. For the first time that I could recall, I thought I looked beautiful.

I opened the wooden box on top of my dresser and dug around

until I found the fishing-fly ring Seth had made for me. I slipped it onto my finger so he would know where I stood: still his, still hooked.

I had sworn Chloe to secrecy about the fact that I was coming to the party. I wanted to arrive when things were already in full swing so that I could surprise everyone. I took my time getting ready, and when my father finally dropped me off at the Seavey camp, it was just past 10:00 P.M. The main house looked different in the wintertime— more inviting, less boastful. I quaked with nervous excitement, anticipating the moment when Seth and I would lock eyes. I had rehearsed it so many times, it felt like it had already happened. I was even looking forward to seeing Greg himself. Maybe he had evolved just like I had. We were on the precipice of a new year, and I was feeling magnanimous.

"Call me if you need anything. If you want to be picked up or . . ." said my dad as I climbed out of the car.

"Okay, but I'm probably going to spend the night, Dad. It's New Year's. Everyone is staying over. So I'll just get a ride home from Chloe tomorrow."

"Okay. But if you change your mind, I'm just a phone call . . ."

"I know, Dad. Thanks. I'll be fine."

As I watched his car start down the snowy drive, I was hit with a pang of sadness. There was still a part of me that didn't quite want to grow up, that wanted to live within the familiar cocoon of my nuclear family forever, even if that cocoon was quickly eroding. But when I heard the din of the party inside, I remembered all the good things to come. I had this sense that the whole world was about to crack open for me, finally revealing its true richness. So I turned toward the house, walked up the path, kicked the snow off my boots, and pushed open the front door.

Chloe was the first to notice me.

"Cricket!" She rushed in, bear-hugging me and rocking from side to side. "You guys! Look who's here!"

The Seaveys' house had a modern layout, with a huge open kitchen and a soaring great room that overlooked Catwood Pond. Greg was holding forth in front of the fireplace. When he saw me, he looked stunned, but then his face tightened into a grin. He took his time ambling over as others rushed to greet me. When he finally reached the entryway, where I was still taking off my coat and boots, he said, "Cricket Campbell at Catwood Pond after Labor Day? Now *this* is a surprise." He looked me up and down as usual, then asked, "You didn't bike here, did you?"

"Nice to see you, Greg," I said, determined not to let him reel me into a verbal scuffle. My eyes drifted from him and began to scan the room.

"Oh, you're looking for Seth? He's not here." Greg wore an empathetic expression, but he delivered the news like a blow.

I felt my body liquify with disappointment. My face must have fallen, and Greg took a long, satisfied pause before saying, "I mean, he's here, just not *here*. He went out to get more beer. Should be back soon." I felt myself reconstitute. Shaken but relieved, I remembered why Greg was the absolute worst.

I headed to the kitchen, where Chloe was pouring whisky into shot glasses that were affixed to a cross-country ski. I was not usually a fan of shots, but I needed something to settle my nerves, so I joined the others as we formed a line, lifted the ski, and then tilted it toward our faces. A few onlookers cheered as we gulped the whisky down, and I felt my eyes burn.

I spent the next twenty minutes enjoying an exhilarating buzz, catching up with the kids I knew, and meeting a few of the ones I didn't. Greg's parents were technically home, but as usual, they had retreated to their wing of the house so that we could be as unruly as we liked. I was sitting on the rug in front of the fireplace when Greg plopped down next to me. He complimented my green sweater and asked me about school. I knew not to trust him—he was always at his most dangerous when he was feigning cordiality. After a few minutes, I checked my watch. It was already after 11:00 P.M., which meant it was less than an hour until the new year. Surely Deb's Depot would have been closed by now. Maybe Seth had had to go farther afield to find beer.

Greg noticed my concern and said, "Hm, he should have been back by now. I guess they're taking their time."

"They?" I asked.

"Oh. *Oh*, you didn't . . . ?" Greg acted like he had been caught in an unanticipated conundrum, but I could tell he had been waiting for this moment.

"I didn't what?"

"Well, Seth is kind of . . ." He paused as if choosing his words carefully, as if pretending to protect me from whatever it was he knew. "Well, you'll see."

"I'll see *what*?" Now I was agitated, by his withholding and by the fact that I had allowed him to unnerve me. Just then, the front door swung open.

In stepped a girl named Molly, whom I had met but didn't know well. She was a year older than me and represented the trifecta: well-liked, smart, and pretty. She was carrying a brown grocery bag and wearing an expensive-looking puffer coat with fur around the hood, and before I had a chance to notice anything else, I saw who was behind her: Seth. And he wasn't merely following her; he had his hand on her lower back, as if he was guiding her, shielding her from the elements as he eased her into the party. He was regarding her with a look I knew well—eagerness—but I had foolishly thought that particular look was reserved for me.

"Speak of the devil." Greg grinned. I refused to look at him, but I knew he was delighting in my reaction. And I knew everyone could see my heart shudder.

Then things got worse. When Seth finally looked over and saw me, his face froze. This was the moment I had been anticipating for days, if not for months. But instead of the jubilant reunion I expected, Seth seemed paralyzed. Finally, he gave me a panicked smile, then looked at Molly, who was already heading to the kitchen to deposit their acquisitions, and then back at me. Then he looked at the case of beer in his hand as if he had no idea what it was or what to do with it. After a moment, he put it down and slowly closed the door behind him. I thought I saw him take a deep breath, and then he finally turned and came toward me.

I stood up as he approached, feeling like the world's biggest idiot. Not only was he not happy to see me, but he had a new girlfriend. I quickly took off my fishing-fly ring and thought about flinging it into the fire, but I couldn't bear to, so I slipped it into my pocket before Seth noticed.

"Cricket." He exhaled as he reached me, as if his emotions were coming back online after a brief power outage. He shook his head to indicate that he had a million questions he couldn't articulate, but I knew the most pressing one was: *What the hell are you doing here?*

There was no way I was going to admit I was here to surprise him, that I had created an elaborate plan to seduce him (finally) and consummate what I thought was the inevitable next stage of our relationship.

"I had no idea . . ." Seth continued. The Seth I remembered was never ruffled like this, and it made me even more uncomfortable than I already was. "Can we talk for a minute?"

"Okay." It came out squeakily, as if my vocal cords had lost their elasticity.

"Let me just . . . Do you want a beer?"

"Sure."

He held up a finger for me to wait there, and then turned and walked to the kitchen. I assumed he was buying time to figure out what to say to me. But by then, it didn't matter what he said. Whatever fantasy I had concocted was tainted; whatever optimism I had harbored was gone.

"I guess you didn't hear," said Greg, popping up by my shoulder like an imp. "They're kind of a thing."

Kind of a thing. I felt the floor dissolve under me, but before I could react, Greg brushed off his thighs as if his work was done and wandered off to join a group in the far corner of the room. In the kitchen, I could see Molly pluck an open beer from Seth's hand and take a flirtatious sip. I turned around and tried to focus on the flames of the fire while I waited for Seth to return and deliver the death blow.

I felt him approach before he actually appeared at my side. Just like always, I could sense his energy, as if it were flowing a few steps ahead of him, clearing the way. Seth held out a beer to me. I took it but didn't open it; I just let my hand fall limply to my side.

"Cricket." This time, he said my name like an apology.

"I wanted to surprise you. I didn't know you had a girlfriend."

"She's not my girlfriend," said Seth. "Greg set us up earlier this week. I don't even know her that well."

"It seems like you know her pretty well," I said. I felt my eyes start to burn and realized that I would need to make a quick exit in order to avoid a public meltdown. "I need to go."

"I want to talk to you," said Seth.

"I can't talk now," I choked. "I can't talk here."

I put my unopened beer on the mantel and headed for the front door. I caught Chloe's eye on my way. She looked as shell-shocked as I felt. I hazily shoved my feet into my boots and grabbed my coat from the hooks by the door.

As I reached for the handle, I thought I heard Greg say something like, "I mean, what did you expect? You broke his heart."

Once outside, I pulled out my phone to call my father, but I had no reception. I walked further out into the driveway, searching for a signal to no avail. I looked back toward the house, which seemed more imposing than it had when I arrived. There was no way I was going back in to use the landline. I had to think fast. It was probably only a matter of moments before someone—Chloe, or maybe even Seth—came out to try to coax me back inside, and no one here was sober enough to drive me home. I could walk. It was about three miles via the road that wrapped around Catwood Pond, or . . . I looked down toward the water. As the crow flies, it was only a mile across the ice to my house. I figured if I could swim it in the summer, I could walk it in the winter. It would be the quickest path home and was the best way to evade anyone who might try to follow me. Before I could overthink it, I started running down the hill, past the Seavey boathouse, and out onto the ice, my boots crunching the snow. I had forgotten my hat and gloves, but it didn't matter. The intense chill of the past few days had given way to warmer temperatures today. It was noticeable enough that I had heard my father mutter "Damn global warming" that morning. Tonight, it felt like winter had pulled a disappearing act, leaving something milder in its stead.

The sliver of moon in the sky was not bright enough to light my way, so I pulled out my phone and used its flashlight to illuminate the ice ahead of me. In the distance, I could see a faint light coming from the windows of our house, and I ran as far as I could before slowing to a walk. The pond was silent except for the sound of my trudging. My tears turned cold against the air, running down my neck and wetting the collar of my sweater.

As I neared the midpoint between the north and south shores, I heard a buzzing, almost like the sound of a far-off chainsaw. I turned back toward the Seavey house and saw a bright headlight move slowly down the hill and out onto the ice. The engine's roar increased as the light moved toward me, and I finally recognized it as a snowmobile speeding in my direction. I turned and kept walking with increased purpose toward my house, but as my pursuer got closer, I couldn't feign indifference. Eventually, I turned and waited for the machine to find me, knowing it would be Seth.

He slowed, pulling up beside me and cutting the engine. He wore a coat and gloves, but no hat or helmet. He must have left in a hurry, the same way I did.

"Cricket, what are you doing?" Seth asked. "It's pitch black. You could get hurt out here."

"I'm fine," I said. He waited for me to tell the truth. "I'm so embarrassed. I thought we . . ." I couldn't get it out.

"You broke up with me, Cricket," he said.

"I know."

"Will you come back to the party so we can talk?"

"I can't."

"Well, at least let me drive you home. You can't walk across the ice in the dark like this."

I hadn't been on a snowmobile since I was a little kid, and it suddenly seemed scarier than I remembered, but I was too depleted to object. A part of me also welcomed the chance to be physically near Seth again, so I climbed on the back and wrapped my arms around his waist.

"You good?" he asked over his shoulder. He turned on the engine and pulled ahead, first cautiously and then with more speed, the wet air pulling my tears straight back to my hairline. Leaning my right cheek against the back of his neck to block the wind, I inhaled his clean scent, and it broke my heart all over again.

The moon hung delicately above us. From my angle, it could just as easily have been a summer moon, and we could have been zipping through the water in a boat. I clung to Seth and allowed myself to fantasize that the winter was melting away and we were flying back to the warmer season where we met. Soon we would arrive at the time before I had messed everything up.

But when we arrived at my dock, it was still winter. I climbed off the snowmobile and stared at Seth, who looked as wrecked as I felt.

"Can I come in?" he asked. "Can we talk?"

I wanted to say yes. I wanted to cocoon with Seth and let the world around us dissolve. But across the water, the Seavey house was lit up like a lantern, and I knew there was no salvaging this night. "I'm exhausted. You should go. People are waiting for you."

"I don't want to go back to the stupid party. I want to be with you."

I felt my heart lift for a minute, and for the first time since Seth had walked through that door with Molly, I felt like I might actually survive this shock.

I stepped forward and leaned down as Seth reached up for my face with his gloved fingers. It was a chaotic kiss, our cold cheeks blurring as hot tears ran salty streams over our lips. When I finally pulled away, I had to catch my breath and wipe my nose.

"I'm sorry," I said, more in love with him than ever, but still rocked by the image of his hand on Molly's back. "I'm so confused right now. Can we talk tomorrow?"

"Okay," he said, sounding resigned but determined. "Tomorrow."

I watched from the frozen dock as Seth pulled away, first slowly, and then faster until he was flying toward the opposite shore. He cut a straight line for a while, but as he neared the center of the pond, he turned a large circle. All I could see was a headlight gliding around like a firefly. Eventually, he veered toward the east bay. I watched until he passed the peninsula that seemed to extinguish his light; but in the far dark, I could still hear the snowmobile's engine ripping through the night air.

As I turned to go inside, I saw a firework pop in the sky above Greg's house. The *bang* found me a few seconds later as it reverberated across the ice. Then another Roman candle whizzed skyward. Before long, the cadence picked up and a shower of colorful fireworks bloomed in the sky, the sparks and booms creating a cloud of joyful mayhem. I could hear whoops and cheers echoing across the pond as if they were determined to reach me.

It was a new year. I turned and trudged up the snowy slope to my house.

———

"Yes, she's here. Yes. Around midnight." I could hear my father answering questions over the phone as he ascended the stairs, his voice growing louder as he neared my bedroom. I was still scrunched under the flannel duvet, unready to face the world. My father reached the doorway and said, "I don't think so. Let me check."

I heard a faint knock. "Cricket?"

"Come in," I grunted. The door opened and my father stood with the portable phone in his hand.

"Is Seth here . . ." He looked around and tried again. "Do you know where Seth is?"

"Seth?"

He waited, with an uneasy look on his face.

"No, I don't know. He dropped me off just before midnight. On the snowmobile."

My dad relayed these details to whomever was on the line and then said, "Okay, yes. Please do," before hanging up.

Now I was awake. "What's going on?"

It had been Mr. Seavey on the phone. Seth hadn't returned to the party after dropping me off, and his cell phone was going straight to voicemail. Greg had assumed he was with me.

But of course, he was not with me. He had asked to come in, and I had sent him away.

At first, my brain spun theory after theory about how Seth *must* be okay. He was too competent to be anything but fine. Maybe he just went to sleep somewhere unexpected; maybe he left town early this morning; maybe he's out for an early New Year's walk. But as the minutes passed, my body filled with anxiety. I was still fruitlessly trying to reassure myself when the phone rang again. After that, everything blurred.

———

At first, it was just a frenzy of phrases that I couldn't make sense of: *a pressure crack, soft ice in the east bay, must have happened in an instant.* And eventually, the details came into relief. Based on what the snowmobile tracks indicated, Seth had continued to turn ever-widening circles around the pond for quite some time after midnight. Finally, though he was only a few yards from where he had passed earlier, he hit a pressure crack that had formed when the ice shifted during the brief thaw that day. Though the fissure was narrow, it had created a two-foot-high ridge that jutted up from the otherwise smooth surface of the ice. There was no way Seth could have seen it in the dark. When he hit the snow-covered ridge at full speed, he was thrown from the snowmobile. They found the machine around noon, partially submerged in the shallows of the bay where the ice was softest. Not long after, they found Seth: ninety feet from where the crash had occurred, lying on the surface of the ice, his body quiet as if he were merely asleep.

At one point, someone had tried to offer comfort by saying that at least he hadn't drowned, nor frozen to death while incapacitated—he had broken his neck before either of those things could happen. As if this would make us all breathe a sigh of relief. Just a broken neck. Thank goodness.

Even before my shock subsided, the guilt set in. If only I had invited Seth up to the house. If only I had gone back to the party with him. If only I hadn't tried to cross the ice on foot. If only I had never gone to the party. If only I had stayed in the city. If only I had never broken up with Seth. If only I had never met him. If only I had never existed. There was no end to the "if onlys," and I played them relentlessly, backward and forward, until they wore a deep groove in my mind.

My heartbreak doubled back on itself. There was the initial hurt that had sent me running from the party: the loss of my hoped-for love story with Seth. That seemed almost inconsequential in the days that followed, but eventually, I would return to it again and again. It was always amplified and complicated by the larger devastation of losing Seth himself—of having him leave the world entirely.

Chapter 22

———

After the sciomancy incident, I put an immediate stop to our divination experiments and try to convince myself there is no way my father is in conversation with Seth's ghost. I am imagining things, and my projections have spun out of control. It is time to come back to earth, so I return to the schedule that Nina had set forth. She was right. There *is* comfort in rhythm and repetition, both for my father and for me. We have enough going on with his Alzheimer's. We don't need any additional surprises or drama, and we certainly don't need any paranormal activity.

But I can't stop thinking about it.

With Thanksgiving approaching, I wonder if this will be the year that I oversee the roasting of a turkey for the first time. For some reason, being in charge of that task feels like a lunge toward adulthood that I am not yet ready for. Nina is appeasing our mother and going to London—for a quail dinner, I presume—so it is just my father and me. I ask him what he would like to do for the holiday.

"Well, let's see. What does one normally do on Thanksgiving?" He needs a reminder.

"Eat, and then eat some more," I say. "Most people roast a turkey."

"A whole turkey? Why on earth would anyone want a whole turkey?"

So that settles it, and I am relieved. We agree to go out, and we invite Carl to come along.

Sleepy as Locust is in the off-season, Lorne's is always buzzing; and as far as diners go, it's solid. The menus hit the table before you've even settled into your booth. If you want to be in and out in twenty minutes, that's entirely possible. If you prefer to linger at the counter all day, that's fine, too. There's no rush. It's not like in New York City, where turning tables is a science, and if your meal exceeds ninety minutes, you start to feel subtle pressure from your server ("Will that be all?") that eventually yields to not-so-subtle pressure (a check you didn't ask for appearing on your table like an eviction notice). Lorne's doesn't have an agenda; it's a place where everyone can feel comfortably indifferent.

The place is half full when we walk in. Two of the dark-green booths are occupied, and a few solo diners sit at the long laminate counter. A sign above the soda fountain displays a quote from Groucho Marx: *"I'm not crazy about reality, but it's the only place to get a decent meal."* On the radio, Bing Crosby is already crooning Christmas carols. We slide into a booth in the center of the long space, and a familiar waitress named Sandy slaps our menus down and points to the sign indicating today's special—turkey club—before scurrying off. That's when I notice Paula, alone at the counter with a gigantic martini—which must be an off-menu item, this being a diner. She turns and gives me a wink, and I wave her over.

"Well, happy Thanksgiving," she says. "I see we all did the wise thing and let Lorne's do the cooking this year."

"Will you join us?" I ask. Having now worked with her for a few months—and taken her dance class a number of times—I now consider her my second-best friend in town after Carl.

She resists for a moment, but then accepts without any additional prodding. When Sandy comes back, I nod at Paula's martini and inquire, "Could I possibly get one of those?"

"You got it," says Sandy.

Carl, who doesn't drink, orders a Coke, and my father follows his lead, saying, "Coca-Cola—what a treat. When was the last time I had one of those? It must have been years ago." (It has been one week.)

We all order different entrees, and Sandy scribbles so hastily that it looks like she's joking. Then she taps her notepad conclusively. "That it?"

Once she leaves, we settle into comfortable small talk.

"No kids in town this year, Paula?" asks Carl. I knew Paula had a daughter, but I didn't realize she had more than one child.

"Zara stayed out in California. She's with her in-laws this year, god help her. And Max finally took a few days off, so he went to Iceland."

"Max?" I ask.

"My nephew," Paula says with obvious pride. "A little older than you. He's an arborist, so he's always up a tree somewhere. Lives near Long Lake."

"We might need some trees taken down at some point, right, Dad?" I say, trying to involve my father in the conversation, though I fear he may struggle to follow along tonight. "We have lots of trees."

"More trees than we know what to do with," he confirms. Carl and Paula smile. I appreciate their acceptance and ease around my father, which is never a given with Alzheimer's. It's an affliction that often makes people self-conscious, worried about making a misstep, worried about others' missteps, so afraid of awkwardness that they can't help but create more of it. Isolation is often easier than trying to maintain a social life, but tonight, our haphazard foursome feels manageable. More than that: it feels right.

Sandy returns and plops down our drinks. Less than a minute later she is back with our plates. Lorne's is not known for its culinary prowess, but after a few bites of my club sandwich, I am confident that this meal is far better than anything I could have conjured up. Paula orders another martini, and I follow suit. We're now properly tipsy, and I can't resist bringing up my recent fixation.

"So I think my father might be a medium. Or an oracle. Or something like that."

"Oh?" Paula looks intrigued as she plucks an olive from her martini and eats it.

I explain how it started with the loons, and how the tarot reading led to our exploration into divination. My father, still sipping his

Coke, nods along. Perhaps influenced by Nina's incredulity, I stop a few times to hedge: "It's probably all in my mind." But Carl and Paula don't seem to think so, and I haven't even gotten to the Seth sighting yet.

"Do you remember . . . when I was a teenager . . . there was a snowmobile accident?" It's hard to even bring it up.

"Of course, love. Such a tragedy," says Paula, without judgment. I look at Carl, who seems in the dark.

"When I was sixteen, my boyfriend, Seth . . . well, he wasn't my boyfriend at the time, but anyway, he died here. He crashed his snowmobile on the ice on New Year's Eve."

Carl winces but then meets my gaze again.

"And a few weeks ago, my father saw him. We were on the dock, and he said Seth had just slipped around the corner into the boathouse. He was sure of it. It didn't seem like a confused memory; it seemed real."

My father listens intently, as if unaware that I'm telling a story about him.

"And it's not the first time he has mentioned Seth. But it seems to come and go."

"Who's Seth?" my dad asks.

"See?" I say. Then I respond to my father: "He's an old friend."

"Are you sure it wasn't someone else? Like a real person who resembled Seth?" Paula asks.

"I checked. There was no one there."

"Could be a hallucination, but I doubt it," says Carl.

"So maybe Arthur really was visited," adds Paula. "You know, he was always very perceptive. We were on the Conservation Committee together a while back. He could practically predict the day the buds would bloom." Then she addresses my dad directly. "Arthur, remember that year when you rallied everyone to battle the Japanese knotweed? And thank *god*. It's a nightmare, that stuff. Invasive species."

"Knotweed . . ." muses my father with clear hostility toward the plant.

"This is only one dimension of many, you know," continues Paula, circling her hand through the air around us. "There's more to life than meets the eye. There has to be."

"You believe in that stuff? The occult?" I ask.

"What's the alternative—*not* believing in it?" Paula shakes her head. "No thank you."

Sandy slides up to our table and plunks down four fat wedges of pumpkin pie. "On the house."

As we chirp in gratitude, Carl takes a slice and ventures, "Just because we don't have an explanation for something doesn't mean it's not real."

Paula nods, and then adds, "Or maybe *nothing* is real."

I'm emboldened by their open-minded reception. "So you believe me?"

Paula nods enthusiastically as she daintily drags the tip of her pie off with her fork. Out the window of our booth, snow has begun to fall with increasing gusto, lacing the trees and sugaring the tops of the cars in the lot.

"I believe Arthur can sense things before they happen. And I believe he can commune with people who are on the other side," says Carl, pausing thoughtfully.

"You do?" I ask.

"Well, it's not just that I believe it—I *know* it." Carl nods. "I've seen him do it."

———

This is the story he tells us.

Before Carl moved to Locust, he lived near Albany. His mother suffered from dementia, too, and he had spent the better part of his forties caring for her. Though he has two siblings, it was Carl who stepped up and took responsibility for his mother's well-being. It took a toll on him, as caregiving often does, but he stuck with it until he couldn't anymore. His mother had become paranoid and erratic. She escaped their home multiple times, and she regularly woke in the night and got into trouble—turning on the stove, turning on the car, wandering the sidewalk in the dead of winter.

Eventually, Carl had to admit to himself that she was more than he could handle, and he secured her a spot in a home where he could visit her every day. He was torn about the decision, but she settled in, and after six months, it seemed they were both doing better than they had in years. Carl began to allow himself the odd indulgence—weekend fishing trips, a new truck. The future began to open up for him, but then, talk of a global pandemic began to spread. Before he could comprehend what was happening—before *anyone* could comprehend what was happening—the first wave of the virus swept his mother's nursing home. She tested positive on a Sunday and died two Sundays later.

Carl's grief was so immense that he initially wished he could follow her, either by accident or by design. His guilt led him in all directions. First, he leaned into vices—alcohol, gambling, whatever pills he could get his hands on. Then, after bottoming out, he leaned into virtues—sobriety, exercise, meditation, vegetarianism.

Finally, he moved to Catwood Pond, determined to start over and lead a quiet life. But still, he was plagued with the feeling that his own decisions had led to his mother's demise. His rational mind could not outmaneuver the part of his psyche that wanted him to shoulder the blame.

Around this time, Carl met my father. Whether consciously or not, he saw in Arthur an opportunity to make amends, or at least to make conversation. He began visiting every once in a while, and then more regularly. Preoccupied with her PhD, Nina wasn't interested in getting to know Carl in any depth, but she was happy to have him occupy Arthur for a few hours now and again.

At first, that was all it was: keeping company. But eventually, Carl opened up and told Arthur how much he missed his mother. He felt able to reveal his secret shame, knowing that Arthur wouldn't remember it the next day. There was something comforting about being able to tell and retell his story—first one way, then another way. He divulged it over a dozen times, with Arthur listening intently and compassionately each time. Eventually, the past began to lose its sting. Carl started to feel unburdened.

One afternoon when he stopped by, Arthur seemed preoccupied. He said he had just been chatting with a woman—older, frail, with ice-blue eyes and a raspy voice, wearing earrings made of seashells.

He was describing Carl's mother to a T; there was no doubt about it. But Carl had never talked about her in this much detail, and Arthur had certainly never known her. Arthur's account was vague at first: they had talked about the weather, about global warming, about how the loons had all gone north, and about Harry Belafonte. This made Carl smile, because his mother had loved the singer like none other.

He left that conversation feeling puzzled but exhilarated. He wanted more; he wanted to apologize. The next few times he visited my father, there was no mention of Carl's mother. He assumed it had been a fluke, never to be repeated, and he felt he had lost her all over again. But then one day, a few months later, when he and my dad were sitting on the porch, my father said, "That woman keeps coming back. The one with the seashells on her ears. A real spitfire. We have a wonderful time together."

"What do you talk about with her?" Carl asked eagerly.

"Oh, this and that," said my father. "But she talks about you mostly."

Carl's heart leapt, and he held his breath as my father continued. "She says you are a wonderful son. She says you want her to forgive you, but that there's nothing to forgive. She is having the time of her life. And she says you should get a dog."

If it weren't for the Alzheimer's, Carl would have assumed Arthur was messing with him. But Arthur was guileless and sincere, and had no reason to know that these were the exact words Carl needed to hear. No, Arthur wasn't a prankster—he was a channel.

The next time Carl visited, my father had absolutely no recollection of this conversation, and he never mentioned Carl's mother again. But it was enough. Whatever he had transmitted had been sufficient to heal the gaping hole in Carl's heart. Ever since, he had

BEFORE I FORGET 137

felt a peace that he hadn't known since long before his mother's death, and even before her illness.

———————

So, no. Carl doesn't think I am crazy, and neither does Paula. On the contrary, they think Seth is visiting my father for a reason.

I tremble to think what that reason might be.

Chapter 23

January 2016

My mother was livid when she found out that my father had taken me to Catwood Pond for New Year's. She cut her Nicaragua trip short and demanded that we return to the city, all but grounding me. Somehow, she felt that the tragedy proved a point she had been trying to make for years: the wilderness was dangerous, lawless, not to be trusted— and I was the same. We were all better off in the city, especially me.

A few weeks later, there was a memorial service for Seth in Lake Placid. I had planned to attend with my father, but on the night before, a nor'easter blew through New York state. When we woke up and checked the roads, it was clear we wouldn't make it in time for the service. I refused to go to school that day, and my parents knew better than to fight me. Instead, I holed up in my room, listening to Adele and sobbing as the snow filled the city below.

One night that winter, I overheard my parents arguing, which was not out of the ordinary, but this time, the conflict had more teeth. They were in the bedroom they had once shared, before my father permanently moved to the sofa in the den. I sat in the hallway by their door and closed my eyes so I could better focus on their conversation. Since the accident, I had become a detective, diligently hunting for confirmation of my culpability.

"You know I always deferred to you when it came to Cricket," my mother said. "Because you understand her, and lord knows she likes you better than she likes me."

"Tish," my father said, sounding tired.

"Cricket is *your* daughter, through and through." She said it like an accusation. My mother claimed Nina as her own on a regular basis, but she was quick to foist me onto my father, as if all my errors were somehow his fault. "But I thought you had her under control. I thought she was at least safe," my mother continued. "What if she had been on that snowmobile?"

"I've thought about that every day since it happened." My father was quiet for a moment. "We're very, very lucky."

"*Lucky* isn't good enough. Something needs to change. You give Cricket and her friends way too much leeway. They're not harmless kids anymore—they're hazards to themselves."

"I just try to treat them like humans."

"They're not humans—they're *teenagers*." My mother seethed. "They need to be managed."

There was a heavy silence, and I could envision the impatient glare my mother was giving my father as she waited for him to respond.

"Maybe you're right. Maybe I've been too permissive with Cricket," he said. "I don't know. Nina always had such good judgment."

There it was: Nina would never have gotten into this mess. There was no way for me to live up to the standard she had set, so I might as well fail spectacularly, and that's exactly what I had done. I stood up and went to my room, having heard all I needed to hear.

To my face, my parents never suggested that I was to blame for Seth's death. They called it bad luck—the combination of an unstable climate and teenage impulsivity. *No one's fault* was how they described it, but I had heard what they said behind closed doors about my recklessness, so I knew it was someone's fault: mine. It had to be.

By spring, my parents had begun their divorce proceedings. I didn't ask outright whether the accident had fueled their decision to separate; I didn't have to. The timeline spoke for itself. My teenaged brain drew a straight line from one tragedy to the next—the end of Seth's life and the end of their marriage, all within the span of four months.

It wasn't a contentious divorce. My mother named the terms; my father accepted them. She would keep our apartment in the city; he would move to Catwood Pond full time. There was no custody dispute. After all, I was only a minor for one more year, and my parents agreed that I would live with my mother for my final year of high school. The only person who put up a fight was me. Feeling alienated from my city friends (none of whom had known Seth or could comprehend the loss I had experienced), I lobbied hard for permission to spend my senior year in Locust with my father. My mother resisted the idea—the Locust school system was not up to her standards, and my grades had plummeted in the months since Seth's accident. She wanted me to stay put, in the hope that I could salvage my transcript and get into a decent college next year. But I couldn't imagine being apart from my father for a full school year, even though he assured me I could spend my vacations with him. I knew I would miss one of my parents either way, but I preferred to miss my mother and live with my father, rather than the other way around.

I kicked up such a fuss that they agreed to think about it. They could see I was spiraling. Whereas life had been sharp with possibility when I was in love with Seth, it now felt blurry and dull. In the late spring, I turned seventeen and finally passed my driver's test, but neither of those events felt like reason for celebration. I counted down the days until I could escape the city for the summer, hoping that a change of scene would ease my distress. But when school ended and I returned to Catwood Pond, I felt just as adrift as I had in the city. The change of scene didn't solve anything. The problem was within me.

At first, I avoided everyone, even Chloe. Whatever confidence I had wielded the summer before was fully eroded. My father seemed both saddened and relieved by the fact that I had no interest in staying out late, or going out at all. I didn't have a job, and I spent my days sitting on the dock, dangling my feet in the water and letting the minnows peck at my chipped toenail polish. I took long swims—sometimes all the way across the pond, sometimes around its perimeter. There was something about being underwater that helped me disconnect from my pain. In the rhythm between breaths, I could almost convince myself I was in another universe altogether.

After two weeks of solitude, Chloe finally convinced me to come to a small gathering at Sully's dock. She said people had been asking where I was, that they wanted to see me, that no one would bring up the accident.

I showed up that evening in the dirty green sweatshirt I had been wearing nonstop. I figured the less effort I made, the less I would be noticed, but of course, everyone clocked my arrival, and to my surprise, they all seemed genuinely glad to see me. The only person who didn't was Greg, and I knew his coldness was calculated.

On the surface, the night felt like any other night. People complained about their summer jobs, took selfies, and philosophized in the self-righteous way that only teenagers can.

"But don't you think if capitalism were going to work, it would have worked by now?" suggested someone.

"Exactly. I don't think we should engage with it," said someone else. "There has to be a better way."

"A hundred percent."

It had been a long time since I had hung out with a group of peers, and I finally began to unwind. As the sun went down, our friends Becca and Ryan pulled up in their boat. When Ryan saw me, he broke into a wide smile. "Look what the cat dragged in! Where you been, Cricket?"

"She's been hiding," interjected Greg from his seat at the edge of the dock. He threw his empty beer bottle into the pond, then added: "Ever since she killed my cousin."

A hush fell. All I could hear was the lapping water and the rush of blood in my ears.

"Come on, man," someone said to Greg. "That's not cool."

"No one killed anyone," said someone else.

"As good as," insisted Greg, opening another beer from the case beside him. It seemed he was back to drinking unremarkable light beer—in increasing volume. "Seth would be here right now if it weren't for Cricket and her drama."

"Hey," I heard someone else jump in to defend me, but by then, I was floating away on a current of rage and shame.

I barely know how I got home that night. Someone took me by

boat; I don't recall who it was. I don't remember disembarking, or walking up to the house, or falling into bed.

What I do remember: the next morning, my father called me onto the porch. He said he and my mother had come to a decision, and I would need to finish out my senior year in the city.

"You don't want me here?" I asked, feeling like the only thing I had left to hope for had been pulled out from under me.

My father began some kind of even-handed explanation, but I had ceased listening. It was all too much: my grief for Seth, my anger at Greg, my sadness about my parents' divorce, and now what felt like a fresh rejection by my father. In that moment, something in me boiled over.

"I don't want to go back to the city. I hate it there!" I screamed. I needed someone to blame. "But I hate it here even more. *You* let this happen!"

"Let what happen?" my father asked, clearly concerned.

"All of it! You're a terrible parent," I yelled, feeling the poison proliferate and wanting to do as much damage as possible. I thought of Greg's accusation from the night before, and before I could stop myself, I redirected it at my father. "Seth would probably still be here if it weren't for you. You should never have let me come here for New Year's! Mom said I needed to stay in the city to study, and if you had listened to her, none of this would have happened!"

"Cricket . . ."

But I was on a roll, and suddenly, it all seemed logical in my stress-addled brain. Maybe the accident wasn't my fault. Maybe it could have been prevented. "You two would still be married and Seth would still be here and everything would be fine. Last summer everything was *perfect*. Now look at me!"

"Let's just take a . . ."

"I hate it here!" I repeated, before running upstairs, slamming my door, and packing my bag.

The next day, I left Catwood Pond and didn't return for nearly a decade.

Chapter 24

―――――――――

As the darkness of December deepens, we try to make the most of the daylight hours. But with the sky black by 4:00 P.M., it's hard not to feel like we live in a burrow. Ever since Thanksgiving, I have been closely watching my father to see if I can spot any more psychic glimmers. It feels like Seth could show up at any moment, and I want to be ready when he does. The possibility of it infuses my days with excitement, making bearable what would otherwise be a very quiet season.

One afternoon, my father calls to me from his chair beside the fire.

"I want to talk to you about something," he says, and I brace myself for a revelation.

"What is it, Dad?" I hold my breath. "What do you want to talk about?"

"Barred owls." Not what I expected. "They're beautiful, yes, but don't let your guard down." He grows serious and leans toward me, then snaps his fingers softly. "They can rip your face right off."

"I'll keep that in mind. Thanks, Dad."

Midway through the month, I get an unexpected email from Gemma. It's been weeks since I finished my last copy project for her, and I still feel like I'm treading water financially. Dominic's dental bill is finally paid off, but my father's licensing deal ends in a few weeks. After that, all we have to live on is his pension, social security, and the modest amount I make from helping Paula with her website admin. I need more work.

The email reads:

hey mama,

the copy you wrote for us this fall was beautiful. I would love to chat about your career progression. It has been tough finding someone to fill your shoes. I wonder—would you consider returning to Actualize if we gave you a new title? Maybe your Dad could move back with you. Would love to find a way to make it work.

xoxox

G

I can't help but laugh at the irony. Now that I've relinquished my life in the city, I am finally offered the promotion I should have had two years ago. I feel a surge of something unfamiliar. Power? Justice? For a long time, I had regarded Gemma as my savior—the woman who plucked me from the gig economy and gave me a steady paycheck. Now, I can't help but delight in the turning of the tables. *She* needs *me*. Of course, I can't move my father to the city. He belongs here—we both do. For a moment, I am tempted to ask if I can take the position remotely. But the thought of going back to Actualize fulltime makes my stomach twist.

Just then, I hear a frustrated grunt from the kitchen.

I set my laptop aside and go to check on my father, who is at the counter wrestling with a mango. He has hacked the poor fruit from multiple angles but made little progress in separating the flesh from the pit.

"I can't get it off the nut!" he growls, his fingers slick with juice and pulp.

I take the knife out of his hands and reassure him, "Mangos are notoriously tricky." I proceed to show him how to cut off one half, then the other, then make a grid and invert each half so it arches like a hedgehog.

He's the one who taught me how to do this years ago, and now, he shakes his head in bewildered amusement. "Not in a million years would I have thought to do that."

We eat our mango chunks by the fire as the light outside wanes, and I make a mental note to respond to Gemma later. I will, of course, decline. Surely Gemma can find someone else to peddle her snake oil, but there is only one person who is qualified to be my father's aide-de-camp: me. It feels good to be needed in two places, but I am most needed here.

"You know, we better hurry up and get a Christmas tree," I say. "It's only two weeks away, and Nina will be here on the eighteenth." She recently informed me that she will be bringing Nils, a guy who she has mentioned a few times over the course of the fall, but I didn't realize that they had reached the point of transatlantic holiday travel. As my life is becoming quieter, hers appears to be getting more dynamic.

"Nina . . . ?"

"My sister," I remind him.

"Ah, yes. The one who went to Stockholm to have a baby."

I am so astounded he remembers the Stockholm part that I almost disregard the rest. "She went to Stockholm to have a *career*. Not a baby."

"No? Maybe it's too soon. What is the gestation for a human? Probably as much as three months."

"Nine months. Well, actually, forty weeks."

"Forty weeks?" He gasps. "Impossible."

I know my father's cognition is sliding, but it's hard for me to track. Sometimes he is completely cogent; other times, like now, he seems to be pulling from cached memories mixed with conjecture; and occasionally he goes quiet and seems completely lost, unable to get any kind of grip on reality. It's hard to witness, though I know it could be worse. Many with his disease are plagued by panic, fear, paranoia. My father, miraculously, still seems to have faith in the general flow of life. And he appears to trust me completely.

We sit silently as the fire settles. Dominic's huge body is spread over my father's lap like a blanket, and before long, both the cat and my father are asleep. I pick up my laptop to draft what I think is a gracious reply to Gemma. I let her know that while I cherish the memory of my years at Actualize, I am currently embroiled in an exciting new project with my father. He is an oracle, I tell her, endowed with psychic gifts that are only growing stronger as his cognition wanes. It's not a lie, because I half believe it; and besides, Gemma loves this kind of stuff. I tell her I would be happy to continue writing copy on a freelance basis, although I will have to raise my rates, given how busy I am with my new venture. I also tell her she is welcome to come to Locust to meet the oracle, though I know she'll never drive this far. Still, I feel a little thrill as I hit send. In the new world order of my imagination, Gemma will have to come to me.

Chapter 25

———————

As Nina's arrival approaches, my father and I make a run into town to pick up some presents and supplies for the holiday week ahead. None of us is especially gift oriented, but I want to make sure we have a few things to unwrap on Christmas morning. Deb's Depot is the obvious destination, given how jam-packed it is with the most random merchandise imaginable. We choose flannel pajamas for Nina and a buffalo-check work shirt for Nils; then I send my father off to browse on his own so I can find a gift for him. He won't remember even if he spies what I'm buying, but I feel the need to uphold a certain amount of Christmas protocol. I choose a hat with ear flaps, an electric mosquito-swatter in the shape of a tennis racquet, a pack of maple candy, and the extra-long matches that he likes. When I'm satisfied, I go aisle by aisle and finally find my father near the hunting equipment.

"This is the one," he says definitively, holding up something called the EZ Grunter Xtreme, which is a tubelike object that mimics a deer's call. We are not hunters, but he seems enamored, and I figure we'll find some use for it.

"Perfect," I say, adding it to my basket. As we make our way toward the checkout, my father also picks up a block of cheddar cheese, a giant popcorn tin, and a pair of tiny socks with snowmen on them.

"I'm not sure we need these," I say of the socks.

"For the baby?"

"We don't have a baby."

"Do we not?" He puts the socks back.

When we get to the cash register, the woman working it is picking at a hangnail. It's not Deb, but she looks like she could be a close relative.

"How's it going?" I ask.

"You know. Livin' the dream," the woman deadpans. I find her blasé manner both off-putting and refreshingly honest. "You are the only ones who've been in all day."

I grab a few extra items—a moose-shaped lollipop, a pack of batteries, a lighter—in a modest attempt to boost the store's bottom line.

The smattering of businesses in Locust generate most of their revenue between Memorial and Labor Days, when tourists stream through at a steady clip. The off-season represents a fight for survival, and though Deb's Depot has held its own for thirty years, this particular employee doesn't seem optimistic about business.

"Let's get a lotto ticket," says my father. "I've got scratch fever."

I laugh and try to gauge whether he's joking. This is unlike him, but then I feel a frisson of excitement—perhaps this is his next premonition. "Do you think we'll win?"

"Of course not," he says. "Trust me—you don't want to win the lottery. It will ruin your life. But it's still fun to play. Dance with danger."

We buy a few tickets.

"Merry Christmas," the checkout woman says halfheartedly as we gather our things.

"Same to you," says my father with genuine enthusiasm.

Outside the store, a motion-sensor Santa raises its arm and gives us a jerky "HO, HO, HO!" before keeling forward into the snow face-first.

I pull Santa back onto his feet, brush him off, and assure him: "You're doing great."

Chapter 26

——————

From the moment they arrive, Nina and Nils are like puppies at play. I have never seen my sister like this—radiant, relaxed, even a little rambunctious. One afternoon, while I am sorting Dad's medications for the coming week, I look out the window and see them having an impromptu snowball fight. Nils is younger than Nina, closer to my age, and he's not an academic, as her other boyfriends have been—he's a chef. It's a surprising choice for my sister, but it's clear that something has shifted since she left for Europe. A weight has lifted, or perhaps it has been transposed to me. As I have become more ensconced, Nina has become more liberated. Observing the two of them scampering through the snow, I feel a flicker of envy. But my sister deserves this renaissance—she did her time in the woods. Even before she took care of our father, she somehow served as the pillar of our family. From a young age, she always had a seriousness about her. I'm glad she is finally learning to frolic.

On Christmas Day, after we have opened our presents and no one has won the lottery, we all settle into different corners of the house. My father rests by the fire with Dominic, and Nils watches *Home Alone* for the first time, trying to understand why it has such an outsized cultural impact in the US. I am in the kitchen, clearing crumbs and drying dishes, feeling good about the state of things. Nils is easy to be around, and he balances out some of the other dynamics between the three of us. He is easygoing with my dad, and he helps Nina to not take things too seriously.

Nina seizes the moment to pull me aside. She grins but says

nothing. I grin back. She keeps grinning, so I grin more. This is getting weird.

"Cricket," she says, as if it's obvious, "I'm pregnant."

I assume it's a practical joke—a bit of Nordic whimsy to brighten these dark winter days. But then it dawns on me that she hasn't had a drink since she's been home. She keeps grinning and waits for me to respond.

"Seriously?" I say, my disbelief quickly shifting from shock to joy to fear and finally to wonder. I can feel my face move through each emotion.

"Yes! Crazy, right? Obviously it wasn't part of my plan, but I'm so happy. And when I told Nils, he didn't flinch. He is totally on board. Maybe even more excited than I am."

"Oh my god," I say, as it sinks in. "Oh my *god*! But how . . . Where . . . What happens now? Are you going to stay in Stockholm?"

"Fuck yes," says Nina without hesitation. "I mean, for now. I'll have the baby there, so it can be an EU citizen and I can get that sweet, sweet Swedish maternity leave. And with Mom in London, it just makes sense. She can visit when I need help. It's a good setup. Somehow life suddenly feels . . . easy."

Again, I understand her joy. After four years of caring for our father, with very little in the way of medical or government support—because that's not really America's thing—she is now reaping the benefits of a system that actually wants to help its citizens thrive. Swedes don't need to win the lottery; they already have.

I hug Nina as tears start to well in my eyes. I'm thrilled for her, but sad to feel like I am losing her again, this time in a more permanent way. Initially, we thought she would only be in Sweden for a year, maybe two. Now, it sounds like it's indefinite.

"It's still really early. I'm seven weeks," she says, also tearing up. We both look down and admire her nonexistent bump. "And I want to tell Dad, but I don't know if he'll get it. Honestly, it seems like he doesn't really know who I am. Like he vaguely recognizes me, but he doesn't know why I'm here."

"Yeah," I say. "He acts that way toward me, too. I think it's just a new phase that we're in." Then it hits me like lightning. "Wait, Nina. I think he already knows you're pregnant. On some level, I think he knows."

"What do you mean? How?"

"A few weeks ago, we were talking about you, and he said something about your being pregnant. And about how humans gestate for three months."

"What?"

"And when we were shopping last week, he wanted to buy a pair of tiny socks 'for the baby.' Holy shit, Nina. I told you!"

Her eyes widen. Maybe this is the thing that will finally convince her I'm right about his psychic abilities.

"I know you think I'm insane," I go on, "but I swear he's tapped into some larger consciousness. He knew you were pregnant before you even got here, and I had no idea until five minutes ago! You've got to admit that's weird."

"Okay, I'll admit it: you're unusually dense."

I make a semi-amused face, and she relents. "Okay, fine. It is weird."

"Thank you." I'm relieved to finally earn this acknowledgment. This seems like as good a time as any to tell her about the day when Dad saw Seth at the boathouse, and about my conversation with Carl and Paula on Thanksgiving that validated my suspicions. I divulge everything in one long torrent.

When I'm done explaining, Nina is silent.

I wait for her to be fascinated and maybe even impressed, but suddenly, her face hardens and she seems annoyed. "I thought you said you were done with that divination stuff." She sounds stern, like the Nina of yore. Pre-Nils Nina. The Nina who had to keep everyone else on track.

"I *am* done with it," I say. "I'm just trying to fill you in on what has been going on. I can't help it if he keeps having premonitions."

"But you're encouraging it, Cricket." I must look crestfallen, because she softens her tone. "Look, I know life gets boring here, especially in the winter. And I know you really believe Dad has superpowers, or whatever. But this is overboard. He's not channeling Carl's dead mother. He's not communing with Seth. This isn't *Beetlejuice*."

I want to continue to argue my case, but it's clear Nina doesn't want to take this mental leap with me, so I stand down. "You're right. I guess I just got carried away. It felt like something to do."

"I get it. But that's what Netflix is for."

"Right."

"It's just too confusing for him, to play these games. You shouldn't encourage him when he's seeing things that aren't there." Nina pauses, then adds: "You know, he's lost a lot of ground since I left."

This final comment feels like an indictment of my ability to properly take care of our dad. Suddenly my confidence is shaken. Maybe Nina can see things more clearly from her new vantage point than I can from within this closed system. My eyes fill with tears. Maybe I really have been imagining that our dad is a seer to try to keep him vital, relevant. Maybe I'm just trying to ward off his earthly decline by assigning him an otherworldly power.

Nina pulls me in for a gentle hug. "I know this is hard—being a caregiver. Believe me, I know." This would be the perfect opportunity for her to throw in an *I told you so*. But instead, she surprises me: "You're doing such a good job."

"I am?" It feels like getting a positive performance review from a hard-to-please boss.

"Yes," says Nina, rubbing my shoulders. "I mean, you do things a little differently than *I* would, but Dad seems happy. You've really stepped up, and I'm proud of you."

The acknowledgment lands like a yearned-for gift. I hadn't realized until now just how desperate I've been to get some praise, or at least credit, for the time I've put in. From day to day, no one is here to witness my work except my father, which means that my efforts largely evaporate into the wind. I've tried to be at peace with that, to not need a gold star. But earning Nina's praise feels huge; it's something I've sought my whole life.

"But no more prophecy stuff, okay?" She raises her eyebrows and waits for me to comply.

"Okay. No more."

She yawns, looks at the clock, and announces that it's way past her bedtime, but as she leaves the kitchen, she turns. "Oh, and Cricket, why are you still sleeping in that single bed, you weirdo? The mattress is so old it's literally crunchy. Don't you want to move into the bigger room?"

"Your room?"

She laughs, as if she has zero attachment to the room or anything else here. "I'm very happy to relinquish it."

It hadn't even occurred to me to move rooms, but later that night, as I lie in bed with Dandy the one-eyed lion, I have to laugh. Why haven't I upgraded to the queen bed across the hall? Laziness? An inferiority complex? Have I been caught in a psychological sinkhole from childhood? I don't have the answer, but I resolve to claim the adult-sized bed once Nina and Nils leave. It's time to level up. I'm not a child anymore—I'm emerging from the netherworld that comes after childhood and supposedly leads to adulthood, and I deserve a better mattress.

———

The next morning, Nils tries to convince me to do an ice plunge with him. I tell him it's a hard no, but we all agree to bear witness. Armed with blankets, towels, and thermoses of hot coffee, we make our way through the knee-deep snow down to the pond, where Nils has already prepared a large hole in the ice. I must admit, he has done excellent work. The square-shaped opening is tidy and close enough to the dock that the plungee can easily pull themselves out of the water.

Nils sheds his robe—thankfully, he is wearing trunks—and walks out onto the ice. This is the kind of thing my father would have eagerly participated in back in the day. Now, he looks on with wonder, as if Nils is performing a magic trick, as if anything could happen next.

Nils lowers himself to a sitting position, dangling his legs in the frigid water, and then slides like a seal down into the black hole. He remains under the surface for an uncomfortably long moment while we all hold our breath in solidarity. Finally, he pops up, shakes his head like a retriever, takes a fortifying inhale, and says, "What? It's warm!"

He continues to breathe and tread water as Nina times him for three minutes, finally counting down, "Three, two, one! Okay, you're done. You did it."

In no rush to get out, Nils submerges himself once more and then pulls himself up onto the dock so casually that one might think he was emerging from a tropical lagoon. He towels off and begins doing weird stretches.

"I'm impressed," I say.

Nils gestures toward the hole in the ice. "It's not too late, Cricket . . ."

"Next year," I say.

As Nils dons his robe and we start to move in the direction of the house, my father stops, looks back toward the pond, then asks, "What about the other boy?"

"What boy?" asks Nina.

"The younger one who went in first. He's still in the pond."

Nina furrows her brow, perplexed, but I know exactly what is happening. He must have seen him again.

"Seth? Was it Seth?" I ask my father.

Nina looks at me with horror. "Cricket!"

Our dad looks befuddled, as if he is trying to piece something together.

"Don't worry, Dad," Nina reassures him while also managing to shoot me a glare. "You're just a little confused. Let's go up to the house and get warm."

I relent, but this time, I can't be talked out of it. When it comes to our father, I am the authority now. He saw what he saw, and I know what I know.

Chapter 27

2017 and Beyond

Seth's death left a gash through my life. I approached the following years as a punishment, certain that the universe was trying to teach me a lesson about the danger of loving too much, or too recklessly, or both. After limping my way to the end of high school, I enrolled at a big university out west. At that point, I hadn't seen my father for almost year. Feeling both rejected by him and ashamed of the hurtful things I had said, I refused to visit Catwood Pond that summer. But when fall rolled around, my father offered to drive me west and move me into my dorm. Over the course of four days, we crossed the country and did our best to reconnect. It was nice to be with him and it almost felt like nothing had changed, but beneath the surface of our easy rapport, something was different between us—a lingering sadness, a shared sense of regret. I thought about apologizing for the things I had said to him, but it was still too raw. I made a promise to hold myself accountable at a later date, once my hurt had subsided. That felt fair.

In the meantime, I asked, "Do you miss Mom?"

"Very much," he admitted.

"Maybe you can fix things with her. I've heard about people doing that: getting divorced but then getting back together."

He shook his head, then patted my knee as if to absolve me of something.

When we said goodbye outside my dorm, we agreed that these cross-country trips would be our tradition for the remainder of my time at college. He picked me up that spring, and dropped me off the next fall. But our cadence was interrupted when I dropped out halfway through my sophomore year, certain that whatever debt I was racking up in student loans did not justify whatever I was (or wasn't) learning.

My mother was incensed that I had left school, but my father was more understanding. "You can always go back," he said, when I told him over the phone. "But you can learn a lot in the real world, too."

I returned to New York and to my mother's apartment, and a few months after that, my father came to town. He still spent the majority of his time in the Adirondacks, but he had occasional business in the city, and we met for lunch. When I arrived at our favorite coffee shop on the Upper West Side, I almost didn't recognize him, though he sat in our usual booth. He looked older, but it wasn't so much the physical changes that struck me; it was something more holistic. His energy had flattened. Though Nina had told me he was feeling depressed, I hadn't expected it to be so manifest. He rose to give me a hug and tousled my hair, which I had recently dyed electric blue, but didn't pass judgment on the color.

We ordered our usual BLTs and attempted to make small talk. He told me there hadn't been much snow that year. He had only had to shovel a few times. I told him I was looking for work—waitressing or nannying or something like that. I knew he could see how much I was floundering without my having to say it, just as I could see how he was hurting. But by that point, neither of us wanted to talk directly about Seth's accident or its aftermath—the divorce, our respective spirals. And despite my intention to apologize to him someday for the terrible things I had said, it felt too late now. There were too many layers of guilt and loss to sift through, and too much distance between us.

"I'd like to see you more often," said my father. He stayed with friends when he was in the city now, so he usually only spent a few days at a time there. Catwood Pond had been the place where we connected most deeply, where our attachment to each other could flourish in its natural habitat. "Do you think you might come up to Locust this summer? Even just briefly?"

"Maybe," I said, though I knew the answer was no. It was the place where my life had gone off the rails, and I couldn't fathom going back until I felt more stable—until I was a new person. But I also didn't want to deflate his hopes, so I said, "It depends on work. Once I actually find work, that is."

The truth was: I hadn't been looking. I'd been waiting for something to find *me*. In the interim, I'd been lolling about my mother's apartment, and she'd grown increasingly exasperated with my aimlessness.

"Of course, of course," my father said, placing a balled-up napkin on his now-empty plate. "You have a whole life to build. Much to look forward to."

I could tell he was trying to sound upbeat for my sake, but he wasn't good at hiding his gloom. This wasn't the father I had known my whole life. His lightheartedness was gone, replaced by something heavier. On my side of the booth, I felt weighed down as well. Seeing each other in this state was painful for both of us.

"You know," my father said, choosing his words carefully, "most parents say that all they want is for their children to be happy. But that's not how life works, Cricket. I want you to experience happiness, of course, but sadness is part of the equation, too, as you well know. What I want is for you to have a rich, full life that is uniquely yours. What I want is for you to chart your own course. It's all I ever wanted, even when you were little. I think every child deserves that—the space to mine her own thoughts, hear her own voice, be her own person."

"I know, Dad," I say. While my mother had a tendency to impose her ideas and expectations, my father had always provided an important counterbalance. I knew that, fundamentally, they were both motivated by love for their daughters, but it manifested differently. My mother sought control; my father chose curiosity.

"We'll spend time together again when the time is right." My father attempted a reassuring smile. "I just miss you, Cricket."

My throat clenched. "I miss you, too, Dad."

"Do you think you might come up to Locust this summer?" he asked again.

"Dad, you already asked me that."

He looked puzzled, but then nodded. "Right."

It was the first time I clocked his forgetfulness, but after that, I noticed that he had more and more lapses. I only saw him one more time before the pandemic hit the following spring, and we all became house-bound. As the world slowed to a halt, seismic shifts happened within my life: Nina decided to relocate to Catwood Pond; my father received a formal Alzheimer's diagnosis; and my mother moved to London to start a new life with George.

It was all too much. The events of the past few years created a cascade of grief: Seth's death, my parents' divorce, my father's diagnosis, the onset of the pandemic. Not to mention that I felt I had lost one home (Catwood Pond) and then another (our New York apartment). It was like getting hit by a wave each time I tried to come up for air. Before long, I left behind the life I had known and began drifting like a tumbleweed—taking random jobs in Wyoming, Montana, New Mexico, the Florida Keys. Restless and rootless, I searched for myself.

When the pandemic finally subsided, I returned to New York. Broadway had just reopened and I landed the gig selling merchandise at *The Phantom of the Opera*. Not long after, Nina said she was bringing my father to the city for a few specialized cognitive tests, and we agreed to meet for lunch.

I was the first to arrive at our go-to spot on the Upper West Side. I was eager to show them that I was okay, that I had weathered the pandemic and had finally straightened out, that they could stop worrying about me. But when Nina and my father finally walked in, it was clear he hadn't been worrying over me at all. In fact, he seemed like his old self, except for one thing: he didn't recognize me.

Nina gave me a hug and gestured for my dad to take a seat beside me in the booth. He hesitated before saying to her, "Wouldn't you like to sit with your friend here?"

Nina and I both froze. I looked from my father to her, and she looked from me back to him.

"Dad, it's Cricket," she said.

He looked at me. "Hello, Cricket."

It was worse than I could have imagined. It wasn't that he had mistaken me for someone else, or that he couldn't pull up my name. He didn't know me at all. He thought I was simply someone Nina had invited.

In that moment, I had never felt more alone in my life.

We muddled our way through lunch, with Nina scrambling to smooth over my dad's lapses, but there was no denying what had happened. It's not that I had lost my father—it's that he had lost me. I had been erased.

Still stuck in the emotional residue of losing Seth, I now had to face the fact that my relationship with my father would never be repaired. One heartbreak compounded the other, and it was under the weight of these burdens that I drifted into my job at Actualize.

Chapter 28

After Nina and Nils leave, the house is joltingly quiet. We've had so much snow in the past few days that it almost feels as though we're living underground. Carl plows our driveway, thank goodness, so we're not officially snowed in. But still, it feels like my father and I are the last two people on earth—two voles curled up for the winter, hoping we survive until spring begins to crack and chirp around us. For now, it's just the resounding silence of snowfall.

The day after Boxing Day, I am sitting by the fire, wrestling with the fonts on Paula's website, a task that would be simple if Dominic weren't laying across the keyboard. I have pushed him off several times, but he persists. Just as his toes graze the keys and enter *gggggghghhkjl//??LK??mmm,* into the text field I'm working on, I notice a new email in my inbox.

Subj: self-care

Hey lady,

I know this is last-minute, but I'm taking a spontaneous trip to Le Refuge for New Year's. I think it's near you? I totally get that you're not in a position to come back and work at Actualize, and I respect the boundary you've drawn. I really do. But I'm going through some personal stuff, and I'd like to have a session with The Oracle himself. Would January 2nd work? Let me know the address. I'm traveling with a friend who will just hang while I meet with The Oracle.

xoxox
Gemma

Her vacillating tone—deferential one moment, commanding the next—brings me right back to what it was like to work for her. She's manipulative, I remind myself, but I'm no longer in her thrall. And after weathering Nina's skepticism all week, I am refreshed by Gemma's open-mindedness about my father's visions. This is the perfect opportunity to test his skills in a new way, and Le Refuge is only an hour from here. Of course that's her destination of choice—it's an absurdly expensive resort that lures big spenders and celebrities with the promise of rustic-chic luxury and uncompromised privacy.

For a moment, I hear Nina's naysaying voice in my head, but I silence it by telling myself this has nothing to do with Seth. If anything, this is an opportunity to clear the slate and tread new mental territory with my father. No channeling the dead—just some lighthearted prophesying.

In replying to Gemma's email, I do my best to echo her tone—friendly but firm—while letting her know she'll have to play by my rules.

Gemma,
Great to hear from you. We have an incredibly busy schedule at the moment, but we would be happy to make room for you at 2pm on January the 2nd. I hope that works for you. Just a note that you will absolutely need snow tires to get up our road. If you need a place to stay in town, the Locust Inn is your best option. Looking forward to catching up with you!
Sincerely,
Cricket

I hit send and feel a jolt of exhilaration. I know from my years as her assistant that Gemma has tried nearly every wellness remedy under the sun (and moon). She once flew to a spa in the Italian Alps to have her colon blasted with mineral water. I can't compete with her usual haunts, but I don't need to. I just have to create an experience she isn't expecting, and I think we can offer something she rarely sees: simplicity, humility, austerity, an ego-less container in which she will have to face the most profound thing of all—herself. Yes, I can do this, as long as my dad is on board.

I hear clanging in the kitchen, and Dominic hops from my lap to investigate. I follow him and find my father standing in front of the open refrigerator.

"Everything okay in here?" I ask.

He turns, wielding a cucumber, and wonders, "What shall we do with this pepperoni?"

"I'm pretty sure that's a cucumber."

He looks at the object in his hand for a long moment. I can see him realize I am right—of course it's a cucumber!—but I can also sense that he still thinks it might be a pepperoni. He had been so sure of it a moment before.

"Oh, yes," he says without full conviction, mentally caught somewhere between the cucumber and the pepperoni. "Well, what shall we do with it?"

"We should make lunch," I say. Who cares if he thinks it's a pepperoni? Maybe it's possible to be two opposing things at once: a cucumber and a pepperoni; a child and an adult; a tragedy and a triumph; a heartbreak and a healing. Things can be both. We can be both.

A while later, as we crunch our pepperoni salad, I ask my father if he is amenable to having visitors.

"Always," he says cheerfully.

"And they may ask you for advice while they're here," I say. "They're looking for some guidance, some wisdom."

"Happy to give it," he says without skipping a beat. In fact, he sounds confident.

When he goes to sleep that night, I begin my preparations in earnest. First, I turn to my old friend Google to research protocol at the Temple of Apollo at Delphi. I am reassured to learn that the actual prophesizing was only a small part of the fanfare. Just as important was the pilgrimage, the arrival, the welcome experience, and the meditation that took place before visitors actually conferred with the oracle. By then, they were primed to have their minds blown, no matter what she said.

My research suggests that the entryway at the original temple at Delphi was inscribed with three maxims, which have been roughly interpreted as:

1. KNOW THYSELF.
2. NOTHING IN EXCESS.
3. CERTAINTY BRINGS TROUBLE.

Before I go to bed, I shoot Carl a text asking if he can whip up three wooden signs—one for each maxim. I send a second text to Paula to see if she would be willing to lead Gemma in some kind of dancing meditation—the weirder, the better.

When I wake up the next morning, I have enthusiastic responses from both Carl and Paula. Between the three of us, we are confident we can fashion my father into the Oracle at Catwood Pond. It's a wild idea, but I figure there's no harm in experimenting.

Chapter 29

I had been dreading New Year's Eve, my first at Catwood Pond since Seth's accident. But ultimately, it passes me by: I fall asleep at 10:00 P.M. The next day, I wake up to drunken texts from Olivia and Tasha (we love you cricky!!!! come back to us!!!!) and Dylan (HNY babe. Miss u). It's the first I've heard from any of them since Thanksgiving, I realize. I open Instagram and scroll through a dozen photos of the party they attended. In one, I swear I can see Dylan making out with a blonde in the background, although it's hard to tell because, in the foreground, Olivia is brandishing a sparkler whose light flare partially covers up his face. I study the photo and feel a million miles away from my former life.

I text Dylan back: Happy new year. Fun party?

He instantly responds: nothing special. what do you have going on this month? Should I visit?

I screenshot the photo and send it to him with a message that says: that depends. is this you?

I see three dots appear to indicate that Dylan is typing. Then they disappear. In the next minute, they pop up and disappear twice more, but he writes nothing.

A few hours later, Dylan still has not responded to my question, which confirms that he was hooking up with the blonde within an hour of texting to say he missed me. Even in an "open relationship," that's some fancy footwork. This kind of thing might have sent me into an emotional spiral in the past, but today, in this brand-new year, it brings clarity. Dylan is free to keep his options open, but I am no longer one of them.

I block his number and turn to more pressing matters. Gemma will be here tomorrow, and I have to prepare.

When she arrives, we are ready. Carl has outdone himself with the signs, which he hand-carved. He even treated them to make them look weathered, imbuing them with a sense of gravitas, and affixed them to three trees along our driveway—a fitting welcome for our first official supplicant.

For her contribution, Paula has choreographed what I can only describe as a full-body chant. It involves deep breathing, rhythmic movement, and primal vocalizations, and it's exactly the kind of thing Gemma will love.

I need not have worried about Gemma making it up the road. A few minutes before our scheduled meeting time, she arrives in an SUV that is just short of an armored tank. For all her talk about natural products and bodily purity, she doesn't seem too concerned about her carbon footprint. As she exits the vehicle, I see that she is accompanied by a stylish woman who looks familiar.

I step out of the house to greet them, and Gemma pulls me in for a ferocious hug. "Cricket." She inhales me as if I am somehow vital to her, then releases me and turns to her friend. "You remember Inez?"

"Of course," I say, holding out my hand to shake hers. Inez Garcia-Gates is the editor of a prominent culture magazine, and I met her a few times when I worked for Actualize. Her magazine once profiled Gemma, characterizing her as the woman who was "gently, intuitively disrupting the wellness industry."

Today, Inez looks polished and alert. Gemma, I have to admit, looks haggard.

"I really need this," says Gemma. "And I know I look like shit. I feel so inflamed lately. I think it's the snail-mucin serum."

"Could be," I say.

"This place is *gorge*," says Gemma, quickly changing energetic gears. I lead them around the house onto the porch so that we can enter through the official front door. The day is spectacular: the morning's clouds have receded to reveal an azure sky above the fresh snow, which shimmers in the sun.

I lead Gemma and Inez into the house, and Carl greets us at the door with steaming mugs of cinnamon tea.

"O . . . M . . . G," says Gemma as she inhales her mug and then spins around, taking in the great room. She runs her hand over the wooden globe and pets the taxidermy-fox umbrella stand. "Adorable. Very dilapidated chic. Very faded WASP."

I know she means this as a compliment, and I'm relieved that she is charmed by our house. She seems eager to embrace this experience, and she is on board with the eclectic dinginess we have unintentionally cultivated.

The two women remove their fancy snow boots, which look like they're being worn for the first time, and we all sit around the fireplace. My father is finishing a nap and Paula is stretching upstairs, which should give me the right amount of time to set expectations. I throw another log on the fire, plus some dry fir boughs that cause the flames to spit and spark. Gemma gasps in excitement, just as Carl emerges from the kitchen with two shots of a liquid that I have concocted.

"This is our proprietary elixir, made from foraged local ingredients," I say.

The truth is, it's just a mix of lemon juice, honey, and some smashed-up basil. Though in a moment of strange inspiration, I also threw in a few chunks of Crystal Light from the container at the back of the cabinet.

Gemma gulps her shot and then lets out a satisfied sigh. "Amazing."

"Now, I'm not sure if you've seen other clairvoyants," I begin. Inez shakes her head no, while Gemma nods her head yes. "But I want you to discard any specific associations or expectations. What we do here is unique. As you know, my father has dementia, and his grasp of 'reality' as we know it is fading. What is emerging, however, is a heightened connection to Source. An ability to zero in on the truth— that which you, yourself, cannot yet see. Sometimes his prophecies are concise and clear. Other times, they are rambling, circuitous, confusing. Things might not make sense at first; but in time, they will.

Think of this session as the beginning of a journey of discovery that will unfold indefinitely. This is just the first step."

Inez looks a little skeptical, but Gemma is nodding and rocking with readiness. I sense that she's going through something and is hungry for healing—not the kind of healing that she sells, but the real deal.

She has come to the right place. Though I am flying by the seat of my pants, the Adirondacks *do* have a history as a therapeutic destination. In the late 1800s, those suffering from pulmonary disease, specifically tuberculosis, flocked here for what was known as the Adirondack cure. Some combination of the altitude, the balsam-infused air, and the crystal-clean waters worked their magic on many a patient.

While I wouldn't claim to have the permanent cure for any specific ailment, I am confident we can help quell Gemma's nonspecific angst, if only momentarily. I dab lavender oil on the women's foreheads and instruct them to gaze into the fire as I lead them through some simple breathing exercises. The flames pop, and suddenly the room that often feels too quiet (when it's just my dad and me) now feels charged with possibility. I am enjoying being the master of ceremonies, and I feel a little high on my own authority.

After a few minutes, Paula enters the room and I leave Gemma and Inez under her jurisdiction while I go to get my dad. I can hear their exhales as they begin to flail around the space.

My father is awake and sitting in the armchair in his room, staring out at the pond.

"Dad, we have two guests who would love your advice," I say.

"Do we? How nice," he says. I help him up from the chair and offer him his shawl-collar cardigan—the one with the leather buttons that gives him a professorial air. Once outfitted, he follows me out to the great room, where the ladies have just completed their dance meditation.

I make the introductions, and the two women regard my father with eager reverence as he settles into his usual chair by the fire.

Dominic hops into his lap and regards the women warily, his green eyes wide.

"We'll start with some bibliomancy," I say, handing my father the dusty poetry anthology we often read from.

He takes it, contemplates the cover, and then hands it back to me. "I think we've exhausted this one."

I didn't expect this. For a moment, I'm nervous, but I decide to roll with it. I replace the anthology in the bookshelf and begin to run my hands along the spines. "Tell me when to stop, Dad."

When I reach a small gray book, he claps his hands. "Bingo."

"This one?"

He nods. I look down and see that it's an instructional guide called *When Duct Tape Just Isn't Enough*, and I immediately regret not curating the shelves better. I brace myself, fearing that this is when our experiment will go off the rails, but I bring the book to my father nonetheless. He looks at the cover and then flips it around so Gemma can see it. Her eyes widen and she bursts into tears.

We all sit in silence for a moment, allowing her to experience whatever it is that's happening. She looks to Inez, who nods in understanding.

"It's about my marriage." Gemma sniffles, gesturing to the book. "When duct tape isn't enough. Isn't it obvious? It's a metaphor."

"There, there," says my father.

"We weren't perfect, Jared and I, but I always had this belief that we were *fated*. Because we met at Burning Man, and it was beautiful in the beginning. So ever since then, I've told myself that the pain is worth it somehow. But when is enough *enough*? I know relationships are hard work, but is this the right kind of work? Is marriage supposed to feel like this?"

I worry that my father will be overwhelmed by Gemma's outpouring, but he seems steady and engaged. He leans forward and looks at Gemma. "Sometimes the marriage has a problem. But sometimes the marriage *is* the problem."

Gemma gasps and nods, tears falling fast down her cheeks. I look at my father in near disbelief. That was real. He nailed it.

"So what should I do?"

"You already know. Or you will before long." He strokes Dominic's fur and gets a far-off look in his eye. "Kierkegaard said something . . . What did he say . . ."

We're going full Kierkegaard? I hold my breath, praying that my father remains coherent.

He looks at Gemma. "Ah, yes: *Life can only be understood backwards, but it must be lived forwards.*"

Holy shit. Somehow, the abstractness of my father's thinking and speaking has found its natural outlet. He is drawing on recesses I didn't even know were there. Whereas he is often lost in day-to-day conversation, this is a space where he can wax in any direction and still hold authority. We have created an experience, but the supplicant must make her own meaning.

I'm confident that Gemma has already gotten what she came for, but suddenly, I am struck by an idea that might round out her pilgrimage. I excuse myself and run down the path to the pond, where the afternoon light is low. At the end of the dock, I check to see if Nils's plunge hole is still in decent shape after all the snow we've had. A thin layer of ice has formed across the top, but after I poke it with a stick, it gives way. I run back up to the house.

When I enter, the conversation has lulled and Gemma's tears have dried, though she is now smiling. "Gemma, I wonder . . ." I say. "We don't offer this to just anyone, but would you like to do an ice plunge in the pond? The experience was designed by a Swedish consultant, and the Adirondack waters are very healing. It's not for the faint of heart, but I think you would really benefit."

"Say no more," says Gemma. I had a feeling she would rise to the challenge. Extreme wellness is her preferred sport, after all. I offer her a swimsuit but she insists she would prefer to experience the elements in the nude. I give her a robe to change into. When she returns, we leave my father in his seat by the fire, and Gemma, Inez, and I walk down to the water.

Gemma doesn't need much coaching—she's done her share of ice baths—and she drops her robe and slips into the water without hesitation, eager to be baptized by ice. When she pops up to the surface, she is calm. She lays her forearms on the edge of the hole and breathes steadily as I time her. After three minutes, Inez and I help hoist her out of the water and wrap her in her robe. As the three of us make our way back up the hill to the house, the change in Gemma is palpable. The edginess that oozed from her when she arrived is gone, replaced by a centered calm. When we reach the porch, she grabs my arm and pauses before we enter the warmth of the house. She seems unbothered by the cold, though the long strands of her hair have frozen into solid shards.

"This is a magical experience, Cricket," she says. "You're going to change people's lives."

———————

Once Gemma and Inez finally leave, my father turns to me with a befuddled look and asks, "Who were those flibbertigibbets?"

Carl, Paula, and I dissolve into laughter. "Friends from the city. Actually, I used to work for the one with the long hair. She was my boss."

"Your boss? She should be working for *you*," my dad says, and I have to agree.

"So, Arthur, did you enjoy that? Do you like being an oracle?" Carl asks. "I think you really helped her."

"I hope I did. It's always nice to have visitors. Will we have more?"

"Would you like to?" I ask.

"I don't see why not."

So that settles it. I doubt we will be able to lure many others to us out here in the woods, but it's good to know that my father is enthusiastic if the opportunity presents itself again. It was a fun experiment, and a confirmation that my father is indeed as wise as I suspected, Alzheimer's be damned.

Chapter 30

The next few weeks pass quietly, with sun and snow alternating but the temperature consistently below freezing. My father and I take daily walks up and down the driveway, and we go into town once in a while: to Lorne's for breakfast, or the post office, or Deb's for groceries. One day, we make the hour-long drive to the hospital for his quarterly appointments. His primary doctor confirms that he has lost a bit of ground, memory-wise, and his hips could use replacing within the next year or two, but otherwise, he is in good health for his age. It makes me realize that *I* haven't actually seen a doctor in over a year, or is it two? Maybe in the spring, I tell myself. And while I'm at it, I will need a haircut as well. The blond has grown out so much that my hair is now two distinct colors: yellow on the bottom, brown on the top.

One night at the end of January, I am sipping whisky by the fire and perusing job postings online. There is an opening for a vet tech at the animal hospital where Dominic had his teeth removed last summer. Of course, I am not qualified for the job without an associate's degree, but for a moment, I let myself daydream. Maybe there is a way to work toward that goal. Maybe I can find a way to balance taking care of my father, making some money, and going back to school. Maybe there is a future in which I build a career I actually enjoy. After all, that's what Nina has. That's what my mother has. Why not me, too? My thoughts are interrupted by a ping: a new email from Gemma.

Shortly after Inez and Gemma's visit with my father, Inez had asked my permission to publish an article about Gemma's experience, and I had consented without any concern or specific expectation. I figured our culture is so awash in content these days that no one would pay the article much mind, but I knew my father would get a kick out of it. Finally: his fifteen minutes of fame. It would be a nice record for us to have of this phase in our lives. Or rather, a record for me to have once my father is gone.

In her email, Gemma provides a preview link to the piece, which is set to go live tomorrow, and she concludes with: Where should we link so readers can make appointments? Prepare to blow up! Xoxox.

Appointments? Blow up? I'm a little caught off guard as I click through and read the headline.

Fulfilling My Prophecy Meant Choosing Myself

How a visit to an unlikely oracle gave wellness-brand founder Gemma Dwyer the courage to leave her broken marriage—and level up her life.

"Oh wow," I say aloud. I had expected a whimsical little write-up about a girls' trip to the woods, but this angle is far more dramatic than I had imagined. The essay takes the form of an "as told to," meaning it is from Gemma's perspective, but it was written by one of Inez's editors. I fly through the write-up, which is surprisingly moving and vulnerable. I had not realized just how dysfunctional Gemma's marriage to a morally rudderless hedge-fund manager had been, especially in the years when I was working for her. I reach the final paragraph, which reads:

> The oracle at Catwood Pond does not charge for his counsel, nor does he offer virtual readings. So an audience with him will likely require a long journey—nay, a pilgrimage. But if you are ready to unlock your best life, I can confirm the journey is well worth it. After I visited the oracle, nothing was ever the same. ◆

I thank Gemma for the flattering article and tell her they can just link to my email address. For a moment, I worry that this could escalate, but I figure our remote location should be deterrent enough. Yes, people want guidance, but most don't want it badly enough to drive hours to a stranger's house in the middle of nowhere. They can make do with the advice they find during their middle-of-the-night Instagram scrolling.

With that, I close my laptop for the night and take a final look into my father's room. His snores are raspy and rhythmic, and there is a cat-sized lump under the covers at the foot of the bed. Dominic can seemingly spend the entire night without fresh air, if it means being this cozy.

I climb the stairs and enter the large bedroom that is now mine. From my window, I have a direct view of the boathouse. In the moonlight, its angled roof resembles the prow of a lonely ship navigating a frozen sea. But I know that, soon enough, the thaw will come, as it always does.

Chapter 31

By the next evening, I have thirty-seven inquiries from people all over the country who want to see the oracle. There is also an email from Inez—via Gemma—confirming that her essay is already the most-viewed article of the month on the magazine's website. Thanks to her 900,000 social media followers, Gemma helped drive much of that interest, but now the article has officially gone viral.

The volume is already overwhelming—there is no way we can receive thirty-seven supplicants anytime soon. I email Gemma in a panic, but all she writes back is, Congrats! So happy for you! I'm sure you'll figure it out! This is huge!

When I read the article aloud to my father, he laughs nearly all the way through.

"I'm glad you're amused!" I begin to laugh with him. "But what do we do now?"

"Let them come."

I appreciate his openness, but I know he can't grasp the level of interest that is already starting to bubble our way. I need advice, and while Nina is usually my go-to in that department, I can't share this specific conundrum with her. Carl and Paula are my next best option, and they both agree to come by this weekend to help me strategize.

"Just breathe," says Paula, picking up on my stress as we sit around the dining-room table. I've set up the equivalent of a war room, with printouts of the article and the now eighty-nine inquiry emails. Paula and Carl leaf through them.

"Well, this woman has a terminal illness, so you should fit her in quick," says Paula. "But most of these are from people who are wondering whether to break up with their partners or quit their jobs. You can handle those at your leisure."

"This is already out of control," I say. "We can't take responsibility for all these people's dilemmas. What if my dad has an off day? What if he loses interest?"

"Well, aren't the prophecies supposed to be kind of vague and open-ended?" asks Carl. "Doesn't a good oracle show you what you already know?"

"Well, yes. According to Heraclitus, 'The oracle neither reveals nor conceals, but gives a sign,'" I say.

"According to Hera-*who*?" asks Paula.

"He's an ancient Greek philosopher."

"Well, there you go!" says Paula. "I mean, it sounds like Arthur doesn't have to do much. He just makes a little chitchat, which he loves to do. Carl can serve the tea; I can lead the dance ceremony. Then the folks jump in the pond, and we send them on their way. Nothing to it."

"But what if one of them is a psychopath? I mean, should we be worried about our safety?" I wonder.

"I can help with that," says Carl. "And you can borrow Cynthia." His shepherd mix would never hurt anyone, but she does look intimidating if you don't know her.

"Look," says Paula, "forward all the inquiries to me. I'll vet them. I'll send you the ones who seem serious, and you can invite them at your own pace."

"But you hate tech." After all, she had hired me to do *her* admin. Now she wants to do mine for free?

"I hate tech. But I like email," clarifies Paula. "And this isn't admin—it's an adventure."

"Okay. If you're sure," I say. "Let's take two people a week and see how it goes. Weekends only. I don't want to overwhelm the oracle."

Paula and Carl light up with excitement and a sense of purpose.

"Are you sure you have time to help with this?" I ask them both. "I mean, my dad and I have nothing better to do, but . . ."

"It's February in Locust," says Paula. "None of us have anything better to do."

Chapter 32

———

Over the next two months, we receive sixteen visitors. Most come from New York and New England, although one travels from California and another from Vancouver. Nearly all of their cars get stuck in the snow or mud at the base of our road, and they complete their pilgrimages on foot, arriving at our house looking dirt-splattered but eager. Everyone drinks the elixir, does Paula's dancing meditation, takes a cold plunge, and receives a prophecy that appears to satisfy them, and, in some cases, to astound them.

Some are the expected "seekers" looking to broaden their horizons in general ways; but we also get visitors who are hoping to heal specific wounds. There is the would-be mother trying to process her recent pregnancy loss. There is the former executive who was "canceled" for a sexual indiscretion and can't get past the shame. There is the father who is consumed by anger since losing his son to an opioid overdose. And there is the cancer patient who knows she doesn't have long, but wants to see the oracle before her time runs out. We even get a few high-profile visitors, including a YouTube sensation who is suffering from burnout and a recently retired NFL player looking for spiritual direction.

We are upfront that the oracle has Alzheimer's, and some of our supplicants take comfort in that fact. They trust they can divulge their secrets, knowing that he will soon forget them. In my father, these people have found an ideal outlet for their angst—a place to voice their fears, hopes, and shame. In the process, these feelings are alchemized. "So much better than therapy," one woman muses after her session. But to me, the most magical discovery is that nothing seems to shock my father. He receives everyone's story with patience and equanimity; it's almost as if he has heard it all before.

By the beginning of April, Paula, Carl, and I have worked out some of the kinks when it comes to scheduling, and our operation is running smoothly. My job hunt has stalled, and for a moment, I wonder if we should monetize our oracle visits. But it doesn't feel right, and I don't want to put pressure on what is still an experiment. This project feels meaningful, if not lucrative. I place a donation box in the driveway to help cover our expenses. Within a few weeks, we have received $1,200, which I split evenly between my Dad, Carl, and Paula. If we continue at our current rate, maybe the donations will be enough to carry us through the season, and then I can get serious about my job hunt in the fall. What's more: my father has really risen to the occasion. He seems to be settling comfortably into our new weekend routine, and he looks forward to every visitor. Some days, I even think his memory has gotten sharper. I'm not naive enough to think that having a purpose will reverse his dementia, but I hope it can slow its progression. Maybe the best medicine for him is the chance to be taken seriously, despite his limitations.

One morning, I receive a call from the owner of the Locust Inn.

"Miss Campbell, I don't know what you are up to over there at Catwood Pond," he says, and I brace myself for admonishment. "But whatever you're doing, keep doing it. We've had more reservations this April than the last few years combined—and during mud season! It's unheard of. All these folks say they're here to see you. To get their fortunes told or whatever it is you're doing."

"Oh, I'm so glad," I say, instantly relieved. "It's really just for fun, but all the better if it's helping your business."

"Sure is," he says. "And have you seen the Yelp reviews?"

"I haven't," I say. "Are people finally giving the Locust Inn its due?"

"No, not for the inn," he says. "For the oracle . . ."

We hang up and I open Yelp to see what he's talking about. Sure enough, someone has created a listing for "The Oracle at Catwood

Pond." There are a few photos of Carl's signs, and there are already a handful of reviews, all of them five stars.

⭐ ⭐ ⭐ ⭐ ⭐

I can't believe I'm writing this, but this oracle is the real deal. Wise, modest, funny. I felt like I was meeting with an old friend.

⭐ ⭐ ⭐ ⭐ ⭐

Run, don't walk, to see this guy. (But wear good shoes because the road is very muddy.)

⭐ ⭐ ⭐ ⭐ ⭐

I was bereft after the death of my dog who I've had for seventeen years. I went to see the oracle out of desperation. He described my dog in detail, right down to his orange collar. He reassured me that Sweet Potato was living a joyful afterlife. I felt such peace when our visit was over. But the weirdest part might be that the oracle has a huge cat named Dominic . . . and now I think I might want a cat . . . ?!

⭐ ⭐ ⭐ ⭐ ⭐

Worth every penny. (Did I mention it's free?)

⭐ ⭐ ⭐ ⭐ ⭐

I've been struggling to process a trauma for the last twelve years of my life. I've tried everything—therapy, SSRIs, EMDR, ketamine, and every form of woo-woo self-help out there. Nothing made a difference until now. The oracle didn't solve my problems for me, but he helped me reframe them. He gave me hope.

⭐ ⭐ ⭐ ⭐ ⭐

The tea is hot, the pond is cold, and the oracle knows his shit.

We had planned to take a break during mud season, but by the end of April, our wait list has grown to over two hundred people. There is no stemming the flow, so we proceed with our two-guests-a-week schedule.

It's still cold, but the sun is becoming more assertive, slowly winning its battle against the last vestiges of stubborn snow. A few patches lie here and there, but the ground is softening, and the busy birdcalls indicate that we are on the edge of a new season.

One morning, I awake to hear the pond groaning. The ice is thawing, and as usual, it is protesting as it goes. It feels like a victory to have made it to this side of winter, but if I'm honest, it's not really spring that I have been waiting for.

My father's prophecies for our visitors have provided plenty of proof of his abilities—if not to see the future, then at least to offer up significant insight into the present. But despite the influx of visitors that is bringing more variety to our lives, I still find myself anticipating one particular visitor.

My father has not mentioned Seth since the day Nils did his ice plunge, but even so, I am always waiting for his ghost to reappear.

Chapter 33

One morning, as I am brushing my teeth, a spider skitters into the sink. It's not the first time I've seen her. She has been in my bathroom spinning webs for a few weeks. I try not to kill bugs unless it's absolutely necessary (the black fly, mid-bite). Even back in the city, when I came across a cockroach, I would trap it in a jar and release it out a window or onto the sidewalk. I figure you never know who you're dealing with, and it's best to be gracious, lest they return the favor someday. So as I watch this spider flirt with the drain, I decide it's time to usher her to safety. I grab an empty Q-tip box and encourage the spider into it, closing the paper flap to seal her inside until I can find a suitable place to release her.

When I get to the porch, I find my father sitting in his chair.

"What do you have there?" he asks.

"A spider."

"For the serpent to eat?"

I cock my head in confusion. "What serpent?"

My father looks around. "He was just here."

"Who was? You mean a *snake*?" Alarmed, I start to flip over the cushions of the wicker couch with my free hand, bracing myself for what I might find.

"They're gone, I suppose," says my father.

"Who? Who's *they*?"

"The blond kid was here to visit, and he brought a snake. Coconut."

My fingers clench around the Q-tip box as I realize that my father has once again been visited by Seth, this time in the company of the long-deceased snake, whose name, I'm certain, I never shared with my father. This time, I don't waste precious seconds by questioning whether what my dad saw was real. I simply ask: "What did you and Seth talk about? What did he say?"

"He was happy to see the loons are back. Coconut is doing splendidly. Something about a cricket . . ."

"What?" I yell, knowing that means me. "*What* about a cricket?"

"What?" My father looks confused.

"What did he say about Cricket?" I'm practically shouting at him now.

"About a cricket? What do you mean?" It's gone. He has lost the train of thought, and Seth has slipped away again. My heart sinks.

We are quiet for a minute and then my father looks toward the box and asks, "What do you have there?"

"A spider," I repeat. Crestfallen, I lift the flap of the box so the arachnid can make its escape onto the railing of the porch.

I'm frustrated, but with whom? My forgetful father? My ex-boyfriend's ghost? Whatever conversation they are having, I want to be part of it.

———————

That night, I have the same dream I had on the eve of Nina's departure last summer.

Again, I cough up my own heart and catch it in my hand. "Can I live without this?" I ask passersby, who shrug. But this time, a familiar face emerges from the crowd. It's Seth—still floppy-haired, still seventeen. (Always seventeen.)

"Do I still need this?" I ask him with more urgency, shoving my heart toward him.

He just smiles and says, "You'll see."

Chapter 34

On the Friday before Memorial Day, I take my father to brunch at
Lorne's. We've decided to accept four supplicants a week during the
summer, and our calendar is already booked through Labor Day. We
plan to slow down again in the fall, but for now, demand is skyrock-
eting and I see no reason not to embrace it. I haven't felt this kind of
adrenaline for a long time, and it's nice to have a sense of momentum.
It hadn't occurred to me that I was depressed for much of the fall and
winter—and, let's be honest, for the last ten years—but now that I
wake up looking forward to my days, I realize just how low I had once
been. I still haven't told Nina about our enterprise, but given that she
is six months pregnant and due in August, I don't want to disturb the
waters. She is distracted by her own life; and I am finally invested in
mine.

We claim our usual booth by the window and Sandy arrives
promptly, carrying menus but not bothering to put them down.

"Morning, Arthur, Cricket. Same as always?" She lifts her eyebrows expectantly.

I nod. She knows the drill: two BLTs; coffee for me; ginger beer
for him.

She strides off to put in our order. As we wait, we play tic-tac-toe
on a napkin. This is a game Dad can still handle, although I sometimes have to give him strategic reminders to ensure that he will win.
As I wait for him to mark a wiggly X, Paula comes wafting through
the diner's front door. She is waving a copy of *The New York Times*.

"Extra, extra!" she calls out. "Cricket, you didn't tell me it was going to be a *feature*."

"What are you talking about?" I ask, genuinely confused. About a month ago, a reporter had visited us. She said her story was a travel piece about the Adirondacks, and she wanted to include a little mention of the oracle. Her photographer took a portrait of my dad, and I showed her around and explained our process to her. Before she left, my father gave her a prophecy—he saw a career shift in her future: a stint in Hollywood, more money, an Italian car; he warned her to shore up who she was before fame devoured her—and then she went on her way.

Paula slaps the paper down in front of us, and on the cover of the travel section, I see the headline:

The Oracle Will See You Now

In the heart of the Adirondacks, a local Nostradamus is putting a little-known town on the map.

As I begin to scan the article, Sandy sidles up with our plates and cranes her neck to see what I'm reading.

"Oh, that," she says. "Yeah, that reporter came poking around in here."

"Did you talk to her?" I ask, but my question answers itself. On the second page of the article, there is a photo of Sandy leaning against the counter at Lorne's. As I rush through the rest, I see that a number of local business owners in town have weighed in on the "phenomenon" that is the oracle at Catwood Pond.

Deb of Deb's Depot is quoted, saying: "Can he see the future? F-ck if I know. But I *do* know that my sales are up 500 percent since last summer." There's a photo of a rack displaying T-shirts and mugs emblazoned with the words: I CAME ALL THE WAY TO THE ADIRONDACKS AND ALL I GOT WAS A LIFE-CHANGING PROPHECY.

I'm gobsmacked, scared, and delighted all at the same time. On one hand, this article seems to validate that our project is not just a flight of fancy. On the other hand, it feels like a level of exposure that none of us anticipated.

"I knew it," says Paula. "I knew we were onto something."

I turn to my father, who is trying to follow the conversation. "Dad, do you understand that this is about you?"

"Me?" He looks more closely at the paper, and I point to his portrait.

"Well, would you look at that!" He grins. "I've never looked better."

"It's a story about how people are coming to see you for advice. About the effect it's having on the town," I say. "You're sort of a celebrity."

"Ha!" My father laughs explosively at the idea. Celebrity is the last thing he has ever courted, but it has found him nonetheless.

Then I see my name, and I zero in on a line about me:

> While my prophecy is given, the oracle's daughter Cricket looms quietly in the background. When I ask her about her role in the operation, she insists, "I'm just his caregiver." But whether martyr or manipulator, she runs a tight ship, ushering me out the door as soon as the oracle shows signs of fatigue.

"'Martyr or manipulator'?" I read aloud. "God, are those my only options?"

Paula laughs so hysterically that my father catches her enthusiasm and guffaws as well. Curious to see what the online version of the article is like, I fish for my phone in my bag, but as soon as I find it, my screen lights up with an incoming call. It's Nina.

I excuse myself and walk out to the parking lot to answer it. Though I know better, I find myself hoping that *The New York Times* is somehow inaccessible in Sweden.

"Hi . . ."

"Cricket." I can tell from her tone that she has seen the article.

"Okay, let me expla . . ."

But she begins reading from the text. "*If anything, Campbell's dementia only adds to his allure.* What the hell is this?"

"I'll admit, the project has taken off a bit," I say.

"A bit? Cricket, you promised to stop this, and now you've turned it into a regional sensation."

National, I think. But I say: "I'm only just processing it myself. Look, I know none of this makes sense from where you sit, Nina, but this is a good thing. Dad is loving the visitors, and I finally have something that . . ."

"That what?"

That feels meaningful. That is reviving me. That has turned the tide of my despair. There is so much I could say, but I put it in terms I hope Nina will appreciate: "That is keeping me focused. That is giving me purpose."

"You know what else could do that? A job!" She continues to read from the article. "*In a world where other self-styled healers charge upwards of $150 a session, the oracle at Catwood Pond is not a commercial enterprise. Campbell doles out his prophecies free of charge, and a wooden donation box is the only place where visitors can contribute.*"

"We've gotten a fair amount of donations," I say.

"Cricket, this wasn't the plan," says Nina. "You were supposed to get settled with Dad and then get a *job*. A real job."

There's no denying it: my financial outlook is flimsy. But with my father's pension, his social security, and the donations we have received, we are surviving. It's not enough for an emergency, but it's enough to get by for now.

"You don't understand," I say. "I wish you could see it, experience it. It's kind of amazing, what we've built."

"What you've built? Cricket, Dad is not an oracle. He doesn't even know *our names*. Did you ever stop to think you're just using him to keep yourself entertained? Just because you're lost doesn't mean you can lead our father on a wild goose chase."

Her words hit me like a physical blow, and for a moment, out of habit, I assume she is right. But once I take a breath, I realize that in this case, she might not be. I feel less lost than I did a year ago; that's for sure. And I may not know exactly where this prophecy project will lead, but I have enough certainty to know that it's somewhere positive, meaningful, and maybe even magical. I am neither martyr nor manipulator. I am not using my father. We're co-creating something, and I'm tired of Nina assuming that he can't be a willing participant in that endeavor just because he has Alzheimer's. Why should dementia be the end of creativity? Why can't it be the starting point?

Nina goes on. "If I weren't hugely pregnant, I would get on a plane right now and put a stop to this."

"Nina, I need you to trust me," I say with conviction. I'm not used to challenging my sister, and it's a foreign feeling. As I stand my ground, my blood courses through my veins, hot and exciting. "I can handle this. I know what I'm doing."

It's not the first time I've ever said those words, but it is the first time I've believed them.

When we finally hang up, I take a deep breath and make my way across the parking lot. I'm so fired up that I forget to look where I'm going, and a car that has just pulled in stops short to avoid hitting me.

"Sorry," I mouth, wincing and putting my hand up in a gesture of repentance. The driver, a young woman, waves back and then lifts her sunglasses onto her forehead.

When our eyes finally meet, we both freeze. It's Chloe.

Chapter 35

The parking lot is not a conducive place for a catch-up that is a decade overdue, so Chloe and I make a plan to hang out the next day. When she arrives at my house, she lets herself in as she always used to, and I can hear her greet my father, who is sitting on the porch enjoying the afternoon sun.

"Hi, Mr. Campbell," she says. "Don't get up. It's just me, Chloe Zimmerman. It's so nice to see you."

"Chloe! And how are you?" my father says. "Have you ever tried this stuff?"

He is about to offer her a sip of his ginger beer when I join them on the porch. Chloe looks a little unsure of what to do, and I swoop in to save her. "Dad, Chloe and I are going for a swim. We'll be at the dock if you need us."

"Very good!" My father settles back into his chair and studies a catalogue from a company that sells fancy fruit baskets.

Chloe and I grab towels and beers and head down to the water. She looks the same as always, although her hair is a bit shorter and she wears a fat diamond on her ring finger. The sun is blazing today, and as we settle onto the dock, we both slather on sunscreen and put on our hats. Mine is a faded baseball cap that bears the Adirondack League Club insignia; Chloe's is a straw sunhat with a wide black bow around the crown. We would never have given such consideration to sun protection in our youth, but clearly, we have matured.

"Look at us, being responsible," I say.

"So responsible," says Chloe, pulling a vape pen out of her bag and offering it to me. I decline, but I open two beers and hand her one.

As she sips hers, she reaches over and presses lightly on the scar I got from smashing my knee into a rock when we were twelve. "I'm still trying to process the fact that you're here, in front of me. Where have you *been*, girl?"

I shake my head, not knowing where to begin. We were sporadically in touch for a few years after Seth's death, but when I stopped coming here, we naturally drifted apart. I don't remember which of us reached out last—I just know that the line went dead. In those years, I was so focused on what *I* had lost that I never stopped to consider what it must have been like for Chloe to lose me.

When we agreed to hang out today, I had worried it might be awkward, but there is a comfort between us that has endured. After all, Chloe already knows about the darkest part of my life. If she were going to judge me, she would have done that long ago. And if she were still mad that I distanced myself, she probably wouldn't be here now.

I give her the rundown of my last few years, and eventually, I look down at her ring, fearing the worst. "Are you and Greg . . . ?"

She furrows her brow and gives me a stern look. "Cricket, please. Greg was like"—she counts on her fingers—"four . . . no, five boyfriends ago. We're still friendly, but he doesn't come here anymore. Didn't you know that?"

"I heard something."

"His dad got caught up in a financial scandal—shocker—and his parents got divorced. They're trying to sell the house, if you're in the market . . ."

We laugh at the thought of me taking up residence across the pond, and Chloe fills me in on the contours of her life. She's only in town for a few more days because her employer is stingy with vacation time, but she plans to spend a whole month here next summer. She is engaged to a guy named Franklin ("the absolute best"). They live in Boston, and they have a Shiba Inu named Romy. They're getting married next May in Maine—she says I should come.

For the next few hours, we talk as if we are still just kids on a dock. I don't know what I was so afraid of. Being with Chloe doesn't make me feel exposed—it makes me feel known. It's not that I haven't had friendships since abandoning Catwood Pond a decade ago, but they were often fleeting or based on short-term commonalities—a shared job, a shared love of boozy brunches, a shared inability to pay for decent housing in New York City. In the years after Seth's death and my parents' divorce, it was hard for me to process what I was going through, let alone convey it to new friends. I had been close with Olivia and Tasha for a few years, but I had never told them the full story about Seth. I preferred to keep things light, some might say superficial. But in holding parts of my life back from my friends, I ended up disconnecting from myself.

Chloe and I dip in and out of the pond as we talk, cooling down, then drying off, then repeating the cycle until the sun has nearly completed its afternoon arc through the sky.

Finally, Chloe brings up Seth. "You know, no one blames you for what happened." She pauses. "Well, maybe Greg did, for a second, but he was just being an asshole."

I nod.

"Everyone really missed you when you stopped coming here. People still ask me about you. I always wished I had something to tell them. And now I do." She looks at me. "I can tell them you're doing great."

"Ha!" I laugh louder than I expect to.

"What?" she says, serious. "You and your dad are singlehandedly revitalizing the economy of Locust. You're back in the place that you love, doing interesting things. And you look really good. Like, you look hot."

I laugh again, enjoying the view of myself through Chloe's eyes. "I'm glad you think I'm thriving."

"Are you dating anyone?" She looks hungry for some good gossip.

I look around. "Who would I date? I live at Catwood Pond."

"Fair. But Cricket"—she leans in—"you *have* had sex, right?"

"Yes. Of course." I slap some water at her. But after a moment, I add, "I'm not sure if I've ever had *good* sex . . ."

"Oh, well, that's normal. I hadn't either, until I met Franklin. But you will, once you get back out there."

"I don't know if I'm datable anymore," I say. "I've become pretty feral out here in the woods."

"I mean, you could probably use a bang trim." Chloe leans back, sizing me up. "But I like the two-tone hair. It's sort of . . . ungovernable."

"That's me."

I lean my head into her shoulder as we stare across the pond, and she drapes her arm around me. It feels as though we are part of the landscape, just like any other element: the water, the trees, the sky, and the girls on the dock.

I feel more than reassured. I feel rooted.

Chapter 36

That evening, my mother calls. When I see her name pop up on my phone, I brace myself for her to admonish me the way Nina had.

"Hi, Mom."

"Well, I read the article. What a hoot!"

A hoot?

"I mean, you've always been quirky, but this is something else," she says.

"I thought you would be mad," I say. "Nina thinks I'm crazy."

"Well, I can't say I'm *pleased*, but I'm not mad. What I really want to know is: Can you make some money with this scheme?"

I laugh, relieved. "Maybe? But that's not really the point."

"Then what is the point?"

How can I explain to her that the project itself is the point? Its meaning is unfolding day by day—we're not attached to an outcome and we don't expect some kind of payoff.

"It's real, Mom. We're helping people, and besides, I think it's helping Dad."

"I'm just looking out for you. What's happening with your job hunt? How are you for money?"

"We're okay. We receive some donations, and I'm still working for Paula. Then there is Dad's income. So all in all, we are getting by."

"Getting by. That sounds familiar," she says.

I know she's referring to the years I spent drifting during the pandemic, staying afloat but never building toward anything concrete. For a moment, I consider telling her that I want to return to school and work toward becoming a veterinarian, but I worry that she might shoot down the idea, saying it's impractical or out of my reach. It's a dream that makes me feel vulnerable in its honesty, and I am holding it gently, like a baby bird or a fledgling love. I don't want to ask too much of it. It's still too fragile to share, especially with my mother.

"Don't worry about me, Mom," I say instead. "I'll make it work. I always do."

A few days later, a supplicant named Jen arrives at our house. She looks drained and apologetic as I welcome her in the driveway.

"I'm so sorry," she says. "I had to bring my seven-year-old. His dad was supposed to have him this weekend, but . . ." She stops herself, perhaps from saying something negative. "Jasper, say hi."

"Hi." Jasper is wearing a full Spider-Man suit, minus the mask, and has a head of exuberant curls.

"Hi there," I greet him. And then to his mom: "Don't worry. I can hang with Spidey while you meet with the oracle."

"Thank you so much," says Jen. "I really need some good advice."

I set her up to chat with my father, and I walk Jasper down to the dock. He skips ahead of me, his curls bobbing down the path as I try to keep up. When we reach the dock, he walks around thoughtfully, as if assessing the value of the property.

"This is nice," he says. "Our house isn't on a lake. It's on a road."

"Oh," I say, amused by his no-nonsense manner. "Is it a nice road?"

"No," he says. "Just normal dirt."

I like this kid already. I ask him if he wants to skip stones, and we comb the shoreline looking for flat ones while we chat.

"My mom said your dad is a miracle," Jasper says.

"An oracle." I smile. "Yes. It's pretty cool."

"So he knows the future?"

"Sort of," I say. "He helps people see things. He helps them envision the futures they want."

"How?"

"Well, that's the magic," I say. "I don't know exactly. He asks questions. He observes. He uses his special brain."

"What's special about it?" Jasper would make a good investigator someday.

"Well, he forgets a lot of things," I say. "But he seems to remember what is most important. Sometimes his brain helps him to be very wise."

"And it's not bullshit?" asks Jasper. He looks at my shocked expression and says, "What? Because I said *bullshit*? That's nothing. I know all the swears. Ass, fuck, butt . . ."

I turn away so he can't see how hard I'm laughing. Once I've collected myself, I tell him I don't think it's bullshit. I think it's real. We make our way to the edge of the dock with our handfuls of stones, and I ask him if he knows how to throw them so they will skip.

"Not really. I did it once with my dad, but he didn't know what he was doing. He's kind of incompetent. I think that's why my mom wanted to come here. She's at the end of her rope."

"Oh, boy. That sounds hard," I say. This kid is precocious, and whatever is happening within his family, he is clearly tuned in to it without completely understanding it. I think of myself at his age—seven—and wonder how much I was absorbing and comprehending. That was the year my father retired and my mom went back to work full-time. That summer was tense, and my mother abruptly left Catwood Pond halfway through July. I missed her terribly. In later years, when she only came up for a week each summer, the missing morphed into resentment. It's only now occurring to me that maybe I should have been proud of her.

Jasper and I look out at the pond. I show him how to cock his wrist so that the stone will fly at an angle that will allow it to bounce along the surface of the water. He gives it a go. His first stone plunks heavily and sinks. His next few attempts do the same. But on his fifth or sixth try, his stone hits the water and flies, skipping twice more before it disappears into the depths.

He gasps.

"You did it, Jasper."

"I did." He seems shocked. "I thought maybe you were messing with me. I didn't think it would actually work."

"I wouldn't mess with you."

He looks at me with circumspection and then seems to accept my statement as genuine.

I throw one of my stones, and we both watch as it skips seven times before easing gently into the water.

"This place is cool," he says, pocketing the rest of his stones as if they're worth something.

Just then, his mother comes around the corner of the boathouse. Her eyes are red, but she looks rejuvenated. She is carrying herself differently, and her energy has shifted completely.

"Jas, you ready to go?"

Jasper doesn't answer but starts to lunge buoyantly up the path.

"Thank you. This was . . . Thank you," she says to me, brimming with emotion, before she turns to follow her son.

I don't ask her what she talked about with my father, and I know he won't remember. The content is irrelevant at this point, but the exchange has worked its magic. I can tell she got what she was seeking. From the looks of it, she got much more.

Chapter 37

———————

The following Tuesday, I attend Paula's dance class as usual. No longer am I the newcomer on the edge of the group. Now, I am front and center, acting as if I were born to *chassé*. This has become my therapy—the one time a week when I am not responsible for anyone and I can just lose myself.

Even though it is after 8:00 P.M. when we finish class, it's still light out. I'm in no rush to get home, as Carl is watching my father for the evening. I sit on the bench outside the barn and drink some water. As I mop the sweat from my neck, I see a man coming toward me from the driveway. He's wearing a green baseball cap that says GARIBALDI TREE CARE and has a tennis racquet slung over his shoulder. He is sweaty, too, but in a good way. His eyes meet mine, and I'm jolted. Eye contact has never been my forte, and I suddenly wish I weren't wearing a T-shirt with a giant cat face on it. It was my last clean shirt.

"Hey," he says. "Cricket?"

First I worry that he is someone from the past that I can't place, but I would remember someone this handsome. Then words start coming out of my mouth involuntarily. "Hi. Cricket. Yes. I am."

"Max." He touches his chest. "I'm Paula's nephew."

"Oh! Hey," I say. "I don't normally dress like this."

"That's a shame," he says. I laugh and start to loosen up, one millimeter at a time.

"Are you visiting?" I ask. Duh. He's here, isn't he? Of course he's visiting.

"I'll be here on and off all summer. I have some work projects in the area." That's right. He's an arborist.

I must be looking at his racquet because he says, "Do you play?"

"I used to. Not recently."

"Want to hit sometime?"

"Okay. Yeah. I mean, I'm not really . . . socialized." Wow, I'm rusty. It's been a long winter.

Max laughs. "I can guarantee you're more socialized than most of the people in this town."

I laugh but don't know what to say next.

"I'll give you a call." He hands me his phone so I can input my number, which I momentarily forget. I'm relieved to see that there is a tiny crack across the top of his screen, which suggests that he is human. Finally, I remember my phone number.

"Great," says Max, pocketing his phone. Just then, Paula emerges from the barn and pulls the door closed behind her. She notices us talking, raises her eyebrows, and then scoots by us in a fake-discreet manner so as not to interrupt.

Max smiles and shakes his head, as if he is accustomed to being mildly embarrassed by his aunt. "Nice to meet you, Cricket."

Once he is gone, I chug the rest of my water in an attempt to drown my jitters. I had forgotten how unsettling it can be to feel attracted to someone. I'm like a bear coming out of hibernation: disoriented and ravenous, but finally awake.

———

When I get home, Carl and my father are on the porch watching the light fade over the pond. Dominic is splayed on my father's lap, and Cynthia lazes by Carl's feet. I pour a glass of wine and join them.

"And where have you been this evening?" my dad asks cheerfully as I plop down on a chair.

"At my dance class," I say. We have this same exchange every week.

"I met Paula's nephew," I say quietly, as if I'm divulging a secret. "Max."

"Oh, he's here?" Carl asks. "Nice guy."

"He is. He asked if I want to play tennis sometime."

Carl smiles, as if he's relieved I've finally made a friend my own age—or at least risked making one.

"I mean, I don't know if I should. I doubt I'm any good anymore," I say. "And I'm not really emotionally available."

Carl gives me an amused look. "I didn't realize you had to be emotionally available to play tennis. I think I've been doing it wrong."

"I guess I'm overthinking it."

"A tad."

"It's just that I used to play tennis with Seth. In fact, I haven't set foot on a court *since* then. Not on purpose. It just happened that way. But the idea of playing again makes me feel a little . . . guilty? That seems so weird when I say it out loud."

"That's how guilt works. It *is* weird. It's conniving. Especially survivor's guilt."

"Survivor's guilt?" It hadn't occurred to me that I have that. "But I didn't survive anything. I wasn't in the accident."

"Do you wish you had been? Do you wish it had been you and not him?"

"All the time. But I thought that was because I was to blame."

"How could you have been to blame? You were home, weren't you?"

"Yes. I was asleep."

He raises his eyebrows as if that should settle it.

"It's complicated," I say. "When I relive it, I invite him inside and . . . well, we ride off into the sunset or something like that. Like if I had just . . ."

"Just what? Seen the future?"

I smile at the absurdity of it.

"I get it," says Carl. "I felt that way when my mom died. Like if *I* had just . . ."

"But you didn't do anything wrong. She had COVID."

He shrugged. "I was convinced it was my fault. Like I said, guilt is conniving. It befriends your ego and tries to convince you that everything's about *you*—the past, the future. But it's just not true. The only thing we ever have is the present, and we do the best we can with it."

I look over at my father, who has slipped into a light sleep in his wicker chair.

Carl is right, of course. All these years, I've been so eager to punish myself, to somehow embody the tragedy and make myself the center of the story. I've been so focused on the fact that Seth died that I have failed to embrace the other truth: I lived.

I take a final sip of wine. "So how do we beat it? The guilt, I mean."

"Exactly what you're doing. Create something. Make the world a friendlier place. Allow yourself to have a little fun. And it couldn't hurt to play tennis with Max."

Chapter 38

The following week, as I put on a pair of shorts and my least-ratty T-shirt, I try to figure out why I'm so nervous. First, I worry that Max expects something from me. Then, I worry that I expect something from *him*. "It's just tennis," I say to my reflection, as I pull my two-tone hair into a long ponytail. "It's just tennis."

I repeat my mantra during my drive into town, and when I arrive at the community courts, Max is already hitting a ball against the backboard. His strokes are easeful, and I'm relieved that at least one of us is relaxed.

As I shut my car door, he stops and turns. "Hey there!" he calls, walking to meet me by the bench at the side of the court.

"Hi," I call, my pulse quickening. Finally, it dawns on me that this is the exact spot where I first met Seth, so maybe that explains the nerves. This is the place where things begin; and we all know how they could end.

"Penn? Wilson?" Max holds up two new cans of tennis balls.

"Hmmm . . ." I say, as if making a weighty decision.

"Oh no. Don't tell me you're a Dunlop girl . . ."

I laugh. "Let's go with Penn."

Max's playfulness helps to put me at ease, and I remind myself that I am no longer an angsty sixteen-year-old. I'm twenty-seven now, and this is just tennis. Nothing more.

"Just FYI, it's been a while, so go easy on me," I say, heading to my side of the court. "Oh, and I grunt when I serve."

"I'd be disappointed if you didn't," replies Max.

With that, he feeds the ball to me, and we begin to rally. I immediately launch a forehand over the far fence, but before long, I am
hitting competent groundstrokes and volleying with what could be
considered sass. Max is good, but I am good enough to keep up—or
at least he lets me think I am.

"Damn!" yells Max, impressed, after I rip a backhand past him
down the line. "You're an animal."

He seems to delight in me in a way that feels oddly familiar, and
I feel myself loosen up. By the time we decide to quit, I've forgotten
what I was so nervous about. After all, it's just tennis.

Chapter 39

When I get home, my father is at the piano, and Dominic is on the bench beside him, alert and watching my father's fingers skitter across the keys. For all of Dad's forgetfulness, he can still play a dozen or so songs by heart. This afternoon, it's "Maple Leaf Rag" by Scott Joplin—not an easy song by any measure. I pause in the doorway and watch as he plays it in its entirety, his left hand deftly leaping between octaves, the muscle memory still there. It's not uncommon for those with Alzheimer's to retain musical abilities, despite losing ground elsewhere. Perhaps the songs live in a sacred part of the brain that is the last to be breached. Or perhaps the music has its own life force, and my father is merely the channel through which it runs. He plays the final notes with buoyancy and then looks down at Dominic.

"Well, my girl, I think that does it for today."

Without noticing my presence, he gets up and shuffles out to the porch, where he settles into a chair. I consider following him out, but he looks so peaceful, I decide not to interrupt him. Maybe he is awaiting something, someone. Maybe Seth is on his way.

The heat of the July afternoon is starting to build, so I change into my bathing suit and make my way down to the pond for a quick swim. With the sun pressing down, I walk to the edge of the dock and lean over to check the underwater thermometer attached to the ladder. The water is a cool 68 degrees, just how I like it. I stand up, inhale deeply, and dive, cutting into the cold depths. I come up breathless and turn to see how far I am from our dock. Maybe twenty feet. I spin 180 degrees and look to the far shore, where the Seavey camp, all but abandoned, sits still and silent. If I squint my eyes, the house and boathouse blend into the hillside, and it's as if it was never there at all.

I hear a ding come from the dock, where I left my phone. As I swim back and pull myself up the ladder, I find myself hoping it's Max. I quickly talk myself down, take a deep breath, and then calmly look at the screen.

I'm disappointed at who it isn't and surprised by who it is: Gemma. Her text reads:

Hey C! Super exciting opportunity for you. New investor in the mix, so I'm expanding our product offerings at Actualize. Here's a crazy thought . . . a whole line of products from the oracle? Or maybe something even bigger . . . Can you meet next week? I'll be in Locust.

She'll be in Locust? Why on earth would she be in Locust? The vagueness of her text is both intriguing and unnerving, but I don't respond just yet. I need to call in my advisors.

———

"I don't like the sound of it," says Carl, scrutinizing Gemma's text. "It's not in the spirit of the project."

"But what's the harm in meeting with her?" goads Paula.

I glance from Carl to Paula, then over to my father, who asks, "Who is it we're discussing?"

"My old boss, Gemma," I say. "You met her this winter. The flibbertigibbet with the very long hair?"

Not remembering, my father nods anyway and says, "Yes, of course."

"A line of products from the oracle?" says Carl. "I don't see the need. This isn't a product; it's not even a service. It's an offering. That's what makes it so rare: there's no quid pro quo."

"Yes, yes. But see where she says 'maybe something even bigger'?" quotes Paula. "I mean, we've *got* to know what that means."

Carl looks askance, but Paula's curiosity is contagious.

"Carl, you're right to be wary," I say, giving credit where it's due.

"Gemma is an operator, and I've been trying to disentangle myself from her for over a year now."

They wait for me to continue.

"I don't plan to take the deal," I say. "But what's the harm in taking the meeting?"

Chapter 40

A week later, Gemma arrives. This time, she is accompanied by Anthony Gill, the founder of a venture capital firm called Animus Investment. I meet them in the driveway as they climb out of their luxury sedan. This car wouldn't stand a chance during mud season, I think, as I am rushed by Gemma, whose sandalwood scent envelops me as she pulls me into a hug. This embrace doesn't follow the usual rules of hugging—loose and brief. It's a tight hold that persists for a few seconds too long as she rocks from side to side. Then she looks into my eyes as if she has deeply missed me. "Cricket. I'm so excited to co-create with you again."

She says this as if I had never been her underling, as if we're already in business together, as if this project—whatever it is—is a foregone conclusion. But last time I checked, Gemma and I have never actually *co-created*. She used to tell me what to do, and I used to do it.

Still, I try to stay even-keeled and open-minded, so I say, "Me too, Gemma. Me too."

Anthony hits a button and his car chirps obediently.

"You might be the first person who has ever locked their car here," I say.

"Well, it helps to have a car worth locking." He holds out his hand. "Anthony Gill."

"Cricket." We shake and I try my hardest not to despise him. At least, not yet. His hair is slick with some kind of product, and he wears a watch that looks expensive and heavy—the kind that could injure you if you brushed against it wrong.

I lead them through the house.

"So cute, right?" Gemma says to Anthony as he looks around the great room.

"Hm," he responds. It's neither a confirmation nor an objection.

We reach the porch, and I motion for them to take a seat. Anthony smashes a spider and then flicks it off his chair before he sits. It's a brilliant day, the kind I often dreamed about in the depths of winter, and the pond sparkles at a distance. For a moment, I want to get up, run down the hill, and throw myself into the water. But instead, I say, "So, Gemma, what brings you to Locust again?"

She's ready. "It began as a vision. Now it feels like a calling."

Anthony is immersed in his phone, both of his thumbs flying up and down as he types. Gemma pauses, and after a moment, he turns his attention to her, though it's clear he has heard this spiel before.

"I kept asking myself, 'What is the evolution of Actualize?' Once our customer has all the serums, the oils, the pollens, the dews, the supplements . . . what comes next for her? It's something I was turning over and over—for at least a year. And do you know what changed everything?"

"What?" I ask.

"My meeting with the oracle. It wasn't so much what he said; it was the *experience*. It was the journey. And that's when I knew—our next product wouldn't be a product. It would be a place."

"Like Le Refuge?"

"Along those lines, but more heart-centered. This would be a haven where our customer can heal and replenish herself. It's more than a retreat center—it's a space for transformation, transcendence. You check in feeling like yourself, but you come out changed. You come out feeling . . . actualized."

"Wow," I say. "Sounds expensive."

Gemma laughs. "Yes. But that's beside the point. This place is going to be a destination; it's going to change the face of Locust. And we're well on our way—we've got the location, the programming. We're just missing one key ingredient."

"What's that?"

Gemma leans in. "The oracle."

"What do you mean?" I ask.

"You and your father have already laid the groundwork. You have a brand, a following, an aura. We just want to take it to the next level."

"You mean . . . you would charge people to meet with my dad?"

"In a sense," says Gemma. "We'd create an authentic—and scalable— experience that draws on your father's rare gift and his deep Adirondack heritage."

I still don't know what she's getting at, but I already object. "Charging people money isn't really in the spirit of our work."

"But it could be," says Gemma, her energy rising as she begins her hustle. "And look, we understand your father's limitations, so we wouldn't expect him to be available to us more than is reasonable. We see him as more of a . . . figurehead."

She locks eyes with Anthony, and he takes the lead: "We'll get right down to it, Cricket. You've built something really special with your dad. We're prepared to offer you $100,000 for the IP, clean and simple. And we'll take it from here."

For a moment, I am blinded by the amount. It's more money than I had hoped to make anytime soon, and I have to work to contain my astonishment. It would certainly relieve my financial strain and give me more time to find a job. It could even fund my return to school. But beneath my excitement is a muddier feeling of deep unease.

"The IP?" I know what the term means: intellectual property. Ironically, it's exactly what my father once sold in the form of his patents. But I don't see what kind of IP they're looking to extract from a man with advanced dementia.

"Yes," says Gemma. "We want the IP, the access. We want to be able to launch with the oracle as our main offering. And then we would scale from there."

"Scale . . . how?"

"We'd leverage our proprietary AI," says Anthony.

My jaw must drop, because Gemma says, "I know, I know. AI." She rolls her eyes as if she and I are equally offended by the idea. "But Anthony's product is *so* sophisticated, and when in conversation with your father's genius, we could carry on his work long after . . ." She stops herself.

"Am I understanding this correctly . . ." I say. "You want to create some kind of digital dupe of my father, and then charge people to talk to it?"

"Something like that," says Gemma, looking relieved that I am the one to articulate it. "And there would be other offerings, too. We would bring in all kinds of mediums, seers, other oracles. Eventually, we would offer a variety of formats: in-person, virtual, text."

"But there aren't other oracles," I say.

"Not yet," says Gemma. "But there could be. That's the beauty of AI . . ."

I'm dumbstruck, and she changes her tack: "I mean, we're just spitballing at this point. But listen, there's no need to make any kind of decision yet. What I would really like to do is show you around the location we're thinking of."

Gemma seems to be waiting for something.

"Oh, you mean right now?" I ask.

She nods. "It's not far from here. That's why I'm in Locust—to check out the site. And to get your thoughts, of course. You know how much I value your opinion."

Before I have a chance to respond, I notice my father peering through the screen door with a question on his face.

"Here comes the oracle himself," I say, getting up to help my dad out onto the porch. I'm glad to see that he is fully dressed.

"Quite a crowd!" says my father. Gemma and Anthony stand to greet him.

I make the introductions as my mind bounces between the absurdity of their vision and the enormity of their offer. After a moment, my curiosity mounts.

"Okay," I say to Gemma. "Let's do it. Let's go see your site."

Gemma grins. "Great. Shall we drive you? Or you can follow us? It's kind of hard to find, but it's just a few miles from here."

"We'll follow you," I say.

It takes me a few minutes to get organized and get my father in the car, but before long, we are caravanning behind Anthony and Gemma. Anthony drives fast, and we bump along after him in our station wagon, swerving around potholes that he blasts right through.

When we hit the main road, I expect them to turn right toward town, so I am surprised when they veer left and continue on the road that encircles Catwood Pond. Up ahead, there is a turn that would take us up to Baneberry Hill, a well-known lookout in the area, and I wonder if they will head that way. But again, they drive right past it.

As the road veers back into the woods, I am even more confused. But a moment later, they slow and turn onto a familiar dirt road, and it finally dawns on me: they are leading us to the Seavey camp.

Chapter 41

When we pull in, the house looms larger and more foreboding than ever. Whatever luster it once had has now become dusty and out-dated. It has neither the charm of the historic camps nor the subtle style of the newer, more thoughtfully designed homes in the area. It's just a behemoth, past its prime.

"What an atrocity," my father says of the house, as if seeing it for the first time, but ever consistent in his distaste for it.

For a moment, I have the urge to turn around and speed away, but I'm also dying to know how, of all the properties in the world, Gemma ended up picking the Seavey camp as the site for her burgeoning vision. My father and I get out of the car and join Gemma and Anthony in the driveway.

"What do you think?" says Gemma, her eyes wide with excite-ment, seemingly unaware that I know the property well.

"Gemma, this camp is directly across the pond from ours. I've been here," I say. "I mean, not for years. But I used to spend a lot of time here. I knew the family."

"Seriously?" She looks delighted, and she turns to Anthony, and then back to me. "Then you know Greg!"

I furrow my brow. "Do *you* know Greg?"

Before she can answer, the front door opens and I hear a once-familiar voice say, "Cricket Campbell."

It's been ten years since I have seen Greg, and he looks the same but worse: a little older, a little oilier, and, somehow, a little shorter than I remember. He grins at me as if we share some kind of salacious secret.

I had heard that he had made his way to New York to work in finance, and I had always feared I would run into him during my time there. But given that the Seaveys had vacated this property years ago, it hadn't occurred to me that I would run into him *here*.

"So fun that you two know each other!" Gemma lights up.

"We grew up together," I say, suddenly feeling cold.

"Well, we *summered* together," says Greg, then turns his attention to my father. "I didn't realize there would be an oracle among us. Nice to see you, Mr. Campbell."

My father looks at Greg as if trying to place him and says, "And you. Beautiful day we're having."

"But how do you all . . ." I say, trying to triangulate between Greg, Gemma, and Anthony.

"I used to work with Anthony," says Greg.

"*For,*" Anthony says under his breath, as he scrolls on his phone. "Used to work *for* Anthony."

"When Anthony invested in Actualize, and I heard Gemma had recently fallen in love with the Adirondacks, it felt like fate," Greg explains.

My brain is trying to keep pace with these developments, but I have a feeling that Greg is the only one among us who understands the full picture. I didn't know he was entangled in Gemma's business plans, and she certainly doesn't seem to know about his history with me.

"Such a small world," says Gemma, turning to me. "Isn't it perfect?"

"It would be," I say, "but you know there's no commercial activity allowed on Catwood Pond. That's kind of what makes it unique in this area."

Gemma smiles. "Oh, we're on top of that. Greg is working on having it rezoned." Of course he is. The Seaveys had never hesitated to try to remake the world to suit their whims. "Can I walk you through how we plan to use the space?"

Greg holds the front door open, and Anthony, Gemma, my father, and I enter the house. The last time I walked through this door was on New Year's Eve—the night Seth died. Now, it's mostly empty, with just a few pieces of furniture scattered in corners of the great room.

There's a moose head mounted above the fireplace, but otherwise the walls are bare. I'm in such a state of disbelief that I feel numb, and I approach the tour as if I'm just a sightseer. We move through the rooms at a slow pace to accommodate my father and, as Gemma narrates—"So the great room, as the heart of the property, would serve as reception. But through here, I want to create a sanctuary for sound baths and other ritualistic . . ."—I feel my consciousness split in two. I am able to follow Gemma's words while simultaneously traveling back in time. It's as if I am watching two distinct chapters of my life collide; and I wonder what Greg is up to.

Gemma leads us outside, and as we make our way down the hill to the boathouse, Greg hangs back in a way that feels like an invitation. I turn around, and we finally look at each other with frankness.

"Wild coincidence, right?" he says.

"*Is* it a coincidence?"

"Well, you know what they say." He shrugs. "There are no coincidences."

He finishes the latte he is drinking, crumples up the to-go cup, and launches it toward the tree line in a dramatic arc. The Seaveys were never considered stewards of the land, but this is egregious. My disapproval is visible, because Greg says defensively, "What? It's compost."

"Compost isn't just throwing things in the woods," I say.

"Sometimes it is." Greg has always done what he wants and found creative ways to justify it.

"Okay. Well, I hope you like bears," I say, before refocusing. "But seriously, how did this happen?"

Greg squints as if he is trying to remember the chain of events. "I met Gemma by chance through Anthony, maybe a year ago. And right around the time he decided to put money into Actualize, Gemma wrote that article about meeting with 'the oracle at Catwood Pond.' It has a nice ring to it." He gives me a wink. "I had to hear more, so I met with her, and she said she wanted to create a space for retreats. I didn't mention that I knew you, because why muddy the waters? But it doesn't change the fact that I think this property is perfect for what she has in mind."

"And you saw an opportunity to finally sell the place . . ." I say, beginning to understand what Greg might be after.

"From what I can tell, there are only upsides here. We're looking to sell, Gemma is an eager buyer with a shit-ton of funding, and you and your dad could cash in if you can monetize this oracle thing. Not to mention the economic lift it would give Locust. It's a win-win-win. Those don't come along often."

"Isn't this a giant conflict of interest?" I ask.

"It's more like a confluence of interests." When I don't respond right away, Greg takes a long breath and says, "Listen, Cricket . . ."

Here it comes, I think. The apology I could have used a decade ago.

"I know the past is heavy. And I know we drifted apart."

"That's one way to put it."

"But at the end of the day, we're old friends. Let's bury the hatchet and make some money together."

Gemma, Anthony, and my father have exited the boathouse and begun walking down the path that leads to the guest cabins. I start to follow them.

"I have to hand it to you. It's really smart," Greg says, stopping me in my tracks.

"What is?"

"Capitalizing on the fact that your dad is losing it."

Ah, here's the Greg I remember. I feel myself ice over as I quip, "Oh yeah, it's a total win-win."

"Easy, tiger. I meant that in a good way," he insists.

"I know you did. That's the problem." I can't believe I thought for a moment that he might have changed. "Listen, this whole thing is ridiculous. I just came to hear Gemma out."

"Fine." Greg holds up his hands, as if he has no real stake in the matter. "I'm just saying, it would be fun to work with you on this. Put the past behind us."

The other three have disappeared down the path, but before I follow them, there's something I have to ask while I have the chance.

"Did you mean what you said that night?"

"What night?"

"On Sully's dock. The last time I saw you. You said I killed your cousin. You said Seth would still be here if it weren't for my drama."

"I said that?" Greg looks skeptical. "I wouldn't have said that."

"You did."

"Well, I hope you didn't take it seriously. I was probably just . . . you know . . . processing. Plus, that was a lifetime ago. We've all moved on, right?"

Wrong. But I don't want to admit just how much that phase of my life has defined the decade since—how much it still defines me now. It's hard to believe Greg is quite so blasé about it. "You won't be sad to leave Locust once the place sells?"

Greg knits his brow and shakes his head. "This property is just a money suck at this point, and it's too far from the city. I have a place in Montauk now."

Somewhere beneath his veneer, I know that he is still troubled and hurting—probably as much as I am—but I decide to let it be. I'm done sparring with Greg Seavey.

As I walk down the path, I can hear Gemma up ahead saying, "I feel like moss is going to be an important design motif . . ."

When I finally reach the unlikely trio of Anthony, my father, and Gemma, they are standing in front of the guest cabin where Seth stayed that summer. I don't need to peek inside—I know every inch of it. After all, it's the place where I fell in love for the first, and only, time.

Gemma continues to hold forth. "We could create a dedicated space for the oracle right here. It's private, tucked away, and it has a really potent energy, don't you think?"

My father nods, but also gives me a look like he has no idea what she is talking about.

"Excellent! The future home of the temple for the oracle at Catwood Pond," she proclaims, then stands back and cocks her head. "Either that or a sauna. I'm still just spitballing."

As we conclude our walkthrough and return to the driveway, I say, "Well, this gives us a lot to consider. Your offer is very generous, but I'll need a few days to think about it."

"Of course," says Gemma.

"Don't think *too* much," says Anthony, finally pocketing his phone and making eye contact with me. "Remember, there are two kinds of people in the world."

I hate false dichotomies, so I say, "Those who make two-kinds-of-people-in-the-world statements and those who don't?"

Anthony gives a courtesy smile and continues, "Those who capitalize and those who don't."

"I'll keep that in mind," I say, holding the car door for my father as he climbs into the passenger seat and begins battling with his seat belt.

We head up the driveway, and I can see Gemma, Anthony, and Greg in the rearview mirror. As their shapes recede, I wonder whether this is the beginning or the end of something. I figure it's probably both.

Chapter 42

$100,000 for the IP, clean and simple.

You and your father have already laid the groundwork. . . . We just want to take it to the next level.

For the next few days, I keep hearing Anthony and Gemma's voices in my head, reverberating and accelerating like some kind of frenetic TikTok mashup.

IP. Groundwork. Next level. Clean and simple.

IP. Groundwork. Next level. Clean and simple.

IP. Groundwork. Next level. Clean and simple . . .

On one hand, I can think of a dozen reasons to turn them down and never look back. They're calling it an offer, but I know Gemma and I know Greg. These people don't offer. They take; they siphon; they extract. They slurp the nectar and leave a dry husk in their wake. Plus, I know my father would be appalled by the idea of "living indefinitely" through technology. After all, I once heard him say, "I've tried the internet. It's not for me."

But on the other hand: $100,000. I don't see how I can turn down that amount of money—not when we're just barely meeting our monthly expenses and I'm no closer to having a real job than I was at this time last year. With that amount of money, I could fix up the house, hire someone to help with my father, and go back to school without having to worry about taking on more debt. At the very least, I could buy myself more time with my father before we would need to sell the house and move him into a home.

Plus, there's another irony: this is the kind of splashy success story

my mother always wanted for me, and, against all odds, I have manifested it.

I consider calling Carl and Paula to help me think through this,
but I stop myself. I need to clear my head and cut the noise. I need
an escape, and to my surprise, there is only one thing I feel pulled to
do right now.

I want to play tennis with Max.

That evening, we meet at the courts with only an hour of light to
spare.

"Thank you for answering my text so quickly," I say as I lace up my
sneakers. "It's been a weird week, and I need to blow off some steam."

"Happy to heed the call," says Max, waiting for me to choose a
side of the court.

Once we start hitting, I begin to decompress. It's similar to the
feeling I get when I'm at Paula's dance class—a sloughing off of stress,
a remembrance of who I am. We rally for as long as we can before
the darkness encroaches and even the neon of the tennis ball becomes
hard to track.

As we pack up, Max says, "Do you want to talk about whatever is
going on? We could grab a drink . . ."

The idea of filling him in on the backstory of the situation is
daunting. How far back do I go—all the way to Seth's accident? But
I get the feeling that Max is a good listener, and I could use a drink.
Carl is watching my dad, and I give him a call to see if he can stay a
bit later, knowing the answer will be yes.

As Max and I walk over to the Locust Inn, I try to calculate how
long it has been since I have had an evening out on the town without
my father. Not since I left New York, so well over a year. I don't miss
my old life or my old self, but I realize that my new existence might
look a bit strange, from the outside.

"Is it weird for you that your aunt is one of my best friends here?"
I ask.

Max shrugs. "Not really. Honestly, Paula is one of my best friends, too. I never really viewed her as one of the adults. She was always cooler, always more of an equal."

We approach the entrance to the inn and make our way inside. I'm happy to see the place is brimming with tourists. I even overhear someone say something about "the oracle," and I wonder if they'll be on our roster of visitors for this coming weekend.

Max and I choose stools at the bar. It's nothing fancy, but it's the closest thing this town has to a cocktail lounge. Max gets a beer and I order a dirty martini, which seems to amuse him.

"I can see you mean business. So tell me: What's going on over at Catwood Pond?"

I don't know where to begin, so I start with the amount: $100,000. Then the concept. Then my history as Gemma's employee. Then my relationship with Greg. And finally—now that I am two martinis in—I get to the meat of the matter: Seth's death and the fact that I think he is visiting my father in spectral form.

Max listens intently, his head shaking and his eyes widening at the appropriate times. I finally circle back to the matter at hand: Gemma's offer.

"I mean, she is really effective at what she does, and I'm sure her retreat center would be a success. It could breathe a whole new life into Locust. But I don't know. That's sort of why I left New York—I was exhausted by the compulsion to monetize everything; to convert every glimmer of authenticity into a product; to scale small joys until they are so bloated that they wither and droop."

Max's face stays serious but his eyes look amused.

"I think whatever magic we *have* created at Catwood Pond must be tied to the fact that we *don't* charge our visitors," I continue. "But our financial situation is a bit precarious, and this offer has really thrown me for a loop. On the one hand, it feels absurd and categorically wrong. On the other hand, it's a lot of money. And I can't help but wonder if Seth—well, Seth's ghost—has orchestrated all of this. Maybe this is his grand plan, and my job is just to see it through . . ."

I finally take a breath, and Max nods slowly, as if he is trying to figure out how to respond to the deluge I have just unleashed.

"Oh my god," I say, finally realizing how tipsy I am and how crazy my pent-up tale must sound. "You must think I'm losing my mind. Wait, *am* I losing my mind?"

Max laughs. "I don't think you're losing your mind. It's definitely a lot . . . but you have been through a lot, and you've taken on a lot, and you've created a lot. I'm not surprised to hear it's snowballing in a way that feels overwhelming."

I exhale, relieved that he isn't judging me. What's more: he seems to be giving me credit, and maybe even applauding where I have landed.

Naturally, Max has questions, and I spend the next thirty minutes doing my best to answer them. As I do, I feel my anxiety unfurl and then dissipate. My clarity returns.

"It's a lot of money, no question," says Max. "And you've given this a lot of thought. From what I'm hearing you say, it sounds like you already have your answer."

"I do?" I say, and then realize he is right. Like a good oracle, he has helped me to see what I already know.

We ask for the check, and when it arrives, I try to be cool. In New York, I wouldn't have flinched at a $56 tab. But these days, I can't afford this kind of extravagance. Max insists on putting his card down, and before I can push back, the bartender tells us it's on the house. He gives me a sly wink. "Oracles and their relations drink free."

Suddenly, I feel that the wind is at my back, that everything will be okay. As Max and I leave the inn, we're close enough for our arms to brush, and it feels lightly electric. I'm not sure if it's him, or me, or the fact that Locust is suddenly more vibrant than it has been in my lifetime. As we stroll down Main Street, Lorne's looks to be at full capacity, and even the windows of Deb's are aglow with a new vitality. Tourists stroll the sidewalks and occupy the benches, and kids navigate ice cream cones as they chase each other around the green.

We walk for a while, and when we get back to our cars, Max doesn't seem to be in a rush. Fireflies are glinting on the tennis court, and the sound of crickets forms an even vibration in the air. As Max leans against my car, I wonder again if he's flirting with me, but instead of waiting to find out, I lean in and kiss him. For a moment, I can't believe what I just did, but soon his hand moves up to my hair, and he pulls me a little closer. When I finally step back, he smiles as if he is relieved I made the first move. And now that the ball is in play, I begin to think this is more than just tennis.

Chapter 43

When Gemma calls me a few days later to check in, I am ready.

Her tone is ebullient: "We've all been buzzing since the meeting. This feels so aligned, and Anthony was really impressed. He loved you, loved your dad, loved the concept."

I didn't get the sense that Anthony was capable of love toward anything other than his phone and his car, but I say, "Oh, that's nice to hear."

I leave my father on the porch with a glass of lemonade, and I walk down onto the lawn as Gemma continues. "So, where are you on our offer? Is that number going to work for you?"

"It's generous," I say, trying to center myself, "but I don't think it will work."

"No? Hmmm. Okay, throw it out there. What are you thinking?"

"I'm not thinking anything," I say. "I don't want to do a deal."

I think I hear Gemma gasp faintly on her end of the line before she asks, "Really . . . Why not?"

I round the corner of the house and begin to meander up the driveway.

"It doesn't feel right, Gemma. You always told me to tune in to my instincts, to listen to my vessel. Well, my vessel is saying no."

"Okay." I can tell she is trying to think of a way to argue against her own historical advice. "But this is a once-in-a-lifetime opportunity. I mean, you've already developed the perfect brand concept. That's more than manifestation—that's fate."

I near the top of the driveway, where the first of our signs is affixed to a pine tree. KNOW THYSELF.

"It's not a brand concept," I say. "It's just who he is. And it feels wrong to trade on his prophecies for profit. My dad isn't a product."

"That's exactly the point," says Gemma, with new energy. "Your father is an absolute gem, but you need to think bigger than what you're currently doing. He won't be around forever, Cricket."

She says it as if it is just an inconvenient truth we will need to work around, as if I'm not aware of my father's mortality, as if I don't stare it in the face every single day.

"This is a way to immortalize him," she presses. "To build a legacy."

"He already has a legacy."

"But you need to *scale*," says Gemma. "Name your number."

I pass the second of our signs. NOTHING IN EXCESS.

"Gemma, there's no number," I say. And to make sure she gets the message this time, I add: "I've thought long and hard about 'What would my best self do?' And the answer is: she wouldn't sell out."

For a moment, Gemma is silent. When she speaks again, her tone is chillier. "Cricket, I'm moving forward with this project, and I want to be crystal clear: if we're not collaborators, then we're competitors."

"Okay."

When I don't say anything else, Gemma adds, "This is going to be huge, and you'll regret not getting on board. I'm sure of it."

She hangs up just as I arrive at the third and final sign. Hung on a birch tree that arcs over the driveway, it reads: CERTAINTY BRINGS TROUBLE.

"Who was that on the telephone?" my father asks as I return to the porch.

"Just a solicitation."

"Everyone's selling something," he says.

We sit for a while as the calm of late morning slowly builds into the warmth of midday. I am proud of myself, and it's a feeling I'm not used to. However, turning down Gemma's offer means I have to address our finances more urgently. Things are getting dire, and the donation box is not providing enough for us to coast on much longer. But for a moment, I bask in the pleasantness of knowing I have done the right thing.

I know I should call Carl and Paula to share my update, but my first instinct is to tell Max. We have texted a few times since our evening at the Locust Inn, and I know he is eager to hear how my conversation with Gemma went. My pulse quickens as I place the call, and when he doesn't pick up, I feel a pang of disappointment that makes me realize just how much I like him. With Dylan, even at the very beginning, I never cared if or when he responded to me. His presence in my life was entirely neutral. But this is different. It seems like there is a momentum building—or at least, I hope there is. I send Max a text that is meant to sound breezy—Tennis later?—and quickly move on.

First, I call Carl, whose calm tone of voice conceals his deep relief. He congratulates me on making a good decision, for both myself and my father. Next, I talk to Paula, who delights in the details I relay to her. "*What would my best self do?!*" Paula hoots. "You gave her a taste of her own medicine."

When I hang up, I am disappointed to find that Max hasn't responded to my text. I tell myself not to be a crazy person. It has only been thirty-seven minutes since I sent it. I'm not allowed to be truly disappointed for at least another few hours, so I busy myself. I scrub the bathtubs, make lunch, take my father on a walk up and down the driveway, then up and down again. We read some poems from the big anthology, and just as he settles in for his afternoon nap, my phone finally pings. When I see Max's name, my heart flips with excitement. But then I see his response.

Bad news . . .

I brace myself for any number of devastations: *I forgot that I have a girlfriend, I've left the country,* or just simply, *I've decided that I hate you.*

I sprained my thumb at work this morning. So tennis might be tough.

I breathe out, relieved that it's not personal, but still disappointed that I've lost my easy excuse to spend time with him. But then he starts typing again.

What about something less thumb-centric, like . . . dinner?

I nearly faint from relief. He goes on.

I want to hear how everything went with Gemma! And I also just want to see you.

I fling myself onto the sofa with joy and hug Dominic so hard that he squawks and jumps away. Some say technology will eventually destroy us, and I do believe that, but in this moment, I love my phone with all my heart. I love the subtle drama of text flirtation. I even love the roller coaster of emotions I've just been through. Mostly, I love having someone to care about—and maybe even something to hope for.

Chapter 44

I am attempting to apply mascara when Max arrives that evening. I haven't put makeup on since I moved to Catwood Pond, but suddenly I feel motivated to look as good as I am able. Next, I dab lipstick on and then rub most of it off, leaving just a soupçon of color on my lips. Carl has agreed to hang with my father for the evening, and when I get downstairs, they are chatting with Max. All three of them turn to look at me, and I notice that their response is different from what I'm used to. I wonder if I've forgotten to put pants on, but when I look down, my jeans are right where they are supposed to be.

"You look so beautiful," says my father, suddenly emotional. I didn't realize that the change in my appearance would be extreme enough to elicit tears, and I suddenly wonder if I should be making more of a daily effort.

Max smiles at my father's earnestness, and then meets my eyes. "I agree. You do."

"Oh, well, thank you," I say, slightly embarrassed, but also impressed by the ease with which Max seems to be connecting with my dad. After a few minutes, we say our goodbyes and walk down to the boathouse. Rather than go back to the Locust Inn or to Lorne's, we've opted to have a picnic on the water. We hop into our boat, with me at the back so I can operate the motor. Max pushes us out of the boathouse as I stand to pull the starter cord. The engine rumbles and quickly dies. I try again. It rumbles and dies. Max watches with interest, but has the good sense not to try and save the day. On my third try, the motor finally catches and roars to life, and Max gives me a confident thumbs-up, as if he never doubted me. As we accelerate and begin to plane, the wind whips our hair and I start to relax. Part of me feels like a teenager who is sneaking off to do something illicit; another part of me feels like a tired parent who is finally getting a night out. I have to remind myself that, somewhere in between those parts, I am also a young adult who has a life to live. As I push the engine to full throttle, I suddenly feel very clear about who I am and what I want—in this moment at least.

"That's where Gemma wants to build her wellness center," I yell, pointing to the Seavey camp. We cruise by so Max can take a look, and then I swing us toward the west bay. As we approach the little island, I slow down and eventually cut the engine. We drift the last few yards, and Max stands to catch hold of the rocks before guiding the front of the boat toward the inlet where we park. I roll up my jeans and hop out into the shallows to tie us up while Max grabs the picnic bag and uses a tree as leverage to pull himself up onto the shore.

The sun casts a coral light over the pond, and as we settle onto the rocks, it intensifies into an orange fireball that seems to protest as it sinks behind the tree-lined ridge, like a child fighting bedtime.

As Max unpacks the contents of his linen tote bag, I have to ask: "How many of these bags would you say you own?"

Max furrows his brow, as if running the numbers. "There are at least three hanging in my mudroom. And those are just the ones I use to stuff other bags into . . ."

I smile, glad we're in agreement about the overabundance of tote bags in the world.

"So I don't know," he continues. "Anywhere between fifteen and a trillion? But who can say?"

"That sounds right." I smile again and take notice of the spread that Max has laid out: three types of cheese, charcuterie, figs, raspberries, cornichons, two kinds of bread, local honey, a jar of Dijon. "You went all out. I was expecting a bag of potato chips."

"Well, you underestimate me," Max says, opening a bottle of wine and pouring it into two carved-wood tumblers.

I look at him, his hair mussed from the boat ride, his thumb bandaged in what looks to be a homemade splint, and I think he might just be the most attractive man I've ever seen.

"Cheers," he says. "To standing your ground."

Our eyes meet as we sip, and the quiet settles around us. In the distance, the loons are calling to each other, as if playing a game of Marco Polo. But aside from that, it feels like Max and I are completely alone in the world.

"So how does it feel now that the dust has settled?" he asks.

"You mean turning Gemma down? No regrets."

He gives me a gentle high five, and I let my hand rest against his for an extra beat before pulling it back.

"I mean, I wouldn't *mind* having $100K in the bank. But not if it means digitizing my father."

Max shakes his head and laughs. "There must be more straightforward ways to make a living."

"You'd think," I say. "But it sounds like Gemma is hellbent on proceeding with her plan. Can you imagine? Two dueling oracles, on opposite shores of Catwood Pond?"

"It would make a good movie."

"Hollywood, here I come," I say. We stare at the near shore, where a lanky heron takes slow steps through the shallows. "Honestly, I have no idea what I'll do with myself once . . . well, when my dad doesn't need me anymore. I've never really had a clear direction, career-wise."

"Who does?"

"My sister. And my mom. And it seems like you do. How did you choose . . . is it arborism?"

Max smiles. "Arboriculture. It's a mouthful. I don't know that I really chose it. I kind of just grew into it. I knew I wanted to work outside. I'm interested in conservation, so I think I always wanted a job that landed somewhere in between being a scientist and wielding a chainsaw."

"Seems like you found it."

"I started out working in landscaping, and clients were always asking us for recommendations for arborists. So when I was ready to start my own thing, I became one. But it was never a grand plan. I just followed my gut and did the next logical thing."

"But you like it?"

"I love it. I get to work for myself, choose my own jobs, set my own schedule, spend more time with trees than people."

"Heaven," I say, recognizing him as a fellow introvert.

He reflects for a moment. "Now that I think about it, I *did* love climbing as a kid. I was always up a tree. So maybe it was predetermined." He refills our tumblers. "What about you? What did young Cricket like to do?"

"I was obsessed with animals. Always wanted to be a veterinarian. Which is a bit hard when you're a college dropout."

He shrugs as if he's not so sure, and the self-deprecation that has always been my defense mechanism suddenly feels childish. Maybe I've been holding on too tightly to the version of myself that's a failure. I wonder what it would be like to give myself a fresh start.

The sky has darkened, and just a few violet streaks of cloud remain above the horizon. Max lies back on the blanket we have spread over a large slab of rock, and after a moment, he gently pulls me down beside him. I can feel my heart thud as he kisses me, and I wonder how long it has been since I felt like this with someone. For a moment, Seth flashes through my mind, but I have to admit: this is even more intense than whatever I felt that summer. The audacity of teenage-hood has given way to something more considered and powerful. Max touches me with both patience and intention, taking the lead but also inviting me in. He pulls the strap of my tank top to the side and kisses my collarbone. I can feel the heat of his skin, and I lift the bottom of his T-shirt up, letting him pull it the rest of the way over his head. As things intensify, we shift positions on the sloped rock, laughing as we try to find our equilibrium.

"You're amazing." Max exhales.

"You should see me when I'm doing this somewhere other than a rock," I say.

He laughs and pulls me on top of him, creating a buffer between me and the hard surface beneath us. "Is that better?"

"Much." I look down at him, tracing my finger along his chest. I can feel him respond, and for a moment, I can't believe this is really happening. All of my selves begin to chatter—with anxiety, excitement, disbelief—and do their best to hijack my thoughts. But as Max guides my body in a smooth, confident rhythm, I melt into the moment and let myself go.

Chapter 45

The next few weeks fly by in a pleasant flurry, and it feels as though life is moving toward something good. Max and I get together every few days—sometimes we go out, but he is also game for coming to my house when I need to keep an eye on my father. He is always solicitous about chatting with my dad, even when the conversation circles back on itself. There's a steadiness between us, and I am increasingly confident that he likes me just as much as I like him. Then there's Nina, whose due date is approaching; I keep my phone with me at all times in case news should arrive. And as far as the oracle at Catwood Pond is concerned, demand continues to surge. Our wait list balloons, and at one point, I find a gaggle of uninvited TikTokers "creating content" in our driveway. Carl's role quickly evolves into that of bouncer, and we guard our schedule closely, refusing to accept unscheduled visitors so as not to overburden my father. But on a quiet morning in August, we make an exception.

It's just after lunch when a woman arrives at our door. She introduces herself as Anita and explains that she had been on our calendar in June, but had had to cancel because of a complication with her chemotherapy.

"Anita, yes, I remember," I say. I can see that she is not well.

"I'm sorry to just show up, but I happened to be passing through town this weekend, and I was hoping to speak with the oracle if he has time," she explains.

"Of course." I don't hesitate, and I lead her into the great room where she takes a seat in one of the armchairs. "Can I get you something? Water or tea?"

"I'm fine, thank you," she says. "And I won't stay long. I just . . . well, I'm on something of a pilgrimage, traveling while I still can. My cancer is spreading and no longer operable, so I decided to stop treatment a few days ago. I just need someone to talk to. And it's funny, but the first person I thought of was the oracle."

"Well, I'm sure he would be honored to know that," I say. Normally, each session begins with Paula leading her meditation, and I am wondering if I can approximate it when I hear a shuffling behind me.

"Hello, hello!" says my father. He carries Dominic, whose fluffy body is so relaxed that it droops into the shape of a horseshoe. Anita's eyes are lively with anticipation as my father approaches and takes a seat.

"I used to have a cat just like that," she says.

"Did you?" says my father, giving Dominic a firm pat on the head. "This is our little Dawn."

Given the gravity of her situation, I am nervous about what Anita might expect from him, and whether he can deliver it. For a moment, I feel the need to mediate their conversation, to somehow ensure that we make this worth Anita's while. But I decide to put my faith in my father's abilities, and as they begin to talk, I leave the room so as not to interfere.

I wander into the kitchen, where my phone is on the counter. I have a missed call from Nils, and I immediately call back.

"Cricket?" It's Nina who picks up the phone.

"Yes, hi. What's happening?"

"The baby is happening. I'm in labor," says Nina, sounding uncharacteristically rattled.

"Oh my god," I say. "Are you okay?"

I can hear her breathing through some pain. "I'm trying to be. Mom is getting a flight, and our doula is on the way."

"Nina! This is really happening!" I scream. Then I try to calm myself. "You can do this. You were born to do this."

"I sure as shit hope so." She laughs briefly and then growls in pain. "I need to go. Nils will keep you updated."

With that, she's gone. I look at my watch: 2:00 P.M. here, so 8:00 P.M. in Stockholm. I've heard that first babies can take a long time to make their entrance, so I take a deep breath. But how can anyone be Zen at a time like this—when there will soon be an entirely new person in the world?

I pause and turn my attention back to the conversation happening in the great room.

"It's odd. Now that I'm dying, I feel more alive than ever," says Anita, tearfully. "I just keep wondering, what will happen to me? Where will I go?"

"You will go somewhere much better," says my father, in a voice that sounds grounded and certain. "A place that is so beautiful, you can't even imagine it."

"How do you know?"

There is a pause, and then my father says, "I've been there. So have you. It's just that, here, in this human form, we forget all the things we inherently know. I am just now starting to remember."

"What is it that you remember?"

"That life gets much, much bigger on the other side. That there is absolutely nothing to fear."

I lean against the wall as I eavesdrop, hoping that what my father says is true—and hoping even harder that he has learned these truths from Seth, who is already in this bigger, better place.

"But is it lonely there? Once I'm gone . . . will I be lonely?"

"Just the opposite, Anita." He uses her name as if he has known her forever. "And you won't be gone. No one is ever truly gone."

———

After Anita leaves, I join my father in the great room. He is running his hands along the cribbage board as if trying to recall something. He was still capable of playing the game when I moved back here last year, but now he can no longer remember the rules. At some point this winter, we must have played our final game without even realizing it.

"It's a beautiful day," I say. "Shall we go sit by the water?"

I help him up, and we walk out to the porch, where we ease our way down the stairs toward the path. It's slow going, and my father leans on me more heavily than in the past. I'm keenly aware of his frailty lately. Even a year ago, this walk used to culminate in a swim or a canoe ride. But my father has not wanted to swim this summer, and he doesn't have the dexterity to get in and out of boats anymore. So we just walk down and sit on the dock, which is enough of an adventure for now.

"What a day, what a day," my father says once he is seated in his rusted folding chair. Alzheimer's may have eroded his sense of context, but it has given him the gift of extreme presence. "The happiest day of my life . . ."

I wait for him to go on, curious as to when that day might have been. When he stays quiet, I ask, "When? When was the happiest day of your life?"

"Today, I think."

"Today is the happiest day of your life?" I look at him, wondering if he can somehow sense that he is soon to become a grandfather.

He closes his eyes and lets the sun hit his face. "I can't see why not."

I happen to know that he has difficult days—hours when he is disoriented, worried, frustrated, or uncomfortable. When he gets agitated with me and I lose my temper with him. But he sheds them easily and we try to revel in his better moments. If he says these are his happiest days, I have no reason not to believe him.

The loons are back this year. At least, I assume they're the same ones who laid claim to the pond last summer. They have a new loonlet with them this season. In June, when we first spotted them, the baby was always riding on its parents' backs. But before long, it began to swim and keep up with them. It has spent the summer absorbing as much wisdom as possible before it is left to make its own way.

Last year, it was a shock to me when the adult loons took off at the end of the summer and left their baby behind. I was frantic, thinking they had made a mistake, but it turns out this relinquishment is how loonlets come of age. Left to their own devices, they must survive on their own and, ultimately, figure out how to make their first migration solo. It seems too much for a three- or four-month-old to manage, and yet, they do.

I look at my father as he watches this year's loonlet pass our dock unaccompanied. It navigates the waters with eagerness, and after a few minutes, its mother surfaces beside it.

"They're such good parents—the loons," I say. "The way they guide the baby with such a soft touch."

"Indeed." Then he looks at me quizzically. "What about you? Are you a parent?"

I smile. "No. Maybe someday. Although it seems like a hard job—especially the teenage years. I wasn't exactly an easy child."

"No? What were you like?"

It's clear he has no idea that he raised me, but I go with it. "Well, as a little kid, I was inventive and exuberant and rambunctious. I loved animals and I wanted to be a veterinarian, and my father always encouraged me in that idea. I was very close with him. He taught me how to do everything."

The two loons turn a large circle in the water, and as they swim back toward our dock, the male joins them. After a moment of preening, they increase their speed and glide past us as a threesome.

"But once I became a teenager, I was a little more ornery and wild."

"Ha!" My father seems to appreciate these qualities.

"I thought I had life figured out, as teenagers do. But then there was an accident, and a friend of mine died. After that, my parents got divorced. I was very mean to my father, and we drifted apart. Then he got sick, and I still feel guilty for how absent I was."

"Oh, dear. You should talk to him about it," says my father.

I feel a tear slide down my cheek. "You're right. I should, but after all this time, he may not be able to forgive me. He may not have the capacity."

"Of course he does," my father says with conviction. "I would have forgiven you long ago, if you were my child."

Chapter 46

By the time I go to bed that night, Nina has been admitted to the hospital in Stockholm, but there is still no baby. I am buzzing with anticipation, but I tell myself I have to sleep. I send Max a text, promising to keep him updated, and then turn out the light. I lie in the dark, letting my senses adjust to the blackness. There is no moon tonight, and the loons are making a racket. I now know that they have multiple calls. There is the playful cackling that evokes a cocktail party. There is the agitated wail that sounds territorial. There is the gentle calling to locate a nearby mate or loonlet. And then there is the mournful, middle-of-the-night song—the one that feels like a meditation unto itself, otherworldly in its timbre. That's the one that is in my ears as I drift into sleep.

I have the dream again. This is the third time, and it begins much the same way—with me coughing up my own heart and catching it in my hand. It thuds urgently, and when I look up, the crowd has thinned and Seth is standing right before me. I hold up my heart as rivulets of blood begin to trickle down my forearm. "Do I still need this?" I ask.

Seth crosses his arms and says, "You tell me."

I jolt awake with a feeling that something has happened, and I paw around for my phone. There is a text from Nils:

He's here! Everyone doing well. Call us when you can.

I FaceTime Nils and he doesn't respond. Then I try my sister. No response, so I leave a message. I think about calling my mom, who must be there by now, but I'd rather hear the news from Nina. I tell myself to be patient and go downstairs, where I find my father rummaging around in the cabinets. He has completely emptied one, and its contents are all over the counters.

"Where do we keep the waffles?" he asks in frustration.

We haven't made waffles since I moved back, but now that he mentions them, I'm in the mood as well.

"It's okay, Dad," I say, closing the cupboard to put a stop to his raid. "We don't have waffles here, but I know where we can get some."

We get dressed and head to Lorne's for breakfast, where I try not to obsess about hearing back from Nina. She's learning how to navigate a newborn, after all. We play tic-tac-toe as we wait for our waffles to arrive, and as I am contemplating my next move, a little girl walks up and pats my father's elbow, smiles, and then runs off. A moment later, her mother comes up to us and says, "Sorry about that. She just wanted to touch your arm."

"Very good," says my father, affably.

As the family files out the door, I hear her explain to her little one, "Yes, that's the oracle. But you should always ask before touching people . . ."

The fact that my father is a local celebrity never ceases to surprise me. He finds it amusing as well.

"What's next, a paparazzo waiting on the curb?" He laughs as I pay our bill. It's not as unlikely as he thinks, if we continue at our current clip.

We get in the car and drive the short distance to Deb's to get some groceries. We could have walked, but my father's hip has been bothering him more and more, and I do my best not to overexert him. Once inside, I head for the dairy aisle and my father browses the cereals. I am contemplating a pack of shredded cheese when my phone finally lights up with a FaceTime from Nils.

I answer the call and the screen fills with my sister's bleary but beaming face. "Look who's here!" she sings as the camera moves to a swaddled lump in her arms. The lights are low where they are, but I can make out the outline of a sleeping baby with squinched eyes and pouty lips.

I squeal from inside the door of the cheese refrigerator. "Nina, he's magical! Do we have a name?"

"We do. Anders Arthur Gunnarsson."

"Now we're talking," I say. "I'll have to let Dad know he has a namesake. But first, tell me everything. Are you okay?"

For the next ten minutes, Nina regales me with the details of her delivery, while I alternate between shock and admiration. As has so often been the case, Nina has crossed a major threshold and left me on the other side in awe. While I am in no rush to pursue mother-hood, I do envy whatever it is I think I see in her eyes—a mixture of pride, joy, relief, and peace. Eventually, she needs to attend to her son's squeaks, and when we hang up, I have to lean on the refrigerator door to steady myself. I am an aunt.

After a moment, I walk to the cereal aisle to tell my dad the news, but it's empty. One by one, I check every aisle, then each corner of the store. I hurry over to the cashier woman.

"Have you seen my dad?" I ask. "Old guy. Wispy hair."

"The oracle?" she says. "Yeah. He stepped outside a while ago."

I drop the basket of groceries I've been lugging and run out the door. The asphalt is cooking in the noon sun, and I sprint to our car. It's unlocked, but he is not inside. I dash past the gas pumps and then around to the back of the store, where there is nothing but a dumpster. I scan my surroundings. My dad has wandered off before, but usually stays within my line of sight. This time, he could be anywhere. Finally, I run back into Deb's and inquire about him again.

"Haven't seen him," says the woman, finally showing a modicum of concern. "Not since before."

Now I am starting to panic. Whichever way he went, he is now getting farther and farther from me. If he turned left, he is likely wandering in town. If he turned right, he could be in the woods or maybe even down by Locust Lake. And if he went straight, he might be in someone's yard by now. I start to run one direction, then change my mind and go the other. Finally, I realize I need to call for help so I can cover more ground, more quickly. Carl will know what to do, and I can always call Max. But as I fish around for my phone, I realize I must have left it in my grocery basket. I circle back and enter Deb's one more time.

"Still no," says the woman. I riffle through my discarded basket, find my phone, and start to call Carl. But then I notice a woman in the parking area, holding her keys and staring through her car window in confusion. I run out of the store toward her, and sure enough, my father is there in her passenger seat, calmly eating a stick of beef jerky that he must have stolen.

"Oh my god. I'm so sorry," I say to her. She's clearly a tourist and seems totally discombobulated.

"Is that the oracle?" she asks.

"He has dementia," I explain, opening the door and startling him. "Dad! Dad, this isn't our car."

He looks at me as if he doesn't believe me, then looks around at the interior of the vehicle.

"Come with me." I help him out and lead him to our Subaru, where I buckle him in. But even after I crawl into the driver's seat and start the engine, he still doesn't seem convinced he is in the right car—or with the right person.

There is something off, and not in the usual way.

"Dad?" I say. "Arthur?"

But by now, his face looks slack, and I know something is wrong.

Chapter 47

———

A few hours later, a doctor confirms that my father had a TIA.

"A what?" I ask.

"A transient ischemic attack," she explains, holding the MRI results to show me the area of his brain that was affected. "It's sometimes referred to as a mini-stroke. The symptoms are similar, but it typically resolves on its own, as was the case here. But it can be a warning sign, so it's good that you brought him in."

My father is listening with as much concentration as he can muster, and he looks scared as he asks, "Is it cancer?"

The doctor shakes her head decisively. "No, Mr. Campbell. It's not cancer."

"Thank god," says my father, relieved even though there was never any threat of cancer.

She continues, "It was a brief blockage of blood flow to your brain. But you should be fine. Your daughter is going to take good care of you."

"My daughter?"

"That's me," I say. "I'm going to take good care of you."

He looks comforted, and I hope that my own panic isn't visible.

———

I decide to put our prophecy project on hold indefinitely. Even though my father is expected to recover, I don't want him to spend his energy on the existential queries of strangers right now. We cancel all of our remaining appointments through Labor Day, and although it's the right decision, we both feel the void.

"Any visitors today?" my father asks every morning.

"Not today," I say, longing for the novelty that his supplicants brought to our lives, the rhythm they brought to our days. And we're not the only ones who have to recalibrate. Paula and Carl both seem mildly adrift now, too. Of course, they have the lives they led before we were all swept up in the oracle operation, but after what we created, none of us can simply pick up where we left off.

One day, Carl stops by just as a thunderstorm rolls in, with Cynthia at his heels.

"We were out walking, but I'm not sure we can make it home before this cracks open," he says of the ominous sky. "Do you mind if we sit for a while?"

"Of course not," I say. "When have we ever minded? You know you can stop by anytime you like, Carl."

He sits and Cynthia wedges herself under his chair, shivering.

"She's not a fan of thunder," he explains, stroking the dog's head to soothe her.

We watch the storm roll in, and within a minute, there is a deep rumble. As the rain begins to fall, my father starts to snore softly in his chair.

"There he goes," I say.

"Like clockwork," agrees Carl.

I lean down and scratch Cynthia's back. "Carl, thank you for being so good to my dad. Even though . . . I mean . . . you've probably noticed. I don't think he really knows who you are anymore."

Carl shrugs. "As far as I'm concerned, you don't abandon your friends just because they don't remember who you are. Hell, that's when they need you the most."

I smile. "I wish I were as equanimous. I try to be. But it hurts that he doesn't know me."

"Of course it hurts," Carl offers. "But he knows you. Maybe his *mind* doesn't recognize you, exactly. But some part of him does. He's still him; and you're still you. You're just in a new phase; you can't rely on your old shorthand anymore."

"Our old shorthand—like my name?"

Carl smiles and nods. "This is the part beyond words. This is the part where we are all fumbling in the dark, writing the book as we read it."

I look at Carl and wonder what he was like before his mother's illness, before his personal crisis, before his renaissance.

"You know, I'm a bit scared," I say. "Without our project, I feel kind of lost again. It makes me afraid for when my dad is finally gone. Without him, I'll have no purpose."

Carl gives me a skeptical look. "I don't believe that for a second."

"I'm serious. I'm sort of . . . aimless. I have been for a while."

"Well, what did you like to do when you were a little kid? Like seven, eight, nine. How did you spend your free time?"

It's not lost on me that Max asked the very same question. "I ran an animal hospital right over there." I point through the wall of rain to the clearing in the trees. "Very important work. I saved imaginary lives, day in and day out."

"There you go. That sounds like purpose," says Carl. "You didn't end up wanting to be a vet?"

"I did, actually."

He picks up on the regret in my voice. "You know there's a great veterinary college just forty miles from here, right?"

"I know," I say.

"So what's stopping you?"

"Well, I never finished undergrad, for one. I had bad grades." I start counting the reasons on my fingers. "I didn't take any premed classes. I can't afford vet school. I'm twenty-seven. It's too late."

On some level, it feels safer to rattle off excuses than to reveal I've already been considering the idea. But on another, I realize that I've come to value Carl's opinion as highly as anyone's. His validation could be just what I need to stop talking myself out of my dream.

"I don't hear any actual reason why you couldn't become a vet." Carl looks at me with a mix of sternness and care. "I want to know why, at the ripe old age of twenty-seven, you have already given up on yourself."

His assessment startles me. It hadn't occurred to me that's what I had done, but of course it's true. It happened after Seth died—a slow atrophy of confidence and ambition that I never recovered from.

"It's not too late," says Carl. "And I'd be saying that if you were thirty-seven or forty-seven or fifty-seven. Do not ever give up on yourself."

I wonder if someone gave him this same pep talk when he was faltering, or if he had had to summon the strength to give it to himself.

"Well, I'd need loans," I say, still hedging. "I'd have to go into debt."

"Who cares? That's the American way."

I smile. He's not letting me off the hook.

"Remember a year and a half ago? You weren't sure you were up to the task of taking care of your father. Look at you now. Look at how many great decisions you've made on his behalf."

Carl was the first person who seemed to think I could step into Nina's shoes, and his vision of me was the one I tried to live up to when I quit Actualize and moved back here. I never thought about it that way until now. And he's right—for all my insecurities, I think I've done well by my dad. In taking things one day at a time, I somehow fumbled my way from one life into another—one that's smaller yet fuller, less flashy but infinitely more meaningful.

Carl meets my eyes. "Don't give up on yourself, Cricket."

A lightning bolt splits the clouded horizon in two, and a moment later, a heavy thunderclap seems to underline his point.

"Okay, okay," I relent. "I won't give up on myself."

Chapter 48

I had held out hope that Seth might return again to talk to my father and give me some kind of resolution. But as summer dwindles, so, too, does that hope. For a moment, I worry that my relationship with Max might have angered his ghost, but I remind myself that Seth was never the jealous type.

Labor Day comes and goes, and the activity in Locust begins to ebb. My father has quieted as well, speaking less and less, eating less and less, walking less and less. One morning when he isn't interested in breakfast, his favorite meal of the day, I take him to the doctor to have him checked out. This time, his MRI shows evidence of two additional TIAs.

"Likely in his sleep," she explains. "They can be very subtle."

For a moment, my instinct is to feel guilty about not noticing sooner, or not being more vigilant. But this time, I stop myself from indulging in self-blame.

"What's causing them?" I ask.

"In his case, it's likely a combination of age-related factors." None of them are dire, she tells me, but none of them are good. She advises me to keep his stress level low, prescribes a few new medications, and sends us on our way.

On our drive home, my father hums softly as I roll down the windows to let in the last gasp of summer. There is a particular richness to early September, when the sunlight is broad and lazy. Everything is holding on to life, but not as resolutely as it did in the earlier months of the season. Even the birdsong that sparkles through the canopy is a little off-tune, as if the birds are relaxed and tipsy after a spring and summer of diligent work (nest building, egg laying, chick rearing). It's the end of the party, and all of nature is stumbling home, spent and satisfied. A breeze rustles the ferns along the road, and every once in a while, I get a quick whiff of decay, a reminder of the inevitable.

For the next while, we carry on gently, taking things day by day, night by night. My father doesn't seem to be getting worse, but he is more subdued than he was even a month ago. I hope the halting of our project hasn't dampened his spirit.

One evening at dusk, I hear the crunch of tires in the driveway. Though we have stopped accepting visitors since my father's first TIA, a few have showed up unannounced, and I've had to turn them away. This evening, I leave him sitting by the fire and go out front to shoo away whomever it is.

When I open the door, there is a woman getting out of a black pickup truck. She is pretty in a plain way: no makeup, comfortable-looking wrinkles on her face, and thick hair that is somewhere between blond and gray.

"Hi there," I say. "I'm so sorry, but we're not accepting visitors anymore."

"Cricket?" She looks hopeful.

"Yes, that's me."

"Oh," she says, with a bit of apprehension. "I'm not here for the oracle. I'm actually here to see you."

This is a shock. No one comes to see me.

"I'm Jill," she says, touching her chest lightly. There's something familiar about her, but the name doesn't ring a bell. "Atwater. I'm Seth's mom."

My breath catches in my throat. With her wavy hair and simple features, there's no question that this woman is where Seth originated. It takes me a minute to gather myself before I invite her in.

I offer her a seat by the fire and introduce her to my father, discreetly explaining that he isn't doing very well lately. She gives him a smile, which he reciprocates before turning his attention back to the cat on his lap. I retreat to the kitchen to make tea and collect myself.

Jill's visit feels both unforeseen and inevitable. Maybe all this time, while I thought I was waiting for Seth to come back, it was actually Jill who was on her way.

When I return to the great room, I settle into a chair and set our tea down on the side table between us.

"Mrs. Atwater . . ."

"Jill," she corrects me with a smile, as if I've told a joke that she appreciates.

"Okay. Jill. I barely know what to say."

"I should have given you some warning, but honestly, this wasn't something I planned," she says, clearly trying to put me at ease. "I've always wanted to meet you, and I thought about seeking you out a few times, but I didn't want to intrude on your life. I'm here this week to help my sister clear some things out of her house. Did you hear they finally sold it?"

"I didn't know it was official," I say. "So Gemma is really doing this . . ."

Jill wrinkles her brow, confused.

"The woman who bought it. Her name is Gemma Dwyer, right?"

Jill shakes her head. "I think she bid on it, but there was something about her funding falling through. In the end, it sold to a family who plans to restore it in the old Adirondack style."

"Really?" I can't hide my relief. "I'm so happy to hear that. It always had the potential to be really beautiful."

"In the right hands." Jill smiles knowingly. "Anyway, I found a few things I think might be yours. And I'm leaving tomorrow, so I finally mustered the courage to drive over here. I'm sorry I didn't call first. We couldn't seem to find a number for you."

"That's okay," I say, reassured by her gentle manner. "I'm glad you came."

Now she looks reassured by me. Memories start to slosh around my mind like waves, and I say, "I didn't realize you and your sister were . . ."

"We weren't close for a long time. But we reconciled—eventually—after she divorced her jackass husband."

I smile. My father used to describe Rod Seavey the exact same way.

We begin to settle into what feels like a shared understanding. The thing that exists between us is delicate but defining. We dance around the topic of Seth's death for a while, but eventually, it must be faced.

"I'm so sorry," I say. "I've gone over it a million times in my head. I've tormented myself with all the ways I could have prevented the accident if I had just done this or that differently."

"Oh, Cricket," says Jill. "Please don't torture yourself with that. It was in no way your fault. It was a tragedy, plain and simple."

"I know that's what the adults have to say." I keep forgetting that I am supposedly an adult now.

"Well, I'm saying it because it's the truth. I hope you don't think I came here to forgive you." She holds my eye contact to make sure I'm listening. "I came here to thank you."

"Thank me? For what?"

"I don't know the extent of what went on between you and Seth that summer, but I know that it was something really special. It changed him, and I'm so glad he got to experience it."

She hands me the box she brought with her, and I open it. Inside are a handful of photos: Seth and me in a canoe, Seth pulling me off our dock into the water, Seth and me curled up in sweatshirts by a bonfire. At the bottom of the pile is the Polaroid Seth took of me jumping off the boulder. I am airborne and ecstatic, plummeting toward the water below, my brown hair flying.

"I had never seen these until this week," she said. "But they made me realize how far I've come, how well I've healed. Looking through them didn't break my heart, like it would have years ago. Instead, it brought me joy. It gave me a glimpse of the happiness Seth experienced with you that summer."

I look at her in near disbelief, searching for at least a modicum of resentment or regret, but there is none.

"And I found this." She hands me a list, written in Seth's scratchy handwriting. He must have scrawled it just before he left at the end of that summer.

- *pack stuff*
- *pick up final check from mr. fisher*
- *introduce cricket to mom (?)*

We both laugh at the hesitation of the final line.

"But we never got to meet, because I broke up with him." I put my hands over my face and shake my head. "I was such a mess."

"Have you ever met a sixteen-year-old who isn't?" asks Jill.

"I didn't mean to break his heart."

"Oh, Cricket. I know. He knew it, too, by the way. He was sad, but certainly not deterred."

"What do you mean?"

"He was confident you'd find your way back to each other. You were his first love."

"Oh, I don't think I was. He was mine, but I wasn't his."

She bats my comment away. "Of course you were. You were the only one I ever heard about, anyway. And when I found this list in his cabin, it made me want to meet the person that Seth cared so much about. So here we are, and you're everything I hoped you would be."

I touch the ends of my unwashed hair and look down to see that I am wearing the cat-face shirt again. Damn it.

"I really admire that you are taking care of your father. It must be challenging," she says, looking around at our house. "But this is love in action. You're a good daughter."

I feel the tears start to come. Jill is saying the kinds of things that I wish my own mother would say to me, or at the very least think about me. It's so unexpected to receive this type of affirmation from anyone, let alone a stranger—though in some ways, she isn't one.

We end up talking for over an hour. Jill tells me about the harrowing years immediately after Seth died, how she could barely function from grief, how she wasn't sure she would be able to live without him.

"I had all this mom energy and nowhere to put it, and I felt completely stuck. I had had Seth when I was so young—just twenty-four—and hadn't thought much about a career yet. I was an administrative assistant at a law firm for most of his life, and just assumed that's what

I would do forever. But at one point, Seth began to say, 'Mom, you work just as hard as those lawyers. You might as well become one.' It was sort of our joke, but once he was gone, I started to really consider it. Eventually I did go to law school, and now I'm a real estate attorney."

"Wow. I really admire that," I say. "I can't seem to find my own professional footing."

"It takes time. For me, it took a tragedy to really light that fire. Not that I wouldn't give it all up to have Seth back, but in a way, his death forced me to reinvent myself. I had no choice. When something dies, something else needs to be reborn. I had to use all the love I had for Seth and turn it toward myself. And I realized that even though I will always be devastated, I can be happy, too. I can be both."

"Wow," I say again. Despite the unthinkability of losing her only child, Jill has used these ten years to heal more effectively than I have. "I could use a rebirth."

"Who's to say you aren't having one right now?"

Initially, I'm not sure if I should tell Jill about my father's visits from Seth, but now that she has shared so much with me, I see no need to hold back. I tell her everything—my father's visions, my recurring dream. As I speak, Jill nods slowly and patiently. When I finish, I can't tell whether she is convinced or concerned.

"You don't have to believe me," I say. "I know it's far-fetched."

"Of course I believe you. He's here. I can feel it." She doesn't strike me as the woo-woo type, and she says this matter-of-factly. "It's the energy. I can't explain it, but I've been across the pond all week, and even though his stuff was there, he wasn't. And now I know why." She looks around. "My boy is here."

I am overcome by a feeling of tranquility and completeness—the opposite of FOMO. In this moment, it seems everything that matters is coalescing in this room, only some of it visible.

Neither of us try to restrain our tears, and we laugh as we see that my father has fallen fast asleep despite our blubbering. When Jill finally leaves, she pulls me in for a long hug.

"Thank you for helping me connect to Seth in this way," she says. "This was such a gift."

As I watch her truck pull away, I know that she has given me a gift, too: the feeling of being both mothered and understood. I hadn't realized how badly I needed those things, and I never knew heartbreak and healing could be so intertwined.

Chapter 49

———

In mid-September, the loons leave their baby. It seems abrupt, but of course they have been preparing since the moment she hatched. There's no stopping it: even the most conscientious of parents eventually take off for the unknown, leaving you to face the mystery of life on your own.

I first see her alone one morning when I am at the dock for an early swim. With Labor Day behind us, I am wringing what I can out of summer before everything starts to turn crisp. The loonlet glides past our dock, taking the familiar path that she has swum with her parents so many times. She looks purposeful, if not quite confident. After a moment, she stops and reverses direction. She begins to glide and flap her wings, first slowly and then with increasing intensity, until she is craning her neck and slapping the water with force. This goes on for yards and yards. I hold my breath, hoping for her to get airborne, but eventually she runs out of energy and flaps to a halt. After a moment, she tries again, with the same result.

"You can do it," I whisper. I so desperately want her to survive and make a successful migration. More: I want her to thrive, wherever she ends up.

For the rest of the month, I remain occupied with my father's care—following his new protocols, administering his new meds, keeping him fed and comfortable and clean, but I am equally fixated on the baby loon. I track her movements; I celebrate when she eats; I relax when I see her dive with skill; I cheer when she practices her takeoff; and I worry if I don't spot her for a day or two.

And then one day, at the end of September, I don't see her anymore. I suppose anything could have happened—it is the wilderness, after all. But I choose to believe she has finally launched and is charting her course south, following her instincts and catching all the right currents. I believe hers is a success story.

Chapter 50

————————

By the time the trees begin to turn, my father is in decline. Over the course of one week, I take him to the hospital twice: first for a fainting spell, and then for a high fever a few days later. They diagnose him with pneumonia and a blood infection, and he stays in the hospital for five nights as we wait for the antibiotics to do their work.

My mother and Nina alternate calling me every day for updates, and I wish I had more to tell them. But for now, we are all holding our breath and hoping that my father is strong enough to fight off his infections.

"What is going on?" I ask his doctor. "He's been relatively healthy for so long. What's causing these new issues, and why all at once?"

It was my understanding that Alzheimer's was a slow-motion disease that could go on for years and years. We are nearing the fifth anniversary of his diagnosis, but I had assumed he had plenty of time left.

"As you know, Alzheimer's is neurodegenerative," explains the doctor. "The pace of it is hard to predict and differs from patient to patient. But at this point, your father has entered what we consider late-stage dementia. As his brain changes, different systems are starting to falter."

"Late stage?" I say, letting it sink in. I had been anticipating my father's death for so many years that it became something of an abstraction—a fact of the future. But now the doctor was indicating that future was here. "What does that mean?"

"He could have six months," says the doctor. "Or he could have a few weeks."

"A few *weeks*?"

She explains that it's not the Alzheimer's itself that is the main threat now. His other systems have begun to give out. His kidney function is deteriorating. There is also concern about his heart and his respiration.

"I would recommend you start hospice care," says the doctor, "if that's something you're considering."

Is it something I'm considering? Is it something I can afford? I try to put my emotions on hold as I consider my immediate next steps. I know I need to loop Nina in, but first, I want to gather some information.

As my father dozes in his hospital bed, I spend the next few hours on the phone with his insurance company, bouncing from one agent to another. Finally, I deduce that they will partially cover in-home hospice care, but we will be on the hook for fifty percent of the fee. I have no idea what hospice costs—I've never thought about it until now. My father's nurse brings me a brochure for an in-home provider that might work, given our immediate need and remote location. When I dig a little deeper, I learn that it will cost us $500 a day—and it's anyone's guess how long the care will be necessary.

My heart sinks. The money I have on hand would only buy us two weeks at most. For a moment, Gemma's offer flashes through my mind, but it's too late for that. I could ask Nina to help, but I don't want to burden her right now. There is only one person left to ask.

My mother picks up the phone immediately. "Cricket? I've been trying to reach you all day. How is Arthur?"

I am hit with all the emotion that I have been holding back. "Mom . . ."

"What? What is it?" She can hear the fear in my voice. "What's happened?"

Her concern brings tears to my eyes instantly. I hadn't realized just how alone I had been feeling until I heard her voice. "Dad isn't doing well. His doctors think we should start hospice."

"Oh, Cricket. I had no idea. Why didn't you tell us it had gotten to this point?"

"I didn't know either. It happened so fast."

She is quiet for a moment, and instinctually, I worry she is going to scold me for something. For a while, I was proud of the way I'd taken care of my father, of the trust everyone had placed in me. I felt I had finally glimpsed adulthood. Yet here I am, as lost as ever. I wait for my mother to say I should have handled things differently, been more responsible.

But she doesn't chastise me. "How can I help? What can I do?"

I don't want to ask for help, but the truth is, I need it. I've done as much as I can on my own.

"I need help paying for it, Mom," I say. "We were doing fine. I just hadn't budgeted for this."

"Of course I'll help, Cricket," my mother says. "Thank you for finally letting me."

By the time my father is discharged from the hospital, the air has cooled and the leaves are a riot of red and orange. The hospice workers will start tomorrow—not a day too soon. When we get home, it takes us five minutes to get from the car to the back door, and though I would love to give my father a shower before tucking him into bed, it's too risky. He is likely to fall, and I can't support his weight on my own. For now, I do my best to keep him comfortable, knowing that help is on the way.

Our two hospice nurses are Nedra (who works the day shift) and Lawrence (who works the overnight shift). It's a relief to have some backup, and it gives me a chance to fill everyone in: Nina, my mom, Carl, Paula, and Max. They all let me know that they are available to help, but I find that in this precarious moment, I want time to myself.

As things progress, I keep everyone as informed as I can, though my father's condition is difficult for me to accurately convey. One day, he seems vibrant and healthy, and I am sure he is bouncing back, that we started hospice too soon. The next, I wonder if the end is imminent. When I speak to Nina, I tell her what feels essential, but spare her details that I know will stress her. She is invested, of course, but she is also distracted—by exhaustion, by wonder, by the new world of motherhood. I don't want to tax her unnecessarily.

One morning in late October, I look at the calendar and realize it has been days since my father last spoke. I don't know what his final words were because I didn't realize, at the time, that that's what they were. *Could the conversation between us really be over?* I wonder, as I feel myself dissolve into sadness. I have to sit down, and I try to remind myself: talking is only one way of relating, and perhaps we rely too heavily on it, forgetting that we can also connect through gestures, sounds, glances. I think about the nonverbal and preverbal entities in our lives: animals, newborns. They don't want our explanations of love; they want to see it in action. *Do you feed me? Brush me? Soothe me? Am I safe?*

I think about Nina across the ocean, building a foundation of trust with her newborn through consistent presence, feeding, cooing, snuggling. The intellect will come into play later, and it will complicate everything. For now, she cares for Anders in the most fundamental of ways, and I try to do the same for our father: dressing him in nice warm sweaters, combing his hair, making his favorite soups, always having a blanket ready to drape over his legs. He rarely leaves his bed now, and Dominic rarely leaves his side.

You can't prepare for someone's death, even if you sense it is coming, even if you have long anticipated it. For many years, I had assumed I would get a call from Nina saying Dad had died in his sleep or had suffered a heart attack or had simply evaporated into the ether. I imagined it as something definitive and already-over-with that I would absorb through my phone. An event, not a process. But once I moved to Locust and realized that I would not only be here for his death, but would oversee it, I developed a new set of assumptions based on what I had seen in Hollywood films. First there would be a sad realization that it was time; then some sentimental words would be exchanged (maybe my father would become lucid and recognize me as his beloved daughter one final time); then he would expel one dramatic final breath before everything would go quiet. In my mind, it was a smooth, two-minute montage that leaves everyone sobbing.

Real death is not like in the movies, and my father's begins on a Tuesday. His energy has been flagging since last week; his blood pressure was low and his arthritis was flaring, but nothing was urgently wrong. Nedra recommended rest: "Let him do his favorite things." Now, his favorite things are to drink ginger beer and pet the cat, so that's what we did. But two days ago, he wouldn't get out of bed. He was tired and in pain. Nedra spent much of that day with us, and she deduced that his kidneys were starting to fail. When I heard this, my thoughts began to deceive me, and I needed her to explain everything two times, sometimes three. I heard her words—"He's starting the process"—but the information didn't stick at first, so I blindly followed her lead.

Now, we sit by my father's bed, his ragged breath beating a steady rhythm that has become our metronome. He is no longer responsive, but he is not gone. Nedra affirms, "He has one foot in this world, and one foot in the next." He is between selves, I think, as I hold his veined hand.

Nedra asks if I want her to stay, or if I'd prefer to be alone with my father. I choose the latter, and she says she and Lawrence will be available, to call if I need them. She leaves me with instructions on how to keep my father comfortable, and once she is gone, I call Nina.

"Cricket? I've been texting you. How is he?"

"It's hard to tell. They don't really give you a manual for this, but I think he's almost gone. Can you come?"

"Yes, of course. I'm looking at flights. I can be there in the morning."

I settle in beside my father. I am supposed to give him morphine every two hours, but sometimes those hours seem to pass in a flash, and others crawl. Time is a vapor, impossible to measure. At one point, I realize it must be afternoon because a golden band of sunlight cuts diagonally across the covers of my father's bed, as if holding him in place. There is a lump at the foot of the bed: Dominic. He has been there since last night, and his steadfastness reminds me that this—not the impatient Hollywood version—is the plodding pace of death.

A while later, Paula, Carl, and Max come by to spend some time at my father's side. They ask if I need anything, if I want company. I am grateful to have their support, but I tell them they should go, that Dominic and I prefer to handle this on our own.

On and off, I read to my father. First, it's something whimsical and nostalgic: *The Wind in the Willows*. Mole, Rat, Badger, and Toad. I imagine them all rowing alongside my father, chatting away, accompanying him on this final outing. Then, we switch to poetry. Mary Oliver, Walt Whitman, Richard Wilbur.

They say that hearing is the last sense to go. I want to say something profound before it's too late, but there is no script for this moment. All I can think to say is "thank you," so I say it over and over. *Thank you. Thank you.* "Thank you for loving me, Dad," I say one last time. "I know you don't remember me, but I remember you. I always will."

My father's face has become drawn, and his chest rises and falls. It's so still in the room that each of his breaths is a cataclysm. He sounds like he is working hard to get somewhere, and I think of the Robert Frost line, "The best way out is always through." It's hard to listen to him breathe this way, but I know he is working his way through, finding his best way out. I squeeze his hand, knowing that my only job now is to see him off.

I think about his conversation with Anita, and I remember how much conviction he had about the fact that when we die, we go somewhere much better. Though it breaks my heart, I touch his cheek and whisper, "You can go whenever you want to, Dad. I am launched. I'll be just fine. You go when you are ready."

Chapter 51

In the morning, when the paperwork is done and the funeral-home guys have carried my father out of the house for the last time, I finally sit down. It has been hours since I actually rested, or really even breathed. I'm not yet exhausted—that will come later—but I curl up on the couch and try to settle my nerves. I wonder where my father is now. Not his body, but the more enduring aspects of who he was, is, will continue to be. Maybe he is in a place where he can reconnect to the memories he had lost, or maybe it's a place beyond memory, beyond thought, beyond what I can imagine with my little human brain.

"Where are you, Dad?" I ask aloud. I know he's not here, but I also know he's not gone.

A few hours later, I wake to the sound of tires in the driveway, and I step outside just as Nina is lifting the car seat from her rental. She sets it down and we look at each other. She knows our father is dead without my having to tell her. There are no words for this moment, no reconciling these extremes: within the span of a few hours, I am meeting my nephew for the first time and seeing my father for the last. I pull Nina into a hug that thrums with all of these layers, and then some.

"I miss you so much," Nina cries into my shoulder. When we finally part, she asks, "When did he go?"

"Early this morning." I peek into the car seat, where Anders is asleep. "Oh wow, he's perfect. Nina, you did this. You made him."

She laughs. "I sure did."

Finally, I turn to Nils, who is rummaging around on the passenger side of the car. But when I make my way over to greet him, I stop short. Nina's traveling companion is not Nils. It's my mother.

"Mom?" I look at her, then at Nina. "I didn't . . . Where's Nils?"

"He had a last-minute work thing." There is a slight edge to Nina's voice and she doesn't elaborate, so I don't press the issue for now.

"So here I am!" My mother embraces me, her Chanel handbag driving a wedge between us. When she stands back, I can see how hard she is working to refrain from commenting on the state of my hair—long, unwashed, still two different colors. Instead, she says, "It's freezing out here."

It isn't. It's actually a perfect late-October day, fresh and bright; but we make our way inside.

Nina looks around and then peeks into my father's empty room. When she comes back, she is smudged with tears. "Cricket? Thank you for doing this."

"For doing what?"

"For being here. For taking care of Dad like this. I never could have done it."

"What do you mean? You took care of him for years," I say.

"Yeah, but this part. The end. I always knew I wouldn't be able to face it."

I start to contradict her, but then I stop. Maybe it's true what she's saying. Maybe my sister has limitations after all, even if I could never see them.

"Thank you for handling everything. I'm sorry I haven't been there for you lately."

"Nina, you have a newborn," I say. "I'm sorry I haven't been there for *you*."

"We're both doing our best. There's just a lot of life happening right now."

"There certainly is," says our mother, a bit unnerved by our emotion.

Anders starts to stir, and Nina retreats upstairs to change and feed him, leaving me alone with our mom.

"I would have gotten the cabin ready if I had known you were coming, Mom."

"No need," she says, looking around as if she's in a cabinet of curiosities. "I'm staying at the inn."

"What? Why? You came all this way."

"Well, they have hot water, for one thing." She's joking, but I understand the real reason she doesn't want to stay here. "I came to help Nina with the travel, and to see you, of course. But I think you two should have time to yourselves to . . . do what you need to do."

This is my mom in a nutshell. She wants to be involved, and I know she wants to support us, but she prefers to stay on the fringe, clear of any real emotional intimacy. I can tell that being in this house is confronting in a way that's not easy for her.

"Okay, well, I'm glad you're here." I nod, meaning it now that the shock has worn off. "I'm glad you came."

Chapter 52

The following morning, I wake to the smell of coffee and a quiet house. When I get downstairs, I find Nina out on the porch with Anders.

"I didn't know you two were up," I say, stepping outside. It's a shimmering autumn morning, and warm enough to be outside in just a sweater or, in my case, a tattered bathrobe.

"Oh, we're always up," says Nina huskily as Anders nurses. "And we're always sort of asleep. We live in a haze."

"I'm amazed you even got yourself here," I say. "It's a long way to go with a two-month-old. Was Mom helpful?"

"As helpful as she can be," says Nina. "As you know, our mother isn't actually very *maternal*. No matter what Anders is fussing about, she tells me to rub whisky on his gums."

"Spectacular advice," I say.

Anders takes a few final gulps and then pushes Nina's breast away with a dramatic flourish. He starts to grizzle and she instinctively rocks and shushes and pats him—no doubt things she has done hundreds of times in the two months since he was born. But his fussing increases.

"Want me to take him?" I ask. I barely know how to hold a newborn, but she looks like she could use a break. I pick Anders up gently, getting a feel for his floppy body as I support his head and pull him close to me. I'm scared by his fragility, but once I settle into my chair, his weight suddenly feels grounding. He quiets and stares at my face, transfixed.

"Look at that. You're a natural."

"I could hold him like this forever," I say.

"Please do," says Nina, closing her eyes. "I'm so tired."

"Do you ever get a break? Is Nils pulling his weight?"

"Sort of. Sometimes. I don't know." Nina pauses. "Honestly, I think we may have rushed into things."

I look at my sister, and for the first time, it occurs to me that she might not be superhuman.

"He's a good guy. It's just—we're really different. And now that Anders is here, I'm clearer about what I want and need long-term. I just don't know if Nils and I are all that compatible."

"Whoa," I say. "Are you breaking up?"

"Not yet. I don't know. Maybe we just need a reset." She turns to me and looks as if she is trying to remember something. "Have you ever done that? Taken a break from someone?"

I stare at her to see if she's joking, but she looks back with genuine interest. I can't believe she has forgotten that she played a central role in the chain of events that led to my rupture with Seth.

"Nina, it was your idea," I say. "You said the best way to keep Seth interested was to break up with him."

"What? That makes zero sense. I don't think I would have said that."

I feel rocked, as if the history I thought we all agreed on was now in question. Is she misremembering, or am I? "You said it worked because it was counterintuitive."

"Really? Well, if I did, I was wrong. I wasn't exactly a sage back then."

I look at her again. She seems to have no idea that I've hung on her every word for the vast majority of my life. She is talking to me as if we are equals.

I could attempt to relitigate the past, but why? As I look at Nina, I do not see a fallen idol. I see a new mom who is exhausted but doing her best; I see a daughter who is grieving; I see a human who is trying to find her way, just like the rest of us. I see my sister, in all of her dimensions, and I love her more than ever.

A lazy wind sweeps through the trees, sending the flame-colored leaves flickering.

"I still can't believe Dad's gone," says Nina. "When you came through the door earlier, I thought for a second that it would be him."

"I know what you mean," I say. "It doesn't feel real."

"I guess we should think about a funeral?" Nina looks at me as if I'm in charge.

"Yes. I don't think Dad would want anything too fussy. And now that he's kind of famous"—I glance over to see if this irks her, but she smiles and shakes her head, as if she has accepted my shenanigans long ago—"I think we should keep it low-key."

"Totally agree."

"Maybe we do a little ceremony down on the dock with just us, plus Carl, Paula, and Max."

"Perfect," says Nina, looking relieved that I've already thought it through. "Wait, who's Max?"

I laugh, realizing just how much we have to catch up on. "I have a lot to tell you. But first, can you do me a favor?"

"Of course," says Nina. "What is it?"

"Can you . . . cut my hair?"

That afternoon while Anders is napping, Nina and I haul a chair onto the lawn and set up a makeshift salon.

"You know I've never done this before, right?" says Nina, kitchen scissors in hand.

"It's fine. It can't look any worse than it already does."

"No promises," she says, as she parts my hair in the middle. "I'm just going to cut straight across, and then I'll neaten it up after."

As she circles me, taking careful snips, I fill her in on all the things we haven't gotten to talk about yet: Max, my reunion with Chloe, my non-deal with Gemma.

"So, wait, Gemma bought the Seavey camp?!" Nina is riveted.

"No. It ended up selling to some people who seem reasonable, thank goodness," I say. "But you're not going to believe this . . ."

I open up Instagram and navigate to the Actualize page. I click on a video of Gemma spritzing mist onto her face and monologuing: "Mmmm, I can't even explain how refreshing this is, you guys. If you've ever been to the Adirondacks, you know the water is exceptionally clear and clean. It's got so many yummy minerals—your skin will just drink it right up. Okay so after I mist, I'm going to go ahead and take the Oracle Oil and just work it into the skin, all over my face and neck and décolletage . . ."

"What is this?" Nina asks.

I explain that a few weeks ago, I received a marketing email introducing Actualize's newest product line: the Catwood Collection. Billed as "sacred skincare from the Source," every product is infused with water from Catwood Pond. I pull up another video and hand my phone back to Nina so she can watch.

In this one, Gemma is in a white bathrobe at a marble sink, with six bottles laid out before her. "We distilled the essence of the Adirondacks into six core products, formulated to elevate the whole human vessel—body, mind, and spirit. Because wellness starts from within, we have the Catwood Tonic for gut health. Then we have our Truth Serum, a resurfacing solution that helps you bare your true face to the world. Then there is Future You, a full-body exfoliating scrub that sloughs off dead skin and regenerates new cells. Next, our Best Self Balm is a rich salve for anywhere you want that extra glow. Our Centering Spritz helps lock in both moisture and self-worth. And finally, our pièce de résistance: Oracle Oil. Infused with nutrient-rich Adirondack pine sap, this is the product that will supercharge not just your beauty routine—but your entire existential outlook."

Nina starts to giggle, and then laugh, and before long, she can hardly breathe.

"I know," I say. "Gemma can make a product out of anything—even pond water."

"Should we order some?" Nina asks, wiping away tears.

"We can't afford it!" I yelp, hysterical with laughter. When we finally calm down, Nina circles me once more, takes a few final snips with the scissors, and then hands me a mirror.

For a second, I do a double-take. I look like Nina, with my hair hitting just above my shoulders in a neat-looking long bob. The blond is gone, and my natural brown is warm and shiny in the sunlight. I peer into the mirror. It's not *exactly* Nina who I look like, but it's someone familiar. After a moment, I realize: I look like myself.

Chapter 53

"Oh thank god," my mother says as she comes through the door and sees my new hair. "I wasn't going to say anything before, but . . ."

"I know," I say. "I needed it. I hadn't had a haircut since before I moved here."

My mother puts her hands up as if she can't bear to hear any more on the topic. We gather in the dining room for a simple dinner—pesto pasta and herby green salad—and afterward, we retire to the great room. Nina arranges herself on the couch to nurse Anders, my mother takes my usual chair, and I sit down in my dad's favorite chair, where Dominic hops onto my lap.

"I can't believe that cat is still . . . with us." My mother is more at ease now that we have all had some wine, and she seems to be opening up. She picks up a photo from the side table—one of the four of us in a rowboat, many years before the divorce. "Arthur never took this down?"

"Why would he? It's not like he wanted to cancel you," I said. "On the contrary, he still loved you."

My mother looks skeptical, so I relay a story that makes me smile while also breaking my heart. A few months ago, my father had been studying the same photo. When I walked in, he pointed to my mother's face and asked, "Who is this? I recognize her. She must be an actress or a singer." I answered, "That's Tish. You were married to her." He looked closer and said, "I was? I must have done something right."

My mother smiles when she hears this, and Nina pouts her bottom lip, saying, "That's so sweet."

"You guys look as though you actually like each other in that photo," I say.

"We always liked each other," my mother counters. "That was never the issue."

"What was the issue?" I press. "Did Dad have an affair or something?"

My mother throws her head back in laughter. "Who would he have had an affair with—a trout? No, if he ever had a mistress, it was this place." She waves her hand, indicating the house, the whole property. "Catwood Pond was his great love. He always hoped I would acclimate, and I tried as hard as I could for as long as I could. For twenty-five years, I hauled myself up here!"

"But didn't you know what you were signing up for? Didn't you talk about your expectations before you got married?" I ask.

My mother looks at me as though I'm crazy. "You don't understand. It was different in the eighties. There wasn't all this . . ."—she waves her hand as if conjuring something—"emotional awareness stuff. We fell in love, and we assumed everything would work out. Well, it didn't."

I take a breath and finally ask outright: "I've always wondered if I was the reason that you got divorced. Was it because of Seth's accident and all the stress it caused?"

"Of course not," my mother answers without hesitation. "I just . . . wasn't satisfied. I wanted to reboot my career, expand our life. Your father always seemed so complacent."

"Complacent?" I ask. "Or content?"

My mother thinks for a moment, as if she hadn't considered there might be a difference. "I really don't know. But *I* wasn't content. I wanted more, and I didn't handle that well. I'll admit it. How do I say this without sounding like a bad mother . . ."

Nina and I ready ourselves for a revelation.

"It just wasn't what I expected—marriage, motherhood. And at some point, I realized I only had one life. So why shouldn't it be the one I actually want?"

In a way, it is strange to hear my mother articulate that having children was not the culmination of her life's work. But in another way, it is liberating. I think back to the divorce and the years of dissonance that preceded it. It wasn't all my fault—it never could have been.

"And what about now?" Nina asks. "Do you have the life you want now?"

My mother purses her lips. "Still working on it, but getting there."

I look at my mother who, by all means, has everything anyone could want: a nice husband, a beautiful home, a vibrant career, a grandchild, and two daughters whom she presumably loves. But she is still going for it, still grasping. You could call that insatiable, or you could call it intrepid.

Complacent or content? Insatiable or intrepid? Or perhaps all of the above, depending on whom you ask—and when.

Having said all she intends to on the matter, my mother deftly changes the subject. "So do you know a good realtor? When will you list the house?"

"I don't want to sell it," I say.

My mother puts her hand to her chest. "You're not thinking of staying here . . ."

"Why not?" I ask. "Where else would I go?"

"I thought you didn't really like Locust anymore," says Nina, surprised. Anders raises his tiny fist skyward, like an activist with an unknown cause.

"Things evolve," I say. I point in the direction of the clearing where my imaginary animal hospital once stood. "Do you remember what I used to do over there? Near the stumps?"

"Of course," says Nina. "You dragged all your stuffed animals out there and operated on them. It was bizarre."

"Well, I think that's what I want to do," I say.

Nina looks at me with concern. "What do you mean? Like another prophecy thing?"

I laugh. "No. I want to open up my own animal hospital—but for real this time. I want to go to vet school. But first, I need to finish my degree."

"Now there's an idea," says my mother, lighting up. "Where? Maybe in London?"

"Here," I say. "For now, at least. I can finish my credits at the community college, and then apply to vet schools."

"Okay," my mother says gingerly, liking the concept if not the details. "And do you have enough money to pay for this?"

"Not yet," I say. "But I'll figure it out."

My mother waves her hand. "Enough with the pride, Cricket. I will pay for it. Just get going already."

"Really?" I look at her skeptically.

"Of course. You have a goal, finally. Let's make it happen." My instinct is to resist her offer, but she cuts me off before I can speak. "Don't fight me on this. I regret that I couldn't pay for your undergrad, but the timing was tough with the divorce. Things are different now. Frankly, I have more money than I know what to do with." Nina and I look at each other, happy to hear this, before my mother adds: "I may not have always been the mother you needed, Cricket, but all I ever wanted was for you to find a passion and pursue it."

I am moved by her generosity, but before I can thank her, she adds, "I can't imagine why you would want to finish your studies *here*, but we're different, you and I."

A more obvious statement has never been uttered, and yet this is the point I've been trying (and failing) to convey to my mother for my entire life. After twenty-seven years, we seem to finally be speaking the same language.

She turns her attention back to the photograph, and I see her eyes glaze with tears for the first time since she arrived. "He might not have been the right husband for me, but Arthur was, without a doubt, the right father for you."

Chapter 54

On the night before my father's funeral, I have the dream again: my heart, coughed up, beating in my hand. Again, I turn to the faceless passersby to ask if I need it, if I can survive without it.

This time, there is no sign of Seth, but after a few minutes, my father ambles through the crowd. He is young and vibrant and confident. "Give me that thing," he says, holding out his hand. I put my heart into it, and he puts it in his pocket. "Be patient, Cricket. Your new one is almost ready."

I wake up to darkness and grab my chest. Everything seems intact. I can feel my pulse; my organs are all accounted for, as far as I can tell. Though it's only 5:00 A.M., I decide to get up and work on the remarks I plan to give at today's ceremony.

As I head downstairs and make coffee, the dream keeps tapping me on the shoulder, asking for attention.

It's an interesting idea: the regenerating heart. After all, we do go on, no matter how much we shudder with grief. And maybe our hearts don't ache because they're scarred or broken or because something is wrong. Maybe they ache because they are shape-shifting. Like the growth spurts of our youth, they make us quake with change; but once weathered, they leave us stronger and even more ourselves. Not our final selves, or our best selves, or even our improved selves, but just our *next* selves. As I now know, we are always between selves. It doesn't mean we are lost—it means we are growing.

Throughout our project, I never asked my father to give me a prophecy of my own. At first, it was because I was scared of what he could reveal about me. I didn't want to know what the future might hold. But over time, as I listened to him carve meaning out of other people's lives, I gained an insight here, heard a whisper there. Fear was replaced by curiosity. Even now, I remember the specific prophecies that stirred something within me: the career change, the great romance, the man who finally bought a horse, the woman who felt most alive just before she died. Each of those supplicants went away with a single jewel to polish; but I received the whole trove.

In the end, I never needed my father to tell me what my future *would* hold—I simply needed him to show me what it *could* hold. And now, as his premonitions echo through my memory, I can use those threads to weave my own prophecy.

When I was younger and living in the city, I distracted myself with activity; busyness was a balm. But up here, in the quiet, the truth has infinite patience. It waits until we have run ourselves ragged and are finally ready to come home, to remember who we have always been.

As the sun starts to rise, I make my way into the great room and light a fire. The flames begin to hiss, and I get an idea: one final brush with bibliomancy for old times' sake.

I walk over to the bookshelf and say, "Dad, give me something good."

Closing my eyes, I run my hand along the spines, feeling the paperbacks, the hardcovers, the ones that are so old that pieces of them come off on my fingertips. Finally, my hand stops on a smallish book, and I pull it off the shelf.

I look down and see that it is an original copy of James Herriot's *All Creatures Great and Small.* I remember reading it, somewhere, sometime, but I didn't realize we owned a copy, let alone a first edition. I must have forgotten—we can't remember everything, after all. I open the cover, and inside is an inscription from my father, back when his handwriting was replete with confident swoops and playful flourishes.

> *For Cricket, on her tenth birthday:*
> *The truth is yours to divine; the future is yours to design.*
> *With love from your many animal friends—and of course,*
> *your adoring father.*

I snap the book shut as my body floods with a feeling so overwhelming that it can only be love. Though I have said it many times,
only now do I fully believe it to be true: a good oracle shows you what
you already know.

Acknowledgments

They say second novels are the most difficult to write, and it turns out, they're correct. There were many moments when I feared this book would never find its way, and I am grateful to those who supported me as I figured out how to tell this story.

To all the families, like mine, who have been affected by Alzheimer's: I hope this book provides an escape, a balm, a laugh. Whatever you might need.

To my editor, Sarah Cantin: You elevate everything you touch. I am so lucky to work with you. Thank you for your patience and encouragement as I wrestled with this project. Thank you, also, to my team at St. Martin's Press—Drue VanDuker, Olga Grlic, Michael Clark, Donna Noetzel, Erica Martirano, Jessica Zimmerman—for bringing this book to life.

To my agent, Erin Malone: It is such a gift to know that you're in my corner. Thank you for the pep talks, the feedback, the unflagging belief. My gratitude to the team at WME—Rae Friedman, Suzy Ball, Hilary Zaitz-Michael, Laura Bonner—for helping this story find its audience.

I am much indebted to my cadre of trusted brainstormers, eagle-eyed readers, and steadfast cheerleaders: Frances Denny, Thyra Heder, Serena Roberts Houlihan, Robbie Henwood, Storrs Hoen, Tom Hoen, Darin Kingston, Callie Kant, Lizzie Bildner, Isadora Tang, Ethan Feirstein, Reid Cherlin, and Colin Mort.

Thank you to Rebecca Barry, Mikki Brammer, Jessica George, and Adam White for your kind words and beautiful writing.

Shout-out to my favorite libraries in the Upper Valley—the Howe Library in Hanover, the Tracy Memorial Library in New London, the Dunbar Free Library in Grantham, and the Norwich Public Library in Norwich—where I wrote and edited much of this project.

To Allie Amerson: This book would not exist without you. Period. Thank you for taking the best care of my Avery Girl so that I could get some work done.

To Nick, Oliver, Annie, Asher, and Eli—I love you.

To my mother, Caroline: You housed me, fed me, babysat, and otherwise made it possible for me to finish this book. All writers should be so lucky. Thank you, also, for taking care of Rat when he was sick with Alzheimer's—a job no one wants, but one that you did with humor and grace.

Finally, to my daughter Avery—the big joy in my life. My whole world sparkles now that you're at the center of it.

About the Author

Frances F. Denny

Tory Henwood Hoen is the author of *The Arc*. Her writing has appeared in *New York*, *Vogue*, *Condé Nast Traveler*, and *Bon Appétit*, among other publications. A graduate of Brown University, she currently lives in Vermont.